JAN 1 2
W9-BAL-649

Burning Bright

NAPA COUNTY LIBRARY
580 COOMBS STREET
NAPA, CA 94559

Burning Bright

FOUR CHANUKAH LOVE STORIES

MEGAN HART
JENNIFER GRACEN
STACEY AGDERN
KK HENDIN

This is a work of fiction. Names, characters, places, and incidents are products of the author's imagination or are used fictitiously and are not to be construed as real. Any resemblance to actual events, locales, organizations, or persons, living or dead, is entirely coincidental.

Foreword copyright © 2015 by Sarah Wendell.

Miracle copyright © 2015 by Megan Hart.
A Dose of Gelt copyright © 2015 by Jennifer Gracen.
A Home for Chanukah copyright © 2015 Stacey Agdern.
All I Got copyright © 2015 by KK Hendin.

All rights reserved under International and Pan-American Copyright Conventions. By payment of the required fees, you have been granted the nonexclusive, nontransferable right to access and read the text of this e-book on-screen. No part of this text may be reproduced, transmitted, downloaded, decompiled, reverse-engineered, or stored in or introduced into any information storage and retrieval system, in any form or by any means, whether electronic or mechanical, now known or hereafter invented, without the express written permission of HarperCollins e-books.

Avon, Avon Books, and the Avon logo are trademarks of HarperCollins Publishers.

EPub Edition DECEMBER 2015 ISBN: 9780062464859

Print Edition ISBN: 9780062464842

10 9 8 7 6 5 4 3

Foreword

EVERY HOLIDAY SEASON comes fully equipped with traditions that mix history, food, ritual, food, celebratory music and decorations, and also, if you missed it, food. Lots of food.

And I don't know if you know this, but Chanukah is *awesome*. I mean, just about any holiday in any culture that involves food is automatically awesome, but Chanukah is particularly excellent—and I don't just say that merely because I celebrate it. And it's not merely the culinary awesomesauce that makes Chanukah so fun.

First, because it's a transliterated word from Hebrew, there are about 36 different ways to spell it. It's hard to misspell, really, unless you throw a stray Z in there or something. Chanukka! Making copyeditors gnash their teeth for over 5000 years!

Second, part of the tradition of Chanukah is to enjoy fried foods to commemorate the oil in the temple that lasted eight nights instead of one. You might be familiar with latkes, which are fried potato pancakes. I make both white and sweet potato curry latkes each year, but really, let's be honest, that is nowhere *near* enough fried food. So how about some sufganiyot, which you might recognize as a jelly doughnut. I'll let you in on a secret—I don't like jelly doughnuts, but I think glazed doughnuts, or even the ones filled with icing totally fit the fried-food requirement. Deep fried doughnuts on a stick with a side of latkes? Now we're talking!

Third, the lights of the menorah grow brighter as a candle is added for each successive night. With a group of four or more, you can probably toast marshmallows over your Chanukah candles. I refuse to confirm whether I have personally done this. (Of course I have.)

Most important, however, is that every culture celebrates light and warmth in the darkness of winter. Our traditions vary in the details, but when everyone is included in the welcoming light and in the warmth of family and friends, there's much to celebrate.

In a sense, the romance genre and the women who love it form a family—a loud, geographically scattered but very passionate family. Any reader can likely think of at least eight reasons why romance is important, and why the genre is important. And with readers connecting online and off in greater numbers, each change of season brings a new discussion about how we can help create a romance genre which reflects the lives and experiences of every woman who reads and writes it.

So on behalf of the authors included in this anthology,

I invite you to find a cozy and welcoming place, and some doughnuts or latkes, or both, because calories consumed in the observation of a holiday tradition do not count. Welcome to *Burning Bright*, a Chanukah romance anthology. We invite you to share in this tradition: reading romance, embracing warmth and light, and celebrating joy and love together.

Sarah Wendell

Burning Bright

Miracle

Megan Hart

Chapter 1

THE NEW NEIGHBOR on the ground floor had told Amanda his name was Ben, and the package that had been delivered to her apartment by accident was addressed to B. Schneider. It had to be his. There weren't any other new tenants in the Valencia, and she already knew everyone else. Ben hadn't been home when she tried to drop off the package, so she'd left a sticky note on his door inviting him to come up and get it.

When the soft knock came at her door, Amanda almost didn't hear it. She'd been watching one of the old Rankin-Bass Christmas specials on TV, the one with the Heat Miser. Her guilty pleasure. She loved that guy and his catchy tune. She was still singing when another, louder rap came at the door, and she opened it to reveal the tall, lean man dressed in a pair of black jeans and a matching black hoodie over a gray T-shirt.

"Hi, Ben, c'mon in."

He nodded and held up the sticky note. "Amanda, right?"

"Yep." She stepped aside to let him pass, noticing his hesitation and the way he looked at the mezuzah on her doorjamb before he came through the doorway. "I have it here somewhere, hold on. Let me find it."

Her living room was a chaos of wrapping paper and boxes. She'd been putting together gifts for her family and friends, as well as about a dozen presents she'd bought for the angels she'd plucked off the Christmas tree outside the department store. She kicked aside a plastic bag of bubble wrap, thinking maybe his package was there on the floor, but nope.

"Must've put it on the table," she said over her shoulder. "You know how it is, you put something somewhere to keep it safe, but then you forget where you put it."

He hesitated again before following her around the mess in the living room and through the arched doorway into the dining room. "Thanks for keeping it safe for me."

"Most of the time this place is pretty secure, but this time of year it's not good to leave packages out in the lobby." She lifted a shifting pile of shiny gift bags that slipped from her grasp and scattered.

Ben bent to help her gather them. "Yeah. Christmas. Lots of deliveries, I guess."

Amanda gave him a glance as she found the medium-sized box and handed it to him in exchange for the bags he'd picked up. "Yep. Here you go."

He weighed the box in his hands, turning it to look at the return address with a frown. He tapped the label.

Then he tucked it under his arm and looked around her apartment.

"No tree," he said.

"I'm Jewish," Amanda said with a shrug.

"But you're wrapping Christmas presents."

She laughed. "Well . . . just because I'm Jewish doesn't mean I can't send Christmas presents to friends or family who celebrate. A bunch of them are toys or pajamas and stuff for needy kids that I picked from the angel tree. I try to do that every year."

Ben's brow furrowed. "That's generous."

"It's the most wonderful time of the year," Amanda said, keeping herself from singing the words, but only barely. At the look on his face, she shook her head. "No? All the lights, the goodwill, the cheer? Doesn't do it for you, huh?"

Ben looked surprised. "I didn't say that."

"It can be a hard time of year for people, too," she said, wondering if he were one of them. When he didn't offer up any information, she added, "But welcome to the Valencia."

"Thank you. Amanda," Ben added as though reminding himself of her name. Suddenly, he stuck out his hand. "I don't think we met officially before."

She took it, bemused at his grip and the way he pumped their hands up and down. Very formal, but also like he wasn't used to shaking hands at all. It was the way he pulled his hand away from gripping hers and looked at it for a few seconds before smiling sideways at her.

"Nice to meet you, too, Ben," she said. "I hope whatever's in the package is something fun."

"It's from my mother," he told her. "So, probably not."

Amanda pressed her lips together to keep from laughing. "Oh. Oops. Sorry."

"Don't be." He shrugged. "It could've been from my father. That would've been worse."

There didn't seem to be much to say about that. Amanda had always considered herself blessed that she got along great with her parents, and her siblings, too. A slightly awkward silence fell between them as they both stared.

"Well," she began just as Ben said, "I guess I should—"

"—get going," he finished when she waved him to speak. "Leave you to your wrapping and stuff. Thanks again for getting the package to me."

"No problem." She walked him to the front door. "It's what good neighbors do."

"You're the only neighbor I've met so far."

"Oh . . . well, everyone's all really nice here. It's a good place to live."

Ben's lips pressed together before he answered, "I've been working a lot of hours down at Morningstar Mocha, you know it?"

"Of course. Their lemon scones are out of this world." He looked so serious, she thought, but couldn't figure out why.

"Well, that's why I haven't met anyone. I've been working."

"You met me," Amanda said with a smile meant to tease him into returning it, gratified when he did. In the next moment, though, he was cutting his gaze from hers again and backing out the door.

When the door shut behind him, she shook her head. B. Schneider, she thought. What is your story?

Chapter 2

THE PACKAGE CONTAINED a small metal menorah and a box of Chanukah candles, along with a mesh bag of chocolate gelt and a wooden dreidel. His mother had also included a box of potato latke mix. He'd never known her to ever use such a thing—she'd always cooked the latkes from scratch. For a moment, his mouth watered at the memory of the crisp, oily potato pancakes slathered with applesauce. Then he pushed the memories aside, packed up the box, and put it away on the top shelf of the coat closet.

He wasn't going to be celebrating this year.

Not with a menorah and latkes and a dreidel, anyway. He'd left all that behind, along with his friends, family, and the girl he'd been supposed to marry. The freedom he thought he'd find by fleeing everything he ever knew was a heavier burden than he'd expected it to be. Time would make it better, Ben thought. It had to. Or else he'd left everything behind for nothing.

Dark had fallen by the time he headed down the street to the Morningstar Mocha, where he'd taken the Friday night shift. On purpose. Tesla, the owner, had told all the employees that Friday and Saturday night shifts needed to be shared equally unless you could get someone to switch. For the past couple months since he'd started working there, it hadn't been difficult for him to find someone who wanted Friday nights off.

Jogging a little because the December air was frigid here in central Pennsylvania, Ben blew out breath after frosty breath. He didn't pause when he passed the synagogue, the lights bright and meant to welcome worshippers inside. Cars in the parking lot meant people had driven to services, something forbidden on the Sabbath in his former community. But then, so was working, and he'd gone out of his way to do that. It was supposed to make him feel like he'd broken even further away from what he'd left, but honestly, all it did was remind him how close it all remained.

"Hey, Ben. Thought you weren't going to make it." Tesla, her asymmetrical haircut dyed several shades of blond, waved him behind the counter as he entered.

"Sorry."

She laughed. "No worries. Just glad you got here. I'm going to head out. Marisol's in the back doing some prep for tomorrow. You feel okay handling everything out here?"

He did. The cash register was only a little different from the ones in his dad's store, and he'd had hours of training on that. He liked being out front, talking to people, all kinds of people. People like his new neighbor, he thought, as the bell jangled over the shop's front door and she walked in.

"Ben," she said warmly.

"Amanda," he replied. "Hi."

"Haven't seen you in forever," Tesla said to her.

Amanda laughed. "Yeah, I know, I know. My bad. Been busy, that's all."

The women chatted for a moment longer while Ben rang up a customer's order of coffee and a muffin to go, and then Tesla took her leave. Amanda turned to him with a smile that tugged one out of him—the way it had in her apartment, he remembered. She smiled, and he was helpless to resist returning it.

"Hi there, neighbor," she said. "Good to see you again. How's it going?"

"Fine."

He'd been too abrupt, he thought, watching her smile fade the tiniest amount. She perused the glass case, biting her lower lip. She had thick, dark red hair that fell halfway down her back in curtains of silk. When she straightened and caught him staring, she didn't look offended. If anything, something flashed in her dark brown eyes that made him want to tell her how pretty she looked.

Of course, he didn't. That was the sort of thing that happened in the movies he'd been forbidden to watch but had snuck out as a teenager to see anyway. He was no romantic movie hero, that was for sure.

"Lemon scone," he blurted, remembering that she'd said how much she liked them.

Her smile brightened again, and she tilted her head to study his face. "Yeah. My favorite. You remembered."

"They *are* the best thing here," he said. "Anything else?"

Again, too abrupt. Too formal or something. He'd somehow lost the knack of superficial conversation.

"Sure, I'd love a soy latte. Thanks."

"I'll bring it to you," he told her. "If you want to go ahead and find a place to sit."

There was usually a rush right before closing on a Friday night, but for Ben it seemed as though no matter how many people crowded into the coffee shop, whenever he looked up his eyes went straight to the table by the front window where Amanda sat with her book. Sometimes she chatted with the other regulars, but mostly she sipped her drink and nibbled at her lemon scone in silence.

Engrossed in what she was reading, she didn't seem to notice as the shop emptied and the clock ticked several minutes past the closing hour.

"Oh, sorry," she said when she looked up, with a faint, dreamy look in her eyes that sharpened at the sight of Ben switching the sign to CLOSED and locking the front door. "I'll get out of your way."

"You don't have to," he said, too quickly, but at least this time he was rewarded with another of those slow, sweet smiles instead of a puzzled look and furrowed brow. "I mean . . . I just have a few things to take care of here, and then if you're going to walk home, maybe we could walk together? Just so you don't have to walk alone. For safety. That's all."

Because, of course, he needed an excuse, so that nobody dared think he was offering for the mere pleasure of her company, he thought, giving himself a mental kick. Nobody around here was going to judge them for walking without a chaperone. If anything, that would be considered absurd.

It clearly didn't occur to Amanda that she should modestly refuse him. She nodded, a finger holding her place in the book. "That would be great."

"Give me a few more minutes?"

"Sure. I'll finish this chapter." She handed him the empty plate and mug.

Marisol had taken care of all the next day's prep, and she would also close out the register and deal with putting the cash in the floor safe. All he had to do was get the dishwasher running and mop the back room. Tonight, Marisol was as eager to get out of there as he was.

"Hot date," she told him with a wink and a glance across the front counter toward Amanda, still waiting. "You, too?"

"Me? Oh. No." Ben shook his head, heat creeping up his throat at the thought of it. "She's my neighbor."

Marisol gave Amanda another look. "Uh-huh."

In the two months Ben had been working here, Marisol had gone on dates with so many different men, he couldn't see how she could keep track. She'd tried to set him up with a couple of her friends, though she'd given up when Ben consistently declined her invitations. He knew she thought he was weird. Well . . . he guessed that if she knew him—really knew his background and where he'd come from—he *would* seem strange.

Outside, Marisol gave them both a cheery wave and headed off in the opposite direction, leaving Amanda to blow out a breath of frost as she danced from foot to foot on the cracked pavement. Ben shoved his hands deep into his coat pockets. The temperature had dipped tremendously, stinging the inside of his nostrils and sparking a few tears of protest at the corners of his eyes.

"Smells like snow," Amanda said.

"White Christmas," Ben replied.

She laughed and nudged him with her elbow as they started walking toward the Valencia. "White Christmas, white Chanukah, whichever. I just love it when it snows. Chanukah starts in—"

"I know when it starts."

This time he'd been deliberately abrupt. He didn't want to talk about it. She would ask him if he were Jewish then, he thought. And what would he say? That he used to be? That he wasn't sure what he was anymore?

But if she wondered about it, Amanda kept the question to herself. She chatted about other things as they walked. The neighborhood, mostly, pointing out some local sites of interest. About herself, too. A project she'd been working on with her job.

"So, it's not so much that they are all crazy about doing arts and crafts," she explained with a hop over a split in the sidewalk where a tree root had poked through. "But they don't always have anything else to do, other than watch television. So I try to think of fun and easy things for them to keep busy doing. It's a myth, you know. That all old people love Bingo and soap operas."

Her foot hit a patch of ice and she slipped, arms flailing, and would've gone down hard if Ben hadn't reached out and snagged her around the waist. His reaction pulled her close to him. She ended up in his arms, her face tilted to his, her mouth open in laughter.

"Sorry." Ben let go of her abruptly. "I thought you were going to fall."

"I *totally* was going to fall." She didn't move so much as a step away from him.

The shaft of light from the streetlamp lit her eyes in shades of amber and deep chocolate, the pupils gone wide and dark. That dark red and silky hair had tumbled over her shoulders, and this close, he could smell a faint perfume of vanilla and lavender. Ben cleared his throat and stepped backward to put some distance between them.

This time it was his foot that hit the patch of ice. This time Amanda was the one who held him up so he didn't hit the ground. And this time the saving grip became an embrace.

"I caught you," Amanda whispered.

Ben breathed in the scent of her. Then carefully but firmly, he let her go. Stepped back, avoiding the ice. He could feel her curious gaze on him, but he didn't let himself look at her. She'd see his feelings all over his face, he knew it. She would see him looking like a fool.

They walked the rest of the way in silence. In the lobby of the Valencia, Ben paused in front of his door, key in hand, but didn't put it in the lock. He shifted from foot to foot, wondering if she expected to be invited inside. He thought about how sparse and bare his apartment was; he didn't even have anything to offer her to eat or drink.

"Well," Amanda said after a moment of awkward silence. "Good night, Ben. Thanks for walking me home."

"You're welcome."

She headed up the stairs, one hand gripping the wrought-iron railing. He unlocked his door and pushed it open. She paused at the landing to look down at him, giving a small wave with her fingers. He returned it after a second. Then she kept going, and he went inside.

Chapter 3

THE PROJECT TODAY was making Christmas tree ornaments using clear plastic balls that could be filled with glitter, water, and glue to create snow globes. Amanda had seen the idea on the Internet, and past experience had taught her that anything using glitter was a huge hit with the residents. She'd set up the table with the supplies, and was helping those who needed assistance, when one of the newer residents came over to the table.

"Oh. Tree ornaments." She sounded sad.

Amanda smiled at the woman, who wore a pretty flowered housecoat and had carefully styled her short gray curls with a cute matching headband. "Hi. I'm Amanda. We haven't met yet. Would you like to do a craft?"

"Well," the woman said with a wave of one gnarled hand, "I suppose, but I haven't anyone to give a tree ornament to."

"You could put it on the main tree," offered Betty

from her place at the end of the table. "They never have enough decorations on it."

"I could." The woman smiled, but still looked a little sad.

"I have some felt menorah kits," Amanda offered. "I was going to drop them off at the Temple Beth Shalom synagogue for their preschool. It's just putting the different pieces in these little bags. If you'd rather help me assemble them?"

The woman brightened and took a seat at the table. "Oh! Yes, I think that would be lovely, thank you. I'm Norma, by the way."

"Nice to meet you, Norma." Amanda laid out the pieces for the kits and showed her how to put them together.

The group worked for a while, the residents chatting and joking with each other. Amanda had known most of them for a few years, so it was no surprise when Betty nudged Wanda with an elbow and then lifted her chin toward her with a grin. Amanda started laughing even before the older woman spoke.

"No," she said before Betty could even ask. "No, not yet."

It was a question they asked her frequently enough that she could no longer be sad that the answer was still negative. She caught Norma giving her a curious glance. Amanda shook her head and sorted out the nine multicolored felt candles, one for each of Chanukah's eight nights, plus the *shamash*, the helper candle. She added the yellow fabric flames to the piles.

"They want to know if I have a boyfriend," she explained. "And sadly, or maybe not so sadly, I do not."

Norma nodded and gave the other women a small smile as she added her pieces to one of the bags and tied a careful bow around it. "You're young still. You have time."

Betty sighed and strung a ribbon through the metal hook of her plastic ball. "That's what we all think, isn't it?"

"No prospects at all?" Wanda leaned closer, hands folded on the table. "What about that nice young man you told us walked you home on Friday?"

Amanda's brows rose. "Ben? My neighbor Ben?"

"Yes, that was his name. The one you told us about when you came in on Saturday looking all aglow," Betty added with a grin at her friend. "Didn't she, Wanda?"

"He's . . . my neighbor," Amanda said, thinking of Ben and unable to quite put her finger on what, exactly, was odd about him. His mannerisms. There'd been heat in his gaze during those few seconds when he kept her from falling on the ice, but it passed so quickly she decided she must've imagined it. "He's very polite."

"Nothing wrong with polite," Norma said.

There was more to it than that. Ben had an air of secrets about him that Amanda wasn't sure she was meant to decipher. "His eyes are gorgeous."

"Gorgeous eyes, there's a start!" Wanda patted the table gently and beamed. "My Albert had lovely blue eyes."

Amanda studied the felt pieces in front of her, trying

not to think too hard about her mysterious new neighbor, but now that the older women had got her talking about him, it was like she couldn't stop herself. "They're brown. A dark, rich brown, like chocolate. Dark chocolate. Really yummy, delicious chocolate. And . . . he has a beard!"

Betty laughed with delight. "Oh, my!"

"I know, right?" Amanda sat back in the chair with a shake of her head. "I don't usually go for that lumbersexual look. But it's sooooo attractive. I mean, seriously, strangely attractive. On him, it works."

"Long hair?" Wanda asked. "A . . . whattya call it? A man bun?"

"No . . . he wears it super short. It's dark, almost black." Amanda sighed, thinking about it. "He's very polite, did I mention that? Anyway, he's my neighbor, and aside from a couple conversations in the hall and the time he came to my place to pick up his package—"

"Oh, ho!" Betty grinned and shook her finished ornament. "Hot cha-cha!"

Amanda burst into giggles. "It wasn't like that."

"Next time," Wanda offered, "make him a coffee cake. Or, no. I guess you should offer him a beer. That's what you kids do these days, isn't it?"

"There *is* something about him," Amanda admitted with a look around the table. Of all the residents she'd spent time with here at the nursing home, Betty and Wanda had been the closest to her. They'd unfailingly and cheerfully gone along with whatever wacky crafts she dreamed up, even the ones that ended up being awful. They wanted her to be happy, she thought, and that was never a bad thing for anyone to wish on someone else. "I can't put my finger on it, but . . . yeah. There's something there. But I don't think he's at all interested. Besides, I don't want to try for something with my neighbor. I love my apartment, and he lives on the first floor. Imagine how awkward it will be when it ends and I have to pass his place every day. No, thanks."

Norma let out a slow, soft chuckle. "So determined it will end?"

"Most things do," Amanda said after a moment, not trying to be a bummer about it, but feeling like that was the truth. Every relationship she'd had, so far, had crashed and burned.

"Nonsense." Norma settled the final menorah kit onto the pile she and Amanda had made, and tapped the soft fabric. "I was married for fifty-eight years. It only ended because he died."

The matter-of-fact way Norma announced this left Amanda a little taken aback. "I'm sorry, Norma."

"He would have died anyway," she said, without so much as a break in her voice, giving Amanda a gaze as hard as steel. "But if I'd never agreed to go out on that first date with him, we would never have been married. Never had those sixty years together. So if you're never going to allow something to start because you're too afraid of it ending, I fear you will spend a very long time by yourself. If you want to see where a road will take you, dolly, you have to walk it."

Amanda looked around the table. Everyone else was nodding. "But . . . he hasn't even asked me out on a date, Norma."

"Well my goodness!" Norma rapped her knuckles on the table. "Who says you have to wait for him to ask? "

When the phone rang, Ben almost didn't answer it. He'd installed the landline in the apartment for emergencies. So far it had only rung about three times, each a sales call. He didn't have an answering machine, though, which meant that if he didn't pick up and the caller didn't give up, he'd be listening to the harsh ringing until one of them gave in.

"Yeah?" he barked into the receiver.

"Benyamin?"

His stomach twisted. "Galya. Hi. I didn't think . . . I wasn't expecting you."

Her soft breathing tickled his ear through the phone until he had to switch the handset to his other ear and scratch. She said nothing for so long he was sure she wasn't going to, but neither of them was hanging up. He wasn't going to be the first, that was for sure.

"I wanted to see how you were doing," she said at last.

She sounded different. Tired, maybe. Sad? He hoped at least there was some small portion of grief in her voice, though it made him unhappy, too, imagining Galya as anything but the font of sunshine he'd always known her to be.

"I'm fine."

She laughed, sounding a bit more like herself. "And if you weren't? You wouldn't tell me, would you?"

"I would tell you," he answered, letting himself rest a

hip against the edge of the half wall between the kitchen and the dining room.

"No. You wouldn't. You forget, I know you." They were both quiet again, for a shorter time now, before she spoke again. "Tell me about what you're doing, Benyamin. I've been worried. We all have been."

"Even my father?" He snorted disbelief.

Galya made a small noise. "You know he loves you very much. You're his only son."

"So, you'd think he might have been a little less of a . . ." Ben couldn't bring himself to use an invective, even though he'd been trying out a few here and there on his own. But he couldn't speak that way to Galya.

"Stubborn. Like father like son, maybe?"

Ben frowned and closed his eyes for a few seconds, thinking of the last time he'd seen his father. His mother had been crying. His sisters, too. His father had yelled himself red-faced, fists clenched. It was the first time Ben had ever feared his father would hit him—but in that moment, he'd been more afraid that he would have hit him back.

"Your mother has been worried," Galya said when Ben didn't answer.

"And yours?"

Galya sighed. "She's angry, of course. Because she thinks—"

He knew exactly what Galya's mother thought. The woman who'd been a second mother to him since childhood hated him for running out on her daughter just months before they were supposed to get married. He couldn't blame her, or any of them. All they knew was that he'd betrayed Galya in one of the worst ways a man could.

They had no idea of the truth, and if Ben had his way, they never would. Because that was real love, he thought as he listened to the soft hush of Galya's silence again. Sometimes it meant lying to protect the person you loved.

"How's Levi?" he asked.

The smile was clear in her voice when she answered. "Oh . . . he's good. Really good. He asked me to send his regards. And he wants you to come home."

"I'm not coming home," Ben said. "You know I can't."

"You can *always* come home."

He shook his head, even though she couldn't see him. "You know better."

"How is it, where you are?" she asked him. "Out there, in the big wide world."

"Harrisburg is hardly the big wide world. Not compared to Brooklyn." But he knew what she meant. Their world, the one they'd shared since birth, was not so much small as it was . . . exclusive.

"Have you joined a shul?"

"No."

Galya paused. "Will you?"

"No," Ben said. "I told you before I left, I was leaving and not coming back."

He hated to hear the strangled sob she didn't even try to hide. "Benyamin—"

"I have to go. Thanks for calling. I'm fine. Everything here is fine. And you're fine, you're good, you and Levi are going to be wonderfully happy together." Ben straightened, feeling a tightness in his jaw.

"Because of you!" she cried. "Please, don't let us . . . don't let what you did for us ruin your life! Please, I couldn't bear it if I thought that. We talked about it, you said it was what you wanted, please, please, I can't be happy if you're not all right. And neither can he!"

Ben's shoulders slumped. "You're both going to be very happy, all right? I didn't do anything that I didn't think was the best choice for everyone, okay? You didn't make me do anything, and Levi didn't make me do anything, and neither did my father. I made my choices. You have to accept that."

"You know I will always care for you so much," Galya said.

It was not the first time she'd said those words to him, but Ben couldn't bring himself to return the sentiment. It wasn't that the words would've been a lie as much as a bandage, covering a wound that needed the open air in order to heal. "Good-bye, Galya."

She hung up on him.

He didn't blame her—he'd been unkind at the end, not to give her some scrap of affection. He'd meant what he told her. She hadn't forced him to make any decisions; he'd done everything of his own free will. He could tell her that a million times, though, and she would still feel guilty about everything. He would never be able to change that, as much as it pained him.

He couldn't stay in this apartment right now. There was nothing in it to keep him home, because nothing in it made him think of it as home. It was a place to sleep and eat, and he couldn't even do that right now because he had no food.

Outside, he pulled the collar of his coat up around his neck and breathed in the crisp December air. It smelled different here than it had in Brooklyn. The sky had more stars. Harrisburg was officially a city, but such a small one that it felt more like he'd moved into the country. He wasn't sure he liked it, not being able to hop the subway and head off to wherever he wanted. He needed to save for a car, he thought, and his job at Morningstar Mocha was not exactly going to lead to an overflowing bank account.

He might've made a mistake in picking Harrisburg, Ben thought as he headed down the sidewalk. Philadelphia had seemed too close to home, too easily reachable. The fact that there was a sizable Orthodox community in Harrisburg had meant something, as much as he wouldn't have admitted it. Even though he'd told Galya he didn't intend to join a synagogue, it still seemed impossible for him to live in a place where there wasn't even the option. He hadn't factored in the city's rural setting or the lack of long-distance public transportation, and he hadn't known that despite the Jewish communities centered in the city, there was very little public Jewish presence. Then again, wasn't that what he'd wanted? he asked himself as he left the Valencia. He'd wanted to run away and make a new life, far away and very different from the old.

Chapter 4

AMANDA HAD STOPPED in the Sheetz convenience store meaning to grab a quick salad, but the fancy coffee drinks and a doughnut had worked their sweet, sugary seduction, and once that happened, she'd gone for the fried mozzarella sticks, too. She grabbed a carton of ice cream while she was at it, and a bag of chips. Might as well make it a total junk food orgy.

She'd almost made it out of the store with her bag of shame when she spotted a familiar figure in the parking lot. She paused at her car. "Ben?"

He turned, a bag in one hand. "Oh . . . hi, Amanda."

"Are you walking?"

"Yeah," he said, then added almost challengingly, "I don't have a car."

She gestured toward hers. "Want a ride?"

"I'm fine."

"It's really cold out here," Amanda said. "Don't be a doofus."

Ben paused, turning to face her. "A . . . what?"

"A doofus." She grinned. "C'mon, it's freezing out here. It'll take you twenty minutes to walk home, and I can get you there in five."

She thought he was still going to say no, but then with a sigh, his shoulders hunched, he nodded and went around to the passenger side of her car, waiting patiently for her to unlock it from inside. She watched him slide into the seat as she fiddled with the heat to get the car warmed up.

"You okay?" she asked.

"Fine. Hungry, that's all. Thanks for the ride." He put his seat belt on with a loud click and looked up at her.

When their eyes met, Amanda couldn't stop herself from smiling again. Slow and crackling tension sizzled between them, hotter than the barely warm air puffing from the vents. Ben didn't smile, not at first, but then his mouth quirked the smallest bit on one side. His gaze didn't waver, not even to blink.

"You're welcome."

Ask him out, she thought, remembering what Norma had told her. But she couldn't quite make herself do it. What, just blurt out a date request right there in the parking lot of the gas station, with their breath curling out between them in the cold air and the smell of fried food making her stomach rumble?

The ride home was only a few minutes, then a few more while she circled the block to find a parking spot, and they didn't say much. They didn't say anything, actually. Not even small talk.

Maybe she'd been wrong about that heated, lingering look.

"Thanks for the ride," Ben said again as they stood in the Valencia lobby. "You're right, I would've been an icicle by the time I got home. I appreciate it."

Amanda lifted her coffee toward him. "No worries. Listen . . . anytime you need a ride, if I'm around . . ."

"Thanks. I couldn't, though. Expect you to drive me around, I mean." Ben patted his pockets and looked at his door, then gave a defeated sigh. "I forgot my keys."

Amanda had done that a time or two. "You can call Mr. Schmidt. He has an extra set of keys."

"No phone," Ben said.

"You don't have a cell phone?" Amanda's brows rose before she composed herself.

Ben laughed self-consciously. "No. Weird, right? I keep meaning to get a new one, but I haven't made it to the mall yet."

"You can use mine." She dug it out of her purse, pulled up the super's number and handed the phone to Ben, who called but had to leave a message. She sipped her coffee, her empty stomach still growling. "You want to come upstairs to wait until he calls back?"

"Sure. Okay. I'm really taking advantage of your generosity." He handed her the phone and followed her up the stairs.

Amanda laughed as she slid her key into the lock and opened her door. "It's no big deal. Neighbors help neighbors, right? It's a mitzvah."

From behind her, Ben made a startled noise. "What?"

She glanced over her shoulder as she set her food and drink on the coffee table to shrug out of her coat. "Mitzvah. It means good deed—"

"I know what it means," Ben said. "It just surprised me to hear it."

Again, that look. Heat flared in Ben's gaze. He took a step toward her. Then he looked away, and a surge of disappointment struck her hard enough to make her blink back a rush of unexpected emotion.

Silly, she told herself. It's not like he was going to kiss her or something like that.

"We should eat before the food is stone cold," she told him instead. "C'mon into the dining room."

The kitchens in the Valencia weren't big enough to fit a table, so she waved him toward the dining room table and grabbed some paper plates from the cabinet to set out for them. Settled into chairs on opposite sides of the table, each unwrapped what they'd bought at the convenience store and set it out. Amanda eyed the breakfast sandwich Ben had bought along with a hash brown. He was turning it around, rotating it on the greasy paper wrapping, but not picking it up to eat it.

"Is there something wrong with it?"

He looked up at her, then at the egg, sausage, and cheese biscuit. "Um . . . no."

Amanda dipped a mozzarella stick into the small plastic cup of marinara sauce and bit into the fried cheese. She watched Ben lift the sandwich to his mouth and take a bite. He chewed fiercely and swallowed, then looked at her again with that odd mixture of challenge and defiance.

"It's good," he said. "Have you ever had one?"

Amanda hesitated a second before saying, "A few times, sure. Not for a long, long time."

"But you're Jewish," Ben said. "Sausage is *treif*."

His use of the term, uncommon among people who didn't keep kosher or at least know what it was, surprised her. "Yeah, it is."

"Do you keep kosher?" Again, his tone was sort of a challenge.

A little annoyed now, Amanda sat back and gestured at the food on the table. "Obviously, I eat from restaurants that aren't kosher."

Ben took another bite and chewed. Swallowed. He wiped his mouth with a napkin. "Do you separate meat and dairy? Have separate dishes? If you don't do that, you don't keep kosher."

"I'm a vegetarian," she said, "so none of that is relevant for what I do in my house. I guess the answer is no, I don't keep kosher. And honestly, Ben, it's not really any of your business, is it? Unless there's some reason it matters to you?"

A few years ago she'd made the mistake of going out with a guy she'd met on the Internet. He turned out to be some kind of Old Testament fetishist who was able to quote, chapter and verse, every single law. Conveniently, he'd made sure she knew how many of those laws had been invalidated by the New Testament, and exactly how steep would be her decline into the fires of hell should she not accept salvation.

Ben looked up at her then, eyes going wide as he swallowed the gigantic bite of sandwich he'd taken after finishing his diatribe. "I didn't mean—"

"Do you have a problem with the fact that I'm Jewish? Because you keep bringing it up. And look, I've had some people be jerks about it in the past, so really, if you've got some kind of issue with it, how about you just man up and tell me that. What, you want to see the part in my hair that hides my horns?" Her voice had risen, shaky with anger and tears.

"Someone actually asked you that?" He sounded horrified. He put down the sandwich and wrapped it quickly in the paper.

Amanda had lost her own appetite. "Yes. Someone did. I've also been told that I'm going to burn in hell after I die, and I've been asked why I don't have more money, since 'my people' are all rich."

"I'm sorry."

She wrapped up her own food and shoved it back in the bag, then stood to take it to the fridge. Her phone rang as she did. Mr. Schmidt. He'd be downstairs with Ben's key in fifteen minutes.

"I'll go now," Ben said when she relayed the message. He hadn't finished his food, but instead had shoved it all back in the paper bag, and now clutched it in one hand without asking her to put it in the garbage. "I'm sorry, I shouldn't have brought this into your house. It was disrespectful of your beliefs."

Amanda stood in the doorway between the kitchen and dining room. "If I minded, I'd have asked you what you ordered before I invited you up. I live by my set of rules, Ben. That doesn't mean I expect or demand other people do."

"Too bad more people don't feel that way."

She crossed her arms and lifted her chin, still stung by his behavior. "Yeah. Too bad."

Ben looked as though he were about to say something else, but when his gaze snagged on hers, he seemed to think better of it. Instead he nodded and backed away. He looked back once more before he closed the door, the click of the lock very loud behind him.

So much for that, Amanda thought. At least she hadn't been an idiot and asked him out on a date.

"BEN. HEY. HELLO?" Tesla snapped her fingers in the air a few inches from his face. "You okay?"

He wasn't, really. He was an idiot of the highest degree, and while feeling that way wasn't exactly new, it was disheartening that he hadn't managed to outgrow his propensity for acting stupid. "Sorry. Just preoccupied."

His boss's brow furrowed. "Yeah, I can see that. I asked you to refill the coffee thermoses twenty minutes ago. You made the coffee, but . . ."

"I didn't do the refills. Yeah, sorry." He shook his head, wishing he could shake off his bad mood as easily. "I'll do it right now."

"I had Marisol do it." Tesla leaned against the counter, her arms crossed, and looked him over. "You want to talk about it? Something going on?"

"No. Well. Yeah. Maybe." Ben had been slicing avocados, but now he set the knife aside to face her. "I met someone. And I like her. I think she's smart and kind, and she's been really nice to me."

Tesla smiled. "And?"

"And, I insulted her. More than once. I didn't mean to."

"You don't strike me as the sort of guy who goes around being randomly insulting," Tesla said. "I mean, if anything, you're about the politest, quietest dude I've met in a long time . . ."

Ben frowned. He stripped off his food prep gloves and tossed them in the trash, then moved to the sink to wash his hands. "Why does that sound like you're going to add a 'but' in there?"

"But," Tesla added with a laugh, "you do have a certain . . . umm . . . well it's kind of a demeanor, I guess."

Ben turned. She handed him a clean, dry towel for his hands. "What's that mean?"

"Look . . . you haven't talked much about where you grew up or anything like that, and it's not really any of my business—"

"No," he cut in. "It's not."

Tesla didn't look offended, despite his sharp tone. "When I was a kid, I spent almost every summer on a commune."

This gave Ben pause. "You did?"

"Yes."

"Like . . . a religious commune?" He'd never heard Tesla talk anything about religion. The Morningstar Mocha was decorated with a tree and colored lights, but the signs all said Happy Holidays and there was an electric menorah in the window, waiting for its turn to be lit.

"Yes. Sort of. I mean, it was mostly an excuse for people to sleep with people who weren't their spouses," she said lightly, her gaze scanning his face as though to look for an obligatory show of shock. "And it was a front for a massive drug operation."

Ben shook his head. "Wow."

"Yeah. Anyway, it was definitely an experience that most people I run into haven't had, and they can't really understand. So, I don't talk about it much, but there's no question that it shaped me into who I am and how I view things." She shrugged. "What I'm saying is, Ben, you strike me as a guy who's trying really hard to forget where he came from."

"So? Lots of people leave the place they grew up, their families. Their faith," he added, without looking away from her gaze. "I'm not the first."

"Not at all."

He frowned. "Are you saying it's so obvious that I'm some kind of what, a freak? An outsider? That I don't know how to interact with people out here in the real world, or something? I didn't grow up on a commune. Or in a cult!"

"I'm saying," Tesla said gently, "that you have a way of speaking that sets you apart from the rest of the yahoos who pound their chests and make a show for the ladies, that's all. That I've seen the women come in here and flirt with you, and you barely blink an eye, and I know you're not trying to be insulting or anything, but you don't realize that most women bending over to flash you some cleavage are not used to men not noticing."

"I notice," Ben said.

Tesla laughed, tossing back her head of crazy hair, then looked at him with a wide grin. "You don't react."

"I . . . they're . . ." He was at a loss for words, uncomfortable. "I'm not used to it, I guess. And yes, it's because of how I was raised. Women didn't do that. Good women didn't, anyway."

Women in his community dressed modestly, to say the least. Married women wore wigs so that nobody but their husbands could even see their real hair. Long sleeves, long dresses, thick stockings. A wall between the men and women at the synagogue so nobody would be tempted to look at each other during services, instead of praying. As far as Ben was concerned, the barrier had only ever made it that much more tempting to try to get a glimpse.

Tesla's laughter faded at his words. "Good women, huh? So a woman is bad if she shows off her body?"

"I didn't say that. And I don't think it, just like I don't think women shouldn't be allowed to lead a worship service or that somehow once a month what happens to their bodies makes them unclean." Ben frowned again. "I don't believe most of what I was taught was true, growing up. The stuff about. . . ." He stumbled on the word *Ha-Shem*, knowing Tesla probably wouldn't know what that meant. "God. That stuff, I understand. But all the other rules, I just can't get behind."

She seemed mollified, though her eyes narrowed and she looked at him more carefully. "Ah . . . Amish?"

It was Ben's turn to laugh. He knew very little about the Pennsylvania Amish, but he could see how she might've thought his description meant he'd grown up in that culture. "No. Orthodox Jewish."

"Oh." Tesla didn't seem to know what to say for a second or so, then replied, "But not now?"

"No. Not anymore." Saying it aloud tasted strange.

They stared at each other for a few seconds before Tesla reached out to squeeze his shoulder. "So, you like this woman. But you hurt her feelings. Apologize. Make it up to her? I bet whatever you did wasn't as bad as you think it was, Ben."

"I like her. Yes."

Tesla grinned. "Like her, like her? Like you really, really like her?"

"Yes, I like her." A laugh pushed its way up and out his throat, surprising him how good it felt. Watching Tesla waggle her eyebrows, he laughed harder, and that felt even better. "I like her a lot."

"You gonna ask her out?"

His laughter eased into a sigh. "I don't know."

The idea was too vast to contemplate at the moment. Dating? In this world, where holding hands and kissing and making love were expected, not forbidden until after marriage. He'd spent his entire life expecting to marry Galya. Asking Amanda on a date seemed . . . disingenuous, at the least. Or somehow dishonest.

Tesla nodded. "Yeah. I get it. But listen. If you hurt someone's feelings, isn't it always better to at least try to make it up to them?"

"Yes," Ben said. "Of course."

"You'll feel better about yourself, too," Tesla offered. "And you know what would make you feel good, too?"

He gave her an expectant look that she returned with another wide grin.

"If you refilled all the coffee at the self-serve station."

Ben burst into laughter again. "Yes. All right. I got it. Right away, boss."

Tesla winked at him and gave his upper arm a small light punch. "Hey. Good luck."

"Thanks."

And, when he walked out into the coffee shop's main area, Ben saw he was going to have his chance.

Chapter 5

"Hi," Ben looked especially cute today in a blue button-down shirt with the sleeves rolled up to show off strong forearms. He'd combed his thick dark hair back from his forehead and trimmed his beard. "I didn't think you'd want to come in here, after . . ."

Amanda laughed, feeling heat creep up her throat and into her cheeks. He'd thought about their conversation? About her?

"We live in the same building, Ben. It's not like I thought we'd never bump into each other again. And besides, I'm not about to give up the lemon scones. I could go over to the Green Bean, but they don't even sell lemon scones, they only have plain. And if you're going to eat a scone, you should make sure you get a good one . . ."

She was babbling. Amanda bit back the words that wanted to tumble out of her mouth. Ben carefully put down the jugs of coffee he'd been replacing.

"Amanda, listen. I have something to say."

She waited. He didn't say anything. She'd wait another few seconds, she thought, before she gave up waiting. Then, to save them both the obvious embarrassment of her presence, she'd get out of here. Clearly Ben didn't want to see her around, and while she wasn't about to give up her great apartment because of some stupid misunderstanding with a guy she barely knew, she guessed she could learn to like her scones plain.

"I'm sorry," Ben blurted.

It was not at all what she'd been expecting him to say, but the surprise was a pleasant one. Amanda turned her mug around in her hands, studying the way the liquid shifted from the motion. Then she looked up at him. "Thank you."

"Tesla told me I have a certain . . . demeanor." Ben looked uncomfortable. Then determined. "Is that true?"

"I would agree with her. Yes."

He sighed, shoulders slumping for a minute, before he gave her a surprisingly sweet smile. "Well, there's not much I can do about that, I guess. But I am sorry if I hurt your feelings. I should've known better."

"People make mistakes. It's all good. Thank you for apologizing." Another flush of heat tinged her face. Could he see her blushing? Amanda took a quick sip of coffee to cover up the awkwardness.

"I brought fresh. Let me dump that for you. Grab a clean mug." He gestured at the shelf above the self-serve station where Morningstar Mocha's eclectic selection of mugs were displayed. "And Amanda . . . I was raised Jewish."

She'd been about to hand him her half-full mug and choose a new one, but at this, she stopped, comically holding out the mug. "What?"

"I grew up Jewish." Ben took the mug and handed her a new one from the shelf.

He'd spoken so matter-of-factly that it would've been inappropriate for her to make a big deal out of this, right? Amanda took the clean mug. "Umm . . . Well . . ."

"I just wanted you to know," he said, "that I never meant to sound as though I was judging you."

He was going to kill her with those long, lingering, and tingly looks. If what Tesla had meant by Ben having a certain demeanor was that he was intense, she was definitely right about that. Amanda cleared her throat again, searching for the right words.

She took the first step. "Would you like to go out with me?"

The words tumbled forth a little unsteady, a little louder than she'd intended. She'd turned several heads with the question, but she kept her eyes on Ben, refusing to look embarrassed. Her chin lifted. Norma had been right. If you never took a chance, you could never find out what might happen.

Ben coughed. "Out? You and me? Like . . . on a date?"

"Yes. You and me, on a date." She nodded.

He was going to say no, she thought, already resigning herself to feeling even more stupid than she had at the beginning of this conversation. Ben looked around the coffee shop quickly, then took a step closer to her. He lowered his voice, probably trying to save her feelings . . .

"Yes," he said. "I will."

A DATE.

A date with Amanda, Ben reminded himself as he let himself into his dark apartment and fumbled with the light switch that was supposed to connect to a floor lamp in which the bulb had burned out without being replaced. He'd lived in his parents' house in Brooklyn. His mother had taken care of almost everything. Here, there was nobody but himself to make sure there'd always be a light on, waiting for him.

The phone rang while he was still juggling keys, coat, and the bag of leftover bagels he'd brought home. Morningstar Mocha had them sent in from a Philadelphia area bakery, but they were still nothing like the ones from home. Ben tossed the paper sack onto the table and dropped his coat to grab the phone.

He knew who it was before he answered, of course. The only person who would call him here was Galya, and it had been over a week since they'd last spoken. At the sound of the male voice, however, Ben stopped short, cutting off his own greeting.

"Don't hang up on me," Levi said.

Ben closed his eyes at the sound of his best friend's voice. "I'm not going to hang up on you."

"Good."

Silence. Levi didn't need to say a world. Ben knew what he was thinking. In the past, he might've let Levi off the hook, filled in the blank space between them with words of forgiveness Levi hadn't asked for. Now, though, Ben stayed quiet, too.

"I don't want it to be like this," Levi said finally. "We . . . I . . . want you to come home."

Ben sighed and made his way into the kitchen to flick on the overhead light. He opened the fridge to grab a drink, though he wasn't thirsty. "I'm not coming home. I told her that, and I meant it."

"You can't spend the rest of your life angry at us. It will tear you down."

Ben leaned against the kitchen counter. "I'm not angry with either one of you. I wish you both the best."

"I know you love her—"

"I love you both," Ben snapped, worn thin by this, their need to make amends for what he'd willingly allowed and held no grudge over. "All right? I want you both to be happy, and I left because I wanted to be happy, too. Don't you get it, Levi?"

"You took the blame—"

"I took my way out." Ben ran a hand through his hair, then over the beard he'd been unable to bring himself to shave. Of all the things he'd done so far, that would've been the hardest, harshest break from the past. "I couldn't live that life, Levi. You know that. You knew it better than anyone."

Levi made a low, rasping noise. "You've abandoned your faith. I can't help but feel it's somehow my fault."

"I didn't abandon my faith." It had betrayed him, Ben thought. The way he'd been raised, everything he'd ever been taught to believe was important, in the end it had all let him down.

"What if I came out there and got you? Convinced you?"

"You can't, Levi. You know that."

Levi sighed. "Will you come home for the wedding, at least? It's going to be in eight months. We wanted it to be sooner, but we couldn't . . . you know. Make it so obvious. And the mothers are involved with the planning, so of course that makes it more complicated."

"I don't think I can." Not because it would hurt to watch his best friend marry the woman who'd been promised as Ben's wife. Not because it would hurt to see his father turn away from him one more time, or because his mother would be brokenhearted again when he wouldn't stay. "It would put a focus on something that isn't as important. It would lead people to *lashon hara*."

Gossip. Words whispered behind palms. Wagging tongues, rumors.

"People always talk."

Ben gave a small, humorless laugh. "I don't need to give them reason to. That's all. If you want to visit me, you're welcome, Levi. Of course."

But they both knew Levi wasn't going to make the trip. Levi wouldn't feel comfortable in Ben's nonkosher home, with his secular clothes, with his job working on the Sabbath. Their friendship had been based on commonality, and they didn't have that anymore.

There wasn't much to say after that. They said goodbye, and Levi hung up first. Ben returned the phone to its cradle, then before he could change his mind, pulled the plug from the wall. Tomorrow, first thing, he'd take the bus over to the mall and pick himself up a cell phone.

Moving forward, he told himself. Always forward. Never back.

Chapter 6

First night of Chanukah. Also the night of her first date with Ben, and though it seemed as though that might've been a coincidence, Amanda did allow herself the smallest moment of belief that the universe was in favor of them going out. If she ever got ready in time, though. She'd been held later at work than she intended. Traffic around the mall just a few days before Christmas was insane, and she barely made it home before it was time to light the first candles.

She definitely didn't have time for them to burn out before Ben was knocking at her door, though she had, thank goodness, grabbed a quick shower and changed from her scrubs into a pretty maxi dress and her favorite knee-high boots. Not much she could do about her hair other than twist it into a loose bun, but a bit of mascara and some lipstick made a huge difference. Maybe too much of one, she thought as she opened the door and saw the look on Ben's face.

"Hi . . . umm . . . Wow. You look . . ."

Amanda stepped aside so he could enter. "I look . . . ?"

"Nice," Ben said.

Would they always just stare at each other this way? Ben looked at her as though she were some brand new road he'd discovered, one that wasn't on any map. An uncharted gaze in admiration of the road stretching out ahead of them to some as yet unknown destination.

"Thanks," she said.

He was looking past her to the menorah she'd set up on the windowsill, well out of the way of the curtains. "Oh."

"It'll be another ten minutes or so before they burn out," Amanda said by way of apology. "I got home late."

Ben shook his head. "I didn't realize."

"Oh. I should've waited for you. I'm sorry . . ."

"No. It's fine. I just didn't think about it." He smiled at her, though there was a shadow in his gaze. "We can wait. That's fine."

"Would you like a drink? I have some beer. Wine." She eyed his expression. "Do you drink booze?"

Ben laughed and gave his head a rueful shake. "Yes, Amanda. I drink alcohol, sometimes. But I won't if you're not going to."

"I'm driving, so I'll have soda. Lemonade? Iced tea?"

"Iced tea would be perfect, thanks."

He was still watching the candles burn down when she brought him the glass. They both drank cool, sweet tea while they studied the flames glinting against the window glass. When she looked up at the reflection of their faces, Ben was staring at her. She didn't look away. Shoulder-to-shoulder, Amanda became very aware of the heat of his body against hers.

"I wasn't going to light the candles," Ben said quietly.

There was a story there, and it seemed long and complicated. Keeping her gaze on his in the reflection, Amanda asked, "Why not?"

"It felt wrong, somehow."

She turned then, to face him. "Why wrong?"

"I can't explain it," Ben said. "Because I'm not feeling it, I guess? Because why would I light the candles to celebrate a miracle when I've stopped doing everything else? It seems shallow, maybe."

She thought about that. "You can share mine, if you want."

"What?"

She laughed a little and shrugged. Ben looked at her. "You can share mine. I'll light them every night. I'm not the greatest about doing some of the other things, but I do make sure to light the candles for Chanukah. You don't need to have your own, if you're suffering some sort of . . . umm . . . existential or philosophical difficulty with it."

Ben blinked. "How is it, Amanda, that you've only just met me, and yet you get it?"

"No clue," she admitted with a nudge of her hip against him. "Lucky guess? Or maybe it's because I've done my share of questioning what matters and what doesn't make sense?"

He looked again at the candles, the *shamash* in the center of the menorah now guttering and going out.

"I was taught my entire life to question. To study and debate. To dig in deep to the questions of what mattered, of what was important and how to obey. But now, I guess I just don't know what I believe anymore. Sorry. That's heavy for a first date, right?"

"It's that demeanor of yours," she told him, and grinned at his look of embarrassment. "Relax. Kidding. I like it."

"You do?" He returned her smile.

"Yeah. I do."

It was okay, she thought, if they kept doing that thing. That warm, tingly, lingering, intense staring thing. It had been a long time since anyone had made her feel the way Ben did with something as simple as a look.

IT STILL FELT strange to go into any old restaurant and order whatever he wanted off the menu.

"The food's good," Amanda explained as she dragged a piece of carrot through the hummus she'd dipped onto her plate. "You don't have to be a vegetarian to appreciate it. But I thought you might."

"Just like you don't have to celebrate Christmas to help others celebrate it."

She nodded. "Yep."

And it was kosher by default, even if his father would not have approved of it. Amanda hadn't said so, but Ben knew that was one of the reasons she'd picked this place. To make sure he didn't struggle with the menu options.

They shared the appetizers, and when the entrées

came, those as well. The conversation moved from one topic to the next with ease, covering subjects so varied that Ben found by the time they got to the end of one, he'd forgotten where and how it had begun. Amanda had an easy laugh that lit up her face and urged him to laugh along with her, something it felt like he hadn't done in a long, long time. At least not this way.

She was beautiful.

And smart. Inquisitive. Emotional; he could see it in the way her expressions shifted as they spoke. How animated she became when discussing her passions for books, movies, lemon scones. Watching her, Ben knew he should've felt embarrassed by the wealth of cultural references he missed because he simply didn't have the same background as she did. They were both twenty-five, but no matter how many times he didn't understand what she meant, Amanda never made him feel stupid.

"My television viewing was restricted growing up," he said at last, when she asked him if he was familiar with a childhood TV program she had watched. "We watched only what was considered appropriate, and it was hardly ever what was secularly popular. Movies, books. All the same. We had plenty to entertain us and keep us busy, don't get me wrong. You had *Sesame Street*. We had *Shalom Sesame* on VHS tapes that my mom brought home from the synagogue library. We had *Lamb Chop's Chanukah* special."

"Hey, we watched that one, too!" Amanda grinned. "I loved that one."

He didn't want her to think he'd grown up shut away,

somehow, from the real world, even if at times looking back he felt that was exactly what had happened. "It wasn't that we didn't hear about Christmas or bacon or whatever. We knew about those other things. We just didn't do them. When we got older, my best friend Levi and I would take the subway to sneak off and see movies we weren't supposed to. I had a small radio and we'd tune into the popular stations when our parents weren't around. Small rebellions, really, when you think about what sorts of things we might've gotten into. But our parents would've punished us for them anyway."

"All kids do that," Amanda said with a chuckle. "My parents have no idea about some of the things I did when I wasn't supposed to. To be honest, I hope they never find out."

Ben laughed. "I guess it's universal, no matter where you grew up."

She didn't dig into him about things, no matter how curious she must've been. Ben appreciated that. It made it easier, actually, to open up to her about his past, which was in no way shameful and yet he'd felt was better kept secret. That was *his* baggage, he realized as he watched Amanda's expression while he described to her what Passover was like in their house. Dinner and commentary on the Passover story that lasted for hours, glasses of wine drunk, singing and hilarity and joy until the children fell asleep and had to be woken so they could hunt for the afikomen.

"A piece of broken matzo that was supposed to be dessert, who ever thought that was a good idea?" Amanda made a face as she laughed. "My gramps was always the one who hid it. Whoever found it got gummy rings. You know, the Kosher for Passover kind, those fruit jellies? So gross."

"Disgusting," Ben agreed, letting himself relax into enjoying the way her face scrunched up at the memory.

She nudged the plate of chocolate cake toward him and waved her fork. "The worst part of Passover for me was school lunches. My mom would pack us tuna or egg salad and matzo, but man, it never failed, that was always the week they had pizza and spaghetti and macaroni and cheese. Torture! But we did it. It was important, she said, to remember that even if we're different, it's what makes us who we are."

"I wasn't around anyone who was different. We were all the same. Our schools closed for the holiday. Passover was great. We played a lot of board games." Ben hesitated, remembering. "My mother would spend all day cooking for the seders and tell us we had to eat the leftovers for the rest of the week, but then she always ended up cooking full meals every day. That's funny, how for you it meant problems with the food, and for us it was when we were allowed to eat cake for breakfast. And not those boxed seven-layer deals from the supermarket that were baked months in advance. She made everything from scratch. My mom's an amazing cook."

"Hey, I could get behind that. Cake for breakfast? No problem." She paused, not looking at him as she forked another bite of rich chocolate. "So . . . Ben. You don't have to tell me if you don't want to, but . . ."

She was going to ask him why he left Brooklyn, he thought. He'd have to tell her the whole story. Watch her face twist again, maybe with pity this time, at how he'd spent his life chasing something that didn't exist.

She looked at him with a faint, curious smile. "Floaters or sinkers?"

For a moment he didn't understand. Then he laughed, first softly and then a little louder. "Floaters. Of course floaters. Who likes matzo balls that sink?"

"Me!" Amanda tipped her head back in glee, and he took the chance again to appreciate her reactions. She looked at him sideways. "My mom used to tell me I liked my matzo balls the way I liked my guys. Dense."

His eyebrows lifted. "She didn't."

"Yeah, she did. And she wasn't wrong." Amanda sighed, shoulders lifting, and tucked her hair behind her ear. She caught him looking, fascinated by the way her fingers stroked through the smooth auburn silk. Her smile faded for a second before becoming something else, something echoed in the small slant of her eyes as she looked him over. "I don't have a great track record with guys."

"No?" Mouth suddenly a little dry, Ben swigged from his cooling coffee.

She shook her head. "No. I seem to go for the ones who start off sweet but don't end up that way."

"That's a shame. A woman like you deserves a man to appreciate her. To treat her like a queen. My father used to sing to my mother every Friday night before we ate dinner. It's a prayer called 'Eyshet Hayel.' A woman of valor," Ben said, then added quietly, sadly, thinking of his parents, whom he'd disappointed so much, "I'm sure he still does."

"It sounds really nice. A woman of valor has a price beyond rubies, right? That's it?" He nodded. Amanda smiled. "I didn't know it was a song."

He'd always thought that one day he would sing that prayer to his own wife as they sat down to the Sabbath meal. He'd imagined singing it to Galya, because she was the only woman he'd assumed he would marry. At least he'd imagined it before he began thinking about all of the places he would never see, the things he would never do, as long as he stayed where he was.

"Thank you for asking me out, Amanda."

She looked faintly surprised, then her brows knit. She bit her lower lip and didn't meet his gaze for a few seconds before braving it. Those dark brown eyes, alight from within. He could get lost in them, if he let himself. There was danger there, but Ben couldn't convince himself to mind it.

"A woman who lives at the home told me I should, or else I'd regret it," Amanda said.

"She said you would regret not asking me on a date? She doesn't even know me." Ben laughed, bemused.

Amanda shook her head. "More that she told me to take a chance, you know? Because if I didn't, I'd never know what might've been, or what could happen. If I'd waited for you to ask me . . ."

"You might still be waiting," Ben told her honestly. "I'm not very good at this sort of thing."

Amanda's gaze didn't waver from his this time. "She said if you wanted to see where a road might end, you needed make sure you started walking it. So . . . I'm walking it, Ben."

Impulsively, he reached across the table to capture her hand with his. Her fingers were strong and warm, her skin soft. She gripped him, palm to palm, fingers interlocking as they both squeezed gently. It would've been a forbidden touch where he grew up, but here, with her, it seemed the most natural thing in the world.

"I'm glad I asked you," Amanda said.

"Despite my demeanor?"

"Oh, definitely in spite of it." She squeezed his hand again, lightly. "Hey, I have an idea. Are you busy tomorrow night?"

Chapter 7

THE SECOND NIGHT of Chanukah. Three candles ablaze, the helper candle and then one for each of the nights. She'd invited Ben upstairs to her apartment to light the menorah and then to nosh on appetizers while they waited for the flames to extinguish. And then, on another date. Not dinner this time.

Something else.

"I don't know the songs," he warned as she handed him a small faded booklet from the pile she'd pulled from the closet. "I can try to hum along, but . . ."

The home had more visitors this time of year than any other—church and school and scouting groups often scheduled craft activities or caroling with the residents. Tonight, Amanda had brought Ben in to help her with a large group activity of making reindeer tree ornaments out of candy canes, felt, and google eyes.

"There will be plenty of people singing, so you'll blend

in. It would be great if some of these groups spread their visits out," she told him. "Or at least the cookies and candy deliveries. I always crave a good peppermint chocolate sugar cookie in the middle of the summer, but guess what, all we can rustle up is tapioca pudding."

She looked up to see him staring. "What?"

"You love your work."

She didn't have to think too hard about that. "Yep. I do. It wasn't what I thought I'd end up doing. I wanted to be a teacher. But midway through my sophomore year of college, my grandma moved in with mom and dad. She had dementia. I decided that one of the things I really wanted to do with my life was be there for people like my grandma, at the end. Making crafts might not be the most meaningful thing, but . . . I like to think that it gives people some joy."

"Giving people joy is meaningful. Maybe one of the most meaningful things anyone can do. Don't sell yourself short. I didn't have any aspirations so selfless. I just wanted to travel," Ben said as he sorted out the carol booklets in preparation for the group that would be singing. "See all the places I'd read about in the books I wasn't supposed to be reading."

"Did you go to college?" Amanda dumped half a package of google eyes into a bowl and set it on the long table set up in the rec room, then glanced at the clock. It was almost time for the program.

Ben shrugged. "I went to yeshiva. I had a couple years in business college. My father wanted me to join him in the family business. Get married. Start a family."

"Your father sounds like my mother," Amanda said lightly. "She's very focused on becoming a grandmother. What's your family business?"

He gave her a glance. "He owns a string of kosher supermarkets."

"And you didn't want to work for him?"

The double swinging doors nudged open for the first arrivals, a small pack of schoolkids that already looked sugared up and hyper, followed by a few chaperones and one or two of the residents. Amanda hadn't even finished putting out all the craft supplies. If previous years were anything to go by, she knew she'd better hurry. The kids had a way of swooping in like locusts, decimating the refreshments and tossing everything all over the place.

"I've worked for my dad since I was a kid," Ben told her. "Long enough to know that as much as it meant to him, the last thing in the world I wanted to spend the rest of my life doing was running a supermarket. "And then, as it turned out, getting married wasn't going to happen, either."

Amanda looked up, surprised, but there was no time for her to ask what he'd meant. The first kids were sliding into their places at the table, jabbering, already messing up the carefully arranged bowls of supplies and getting into the glue. The residents who'd come to join the activity were finding their places, some of them laughing with the rambunctious group of children, some looking sour.

"I'll pass out the songbooks," Ben offered.

Amanda gave him a grateful nod, then turned to help start the simple craft. Nothing about it should've been difficult, but in about ten minutes there was glue everywhere, google eyes scattered every open surface, and some of the kids were tearing off the wrappers of the candy canes to eat them without even making them into reindeer.

"Is it time to sing yet?" one of the adult chaperones asked. "Or how about the cookies and punch? We said we'd have the kids home before nine."

With a defeated sigh, Amanda gestured toward the table at the back of the room where the kitchen staff had set out the refreshments. "Sure, you can have everyone grab a snack and then we can start the caroling."

"Miss?"

Amanda turned to see a small boy in a blue sweater and brown corduroy pants tugging at her sleeve. He had glue all over his hands and a google eye clinging to his cheek. She plucked it off gently. "Yes?"

He pointed toward the room's sole window, which was on the far side near the decrepit piano nobody ever played. "Are we gonna light the m'norah?"

She straightened, looking at the electric menorah. It was dark. She hadn't even noticed it was there, honestly, as the Christmas tree mostly hid it. "Sure. Absolutely . . . ?"

"Josh," the kid said.

"Do you light the menorah at home, Josh?"

"No. But my cousin does." The kid gave her a grin missing his two front teeth. "She gets eight nights of presents. I think that's cool, huh? So, can we light it? It's Chanukah now, isn't it? We're going to my cousin's house tomorrow to eat hash browns and sour cream."

"Latkes." Amanda laughed and caught Ben's gaze over the top of the kid's head.

"I like them with applesauce," Ben said.

Amanda grinned. "Yeah. Me, too."

With the refreshment table well on its way to destruction and the candy canes either gobbled or transformed into an army of Rudolphs, Amanda had only a small amount of trouble wrangling the group into place in front of the menorah. Ben, she saw, was great with the kids, encouraging them to settle cross-legged on the floor and hush while she plugged in the menorah. It was brand new, still bearing the price tag, none of the orange bulbs dusty or worn. Much nicer than the older one she'd left in the closet the past few years because she'd been afraid it would short out and start a fire, and because nobody in the home had seemed interested in lighting one.

"Who can tell me about what holiday we're celebrating right now?"

Cries of "Christmas" and "Jesus' birthday" and "Frosty the Snowman" rang out, but the kid who'd asked if they could light the menorah stood up and waved his hands around until everyone looked at him.

"It's Chanukah," he said proudly.

"Who knows the story of Chanukah?"

No hands went up this time. Amanda looked around the room, thinking of how best to condense the story of the Maccabees and the miraculous vial of oil, when Ben stepped up and began speaking, mesmerizing kids and adults alike with his richly detailed retelling. He laced the story with humor and drama, keeping everyone's attention until the very last, when he turned to show them the menorah in the window.

"So, we light the menorah for eight nights to commemorate the oil that burned, and to celebrate the victory of the Maccabees over their enemies."

"And eat hash browns! I mean latkes," Josh cried out.

Amanda stepped aside to let the kid turn the bulbs to light the candles. Then, as everyone grabbed a song booklet and broke off in groups to carol in the hallways, she hung back and snagged Ben's sleeve. He turned with an expectant expression, looking more relaxed than she'd ever seen him.

"That was great. You really had all the kids' interest."

He shrugged. "I like working with kids."

"They're all set to go sing. Do you want to go along? Or head out? I have to stay and clean up here."

"I'll help you."

They worked in efficient and companionable silence to tidy up the leftover craft supplies. She caught him looking at the menorah, its light bright and cheery reflected in the glass alongside the twinkling, multicolored glow from the tree behind it.

"Did you ever wish you could have one?" he asked her with a glance over his shoulder.

She joined him to look at both sets of lights. "What. A Christmas tree?"

"Yeah."

She shrugged, thinking about it. "No. Not really. I had plenty of friends with trees, and it's not like I didn't get my fill of it in school or the mall or, you know . . . everywhere. You don't have to work too hard around here to experience Christmas, not when it's basically the default setting. My parents never made a big deal out of it. Other people had Christmas, and sometimes we went over to the neighbor's house for it, but we had Chanukah, with eight nights of presents and latkes and dreidels and stuff like that. What about you?"

Ben had put his hands in the pockets of his jeans, rocking back and forth on his heels. "No. It never occurred to me that I could have a tree. Just that I definitely shouldn't want one. They're pretty, though."

"This whole time of year is pretty. Everything about it," Amanda said.

Ben, without looking at her, said quietly, "You're pretty."

From behind them came the soft shush of slippers on the tile floor. "Oh! You've lit it."

Amanda turned to see Norma. "Hi!"

"I had my grandson bring it for me. They won't allow burning candles in the rooms, you know," Norma said as an aside to Amanda, though her eyes were focused firmly on Ben. "Hello, I'm Norma."

"This is Ben," Amanda said.

Norma beamed. "Oh . . . Ben. Your neighbor, Ben?"

Amanda laughed. "Yes."

Norma nodded and gave them both a thumbs-up. She waved at the menorah. "It looks nice. I didn't want to keep it all for myself, so I brought it out here. My grandson and his wife are bringing my great-granddaughter here tomorrow so we can open gifts. Will you be here tomorrow night, Amanda? I'd like you to meet them."

She wasn't scheduled for the evening shift, but Amanda nodded anyway. "Sure, Norma. I get off at three tomorrow, but I'd love to meet them. What time?"

"Oh, around seven. The baby's only two, she can't be up too late. And you, Ben. Will you be back with our Amanda?"

Ben let out a small, huffing noise of surprise and shot Amanda a look. "Ummm . . ."

"Say yes," Norma prompted.

"Yes. That sounds great," Ben said with one of those looks at Amanda. "I'll be here."

Chapter 8

BEN HAD MET Amanda at the nursing home to light the menorah and spin the dreidel with Norma and her family. They'd stayed for homemade jelly doughnuts brought by Norma's son and his wife. Now, outside in the parking lot, Amanda was getting ready to give him a ride home.

It was starting to snow.

"Oh," she said, tipping her face up to the night sky and catching a few flakes on her tongue. "I love the snow."

"We're supposed to get about a foot," he told her.

Her eyes widened. "Shut the front door! No way."

"That's what I heard at work." Laughing, he watched her spin, arms stretched out wide. "You're so different from any woman I've ever known."

She stopped spinning, her eyes alight. "Is that a good thing or a bad thing?"

"It's not good or bad," he said. "It just . . . is."

The falling snow shifted in that moment, turning

from spare and floating flakes to thicker, heavier ones. Amanda looked at the ground, where the snow had started to accumulate. "We should head home, before the roads get bad."

Both of them were quiet in the short car ride, the radio playing softly to cover up the silence. He glanced at her now and then, tracing the outline of her face with his gaze. Knowing she could feel him looking at her by the way she'd every so often smile, even as she kept her eyes on the road.

In the Valencia lobby, both of them hesitated. The short walk from the car to the building had covered them both with swiftly melting snow. It glistened in her dark red hair, and moisture clung to her eyelashes. Her cheeks had pinked from the cold. She was laughing at the joke he'd told her, something simple and silly, a play on words he'd thought up at work but had obviously struck her as funny enough that even several minutes later she was still chuckling.

He wanted to tell her, then, everything. About his past, Galya and Levi, about leaving home and why he worked Friday night shifts at a coffee shop instead of for his father. He wanted her to know him, Ben realized, and he wanted to know her.

"Well," Amanda said, when he hadn't gathered the courage to speak. "Good night."

"Night." He paused at his door to watch her climb the first few stairs.

She looked over her shoulder, then turned slowly on her heel, one hand on the railing. "So, tomorrow night, I was going to make latkes. I usually invite everyone in the building. That includes you."

"That sounds great."

She grinned and hopped up the next couple of stairs with a wave. "See you tomorrow night."

"Tomorrow, then."

Inside his apartment, Ben stripped out of his damp coat and hung it on the hook by the door. He shed his jeans and flannel shirt, noting that it would be time to do laundry soon. Another chore he'd never had to think about when he lived at home. He took a long hot shower, letting the water pound away some of the tension in his neck and shoulders, and then he slipped into a bed with chilly sheets.

He thought about Amanda the entire time.

He thought about her until he fell asleep.

He was still thinking about her when he woke up.

BEN HAD BEEN wrong about the snow. Instead of a foot, just over eighteen inches had come down in the night. It sent the city into a flurry of plows and salt and cancellations. As nonessential personnel, Amanda had the choice of not reporting in for work, and she took the snow day without a second thought. She had two bags of potatoes and one of onions, a jar of minced garlic, and a jug of oil. She was ready.

She thumbed the number he'd given her into her phone. "Ben. Tell me you're not going in to work today."

"I'm definitely not," he told her. "Tesla closed the Mocha."

"Come upstairs with me and help cook the latkes for the party. We can watch Interflix and play cards. If you want," she added after a second.

She could hear the grin in his voice. "Sure. That sounds great. I'll be up in about ten minutes. Want me to bring anything?"

"What do you have to bring?"

"Nothing," he said after a second.

She laughed. "Just yourself, then. See you."

Humming, she slipped on an apron and pulled out all the ingredients she'd need, then streamed some tunes to the speakers she'd set up around the apartment. By the time Ben knocked, she'd already launched into an enthusiastic, if off-tune, rendition of "Sweet Caroline" that she was still singing as she flung open the door. " . . . ba-da-da . . . hi!"

To her delight, Ben came through the door to join her in the song, both of them doing a little shuffle step together in her living room just as the tune ended. "Neil Diamond. My mom was a huge fan, even if he did make those Christmas albums. Here."

Grinning, he handed her a small paper sack emblazoned with the Morningstar Mocha logo. Inside were a couple lemon scones.

"Yum, thanks." Without thinking, she pushed up on her tiptoes to kiss his cheek, but she caught him turning and her lips brushed his.

Amanda hadn't meant it to be anything more than friendly, at least not on the surface, but Ben pulled her close. The kiss deepened, but ended when he pulled back without letting go of her. Blinking, Amanda focused on his gaze, which looked cloudy.

"Sorry," he told her.

"No, don't . . . it's not . . ."

He let her go and she stepped back, embarrassed, uncertain. She hadn't meant to overstep but clearly had, that seemed obvious. At least until Ben pulled her into his arms and kissed her again. Harder, this time, one hand on the small of her back and one between her shoulder blades. Their lips parted and she caught the sweetest, briefest taste of his tongue before he withdrew again.

Amanda put her fingertips to her mouth. "Mmmm."

Ben ducked his head, his turn to look embarrassed. "Sorry."

"I'm not sorry," she told him. "So don't you apologize unless you wish that hadn't happened, and if that's true, then you can say you're sorry again, and we can just pretend it didn't. It'll only be a little awkward, but I'm sure we can get past it."

She'd spoken lightly, a touch of sarcasm tinting her words, but Ben must've learned her sense of humor, because he took her hands in his, the fingers linking. His thumbs stroked her palms briefly, that swift touch enough to send warmth trickling all through her. Him, too, she thought by the gleam in his eyes, no matter how many times he apologized.

"Okay. Not sorry."

Stories, everyone had stories, Amanda reminded herself as she studied him but couldn't figure him out. "C'mon. I told everyone to come around four, if they could make it. We have time to make the latkes and still watch a movie or something . . . if you want."

He nodded, following her into the narrow galley kitchen. "I want."

"Good." She glanced at him over her shoulder as he let go of her hand. "Do you want to shred the potatoes or cut the onions?"

AN HOUR LATER, interrupted by laughter and a pause to sample the scones he'd brought, they had a giant mixing bowl of shredded potatoes and onions mixed with some garlic, salt, and pepper. The oil was heating. Neil Diamond had shuffled off to be replaced by Kenny Rogers, who, as it turned out, Ben did not know how to sing along with.

"Neil Diamond is Jewish," he explained when Amanda asked. He was washing the bowls and utensils while she set out a platter for the finished latkes. At her look, he laughed. "Yes, even with the Christmas albums. We didn't listen to pop music, unless it was somehow Jewish. Or classic rock. My dad had a vinyl collection that was out of this world. Original Stones, Zeppelin, The Who . . . He'd listen to them in the basement den only, and we weren't supposed to know. But I'd sneak down sometimes and listen at the door. Great music."

"He had to hide the fact he listened to it?"

"He didn't have to, I guess. But he did. He didn't want anyone outside the family knowing, because there would've been talk. Just like he'd sometimes put on jeans and an old concert T-shirt while he was down there, but you'd never have seen him in public that way. Ever."

Amanda pressed her lips together, trying to think of what to say. Ben's mysterious past was being revealed to her one tidbit at a time, and she didn't want to come off sounding judgmental. "I'm not sure I get it."

Ben set the final bowl in the drying rack and faced her, leaning against her counter with his arms crossed. "My parents met in Israel when they were doing a year course program before college. Neither of them had been Orthodox growing up, but somewhere along the way they decided they wanted to be *frum*. Observant."

"I know what it means," Amanda said.

Ben gave her a small smile. "Do you?"

"I know what the word means," Amanda said. "If you're asking me what being observant means, I have a good idea. Maybe not every detail, but yeah."

"There are a lot of rules."

Amanda nodded. "My dad says that some people thrive on making rules, and some people thrive on breaking them."

"I believe that. Anyway, they thought about making aliyah and staying in Israel, but decided to move home so my dad could come back and take over his dad's store. He made it kosher, opened another in the next town over, then another sometime after that. The family business had been pretty small, but he's made it into something a lot bigger. More successful." Ben frowned, then shrugged and looked past her to the stove. "The oil looks hot."

It sounded like he was trying to deflect the conversation, so Amanda didn't push. Instead, she took heaping spoons of the potato/onion mixture and settled them into the sizzling oil, smooshing them flat so they could fry. Behind her, she felt Ben looking at her.

"He always assumed I would simply jump right in. He never asked me if I wanted to."

She nodded, concentrating on flipping the frying latkes. Spatula in hand, she turned to him. "And you don't want to."

"No. I don't."

"And you don't want to be observant," she said quietly, thinking of the Friday nights she knew he worked and the sandwich he'd eaten from the gas station.

Ben didn't say anything at first. He hitched a breath, shoulders rising and falling. He covered his eyes for a moment with the palm of his hand, but when he looked at her, his gaze was clear.

"To be honest with you, Amanda, I have no idea what I want."

Carefully, so as not to splash burning oil, she slid the finished latkes onto the plate layered with paper towels to catch the grease. Though they were still hot, she took one and tore it in half, blowing on it before handing it to him. "The good news is, you don't have to decide right this minute. Do you?"

Ben tossed the latke from hand to hand before biting into it with a happy sigh. "No. I guess I don't. Wow, this is good. Really, really good."

"Good." She handed him the spatula with a grin. "You take over the frying. I'm going to make some brownies."

BEN HAD MET a few of the neighbors before, but now with Amanda's living room full to bursting with people, he was having a hard time keeping everyone's names straight.

"Quite the party," said the short guy with big dark glasses who'd introduced himself as Damien.

He shared the second floor apartment directly above Ben's with the couple sitting on the couch. Mark and Tina, Ben remembered. They had a dog, which explained the occasional thumping and scratching that he heard overhead.

Ben nodded. "Yeah."

"I love these lat-key things, man. Last year was the first time I ever tried them, and I'm hooked. I actually went out and bought some of that boxed mix from the ethnic aisle in the supermarket." Damien lifted his plate of greasy latkes smothered in applesauce. "They can't come close to this, you know what I mean?"

He sure did. Amanda and he had slaved over the frying pan for hours, taking turns flipping the latkes. They must've fried over a hundred, and most of them were already gone. "Good stuff."

"So, Ben, what do you do?"

The conversation meandered that way, subject to subject, interrupted as other guests mingled. Ben talked about the snow, his job, New York City, applesauce versus sour cream, and his opinion on dogs—and all the while, no matter who he was talking to, he found his gaze wandering back to Amanda. Her cheeks flushed, that dark red hair pulled up into a messy bun, her brown eyes sparkling with laughter. She wore a loose fitting sweatshirt decorated with dancing dreidels and stars of David that said HAPPY CHALLAH DAYS, and she had to keep pushing the sleeves up her arms because they were too long.

He couldn't get the taste of her out of his mouth.

After the latkes but before the party started, they'd turned on the TV to a movie the name of which he could not longer remember, because ten minutes into it he'd found himself pulling her onto his lap to kiss her. Long, slow kisses that had set him on fire, the feeling of her curves beneath his hands, the way her breathing had sighed into his ear when she tipped her head back so he could get to the smooth skin of her throat. It would've gone further had the first guest knocking at the door not interrupted them.

He didn't know how to feel about that.

All he did know was that he couldn't stop his gaze from finding her, or from smiling when she smiled at him from across the room. That was the problem, wasn't it? he asked himself as he tried to drag his attention back to the conversation he was having with Gladys Barnes, who lived in the other ground floor apartment. He couldn't stop himself from focusing on the sensual rather than what was right in front of him. He didn't know what was worse—his inability to keep his mind from wandering to how it had felt to kiss Amanda, or that he couldn't stop himself from figuring out how he was going to get to kiss her again.

"Excuse me," he said to Mrs. Barnes. "It was nice meeting you."

Without waiting for her to reply, Ben pushed through the crowd toward Amanda's front door. The temperature in the room had grown too warm, or maybe it was the flush of embarrassment flooding him; either way, he needed to get out of there so he could catch his breath. She saw him leaving, she knew he did, so he stopped himself on the landing outside her front door.

She came out a few seconds later, her brow furrowed. "Hey. You okay?"

"I got too hot. I think I'm going to head down to my place. The party was great. Thanks for inviting me. And for . . . everything." Great, cue the stumbling awkwardness. How could he explain that he'd been raised not even to shake a woman's hand, much less kiss her until they both couldn't breathe . . . at least not until they were married.

"Ben."

He stopped in his tracks to turn, giving her the courtesy of meeting her gaze.

"Did I do something wrong? Or . . . Look, if you're just not into me, that's cool. But I wish you'd tell me." Amanda shook her head, frowning, and he hated that he'd been the one to make her feel that way.

He hated that he'd made her doubt anything about herself at all, when this was him. All him. So instead of being honest, he messed up again by reacting without thinking. He pulled her against him and kissed her again. Then all at once she was up against the wall with his body pressing hers, and it was amazing and wonderful and he couldn't get enough. He wanted more.

"Benyamin?" The deep male voice pulled Ben out of the kiss and he turned, heart already sinking, already knowing whom he'd see and what a disappointment he continued to be.

"Abba," Ben said, aware Amanda's fingers were still linked through his and his mouth was still half open and wet from her kisses. He let go of her hand, but gently, not moving away. He gestured toward the man in the black coat standing a few steps below them. "This is my father."

Chapter 9

THE MAN ON the stairs did not look like he'd listened to classic rock while wearing an old concert T-shirt. He wore dress pants and a button-down shirt beneath a long black coat, along with a blatant expression of parental dismay. He bore such an unmistakable resemblance to Ben that even if he hadn't introduced him, Amanda would've guessed it was his dad. Instinctively, she stepped forward to offer her hand.

"He won't shake it," Ben said in a low voice.

She'd heard of Orthodox men and women who didn't shake hands with the opposite gender, but this was the first time she'd experienced it. She and Ben's dad eyed each other, assessing, as she withdrew her offered hand. She tried a smile. It wasn't returned.

"I came to talk to you, and you weren't home," Ben's father said, dismissing her. "I heard noise. And this is how I find you?"

Ben glanced at her. "Let's go into my place."

"Why? Are you ashamed of your behavior?"

"No," Ben said sharply. "I'm afraid I might be ashamed of yours."

Amanda winced at the sight of Mr. Schneider's expression—Ben might as well have reached out to slap him. The older man narrowed his eyes, then sighed, looking so sad it hurt Amanda's heart. He put his hand on the railing and shook his head.

"I didn't come here to fight with you, Benyamin."

"No? Then why did you come here?"

Ben's father shrugged. "To see if I couldn't convince you to come home."

"I don't want to come home."

"I'll just . . . umm . . . Ben, I'll see you later?" She hadn't meant for it to be a question, but there didn't seem to be any other way to phrase it.

"Yeah, sure." Without a look back at her, Ben pushed past his father on the stairs and headed down, leaving the older man to stare at Amanda.

She gave him a steady look in return, refusing to look embarrassed. "Mr. Schneider, we're having a Chanukah party with latkes, if you'd like to come in."

"You're Jewish?"

"That's what your son asked me the first time we met, and he sounded just as surprised." She couldn't stop herself from sounding the tiniest bit sarcastic. "But yeah. I am. My latkes are kosher, too, if you want to know."

"You keep kosher?"

"I'm a vegetarian," she said, aware she sounded defensive, and not sure why she cared the least little bit about what this guy thought. Other than he was Ben's father, and she liked Ben a whole lot. "So yes. By default, right?"

"I should go see my son."

"I guess you should." Amanda's smile felt brittle, but she forced it, anyway. She was at her door when his voice called her to turn around.

"I only want what's best for him, you know," Ben's dad said. "If you're a good friend to him, you'd want the same."

She didn't have an answer for that, so they stared at each other a moment longer before Mr. Schneider went down the stairs.

THEY'D ARGUED FOR hours, and now sat across from each other at the battered dining room table Ben had bought from a thrift store. None of the chairs matched. The one his father sat on had one leg a bit shorter than the other, enough to make it rock with every movement.

"We can make it all work all right," his father said now. "That girl, she's going to marry your friend."

Ben rubbed his temples, then got out of the chair to pace. Debating. Lying to his father had been one of the worst things he'd ever done, even if his reasons had felt right at the time. "I know."

"Who told you?"

Ben turned to face him. "I knew before I left."

Understanding dawned on his father's face. More disappointment. Ben thought he should be used to seeing it by now but knew he'd never be.

"Ah."

That was it. Just Ah? No diatribe, no lecture, no guilt trip?

"You could still come home, son." His father sounded weary. Worse, he looked . . . old. "We want you to, no matter what happened with Galya and Levi."

"It's more than that."

His father pressed the palms of his hands to his eyes for a moment before looking at Ben again. "Benyamin, I know you struggle with a lot of things. You question. You study. You argue against the rules. You're a lot like I was, when I was your age . . ."

"When you were my age, Abba, you were listening to hard rock and wearing jeans and eating cheeseburgers," Ben answered calmly. "You went to the prom."

"And when I got older, I realized all those things had done nothing to lead me toward a religious life."

Ben shrugged, knowing that no matter what he said, his father was probably never going to understand. "I think everything that ever happened to you is what leads you toward your life, religious and everything else."

"Are you saying that eating *treif* is going to somehow make you a better person?" His father's voice rose, then quieted with an obvious, concerted effort.

Ben shook his head. "No. But I don't know that being unable to flick a light switch on Shabbat is really going to keep me away from *Ha-Shem*. I don't think that finding the person I want to marry and raise children with means that she is responsible for preparing a huge feast every Sabbath, but has to do it without making her life easier by using the microwave. I think it's about being together with the people you love and spending time in contemplation and prayer, not how strict you are about using electricity."

His father got up to pace. "You know why we set those restrictions—"

"Yeah, the fence around the Torah, to keep someone from accidentally breaking one of the commandments. I get it, but you know what, I guess I believe that if we're supposed to think and study and argue to really understand what *Ha-Shem* wants from us, it's not necessary to add on all those other things just in case we get it wrong. For someone else to have decided what I'm capable of doing or not."

His father turned, looking defeated, shoulders slumped. "I don't want to see you fall away, Benyamin."

"I'm trying to figure out where I fit. That's all. You can't decide for me. Your parents didn't decide for you," Ben pointed out. "You chose. Like I'm trying to choose."

"I moved up the ladder. You're trying to jump off it."

Ben didn't answer that. His father gave a heavy sigh and gripped the back of the chair as though he needed it to hold him up. He shook his head.

"I don't want to work for you, Abba. I'm sorry. And I don't want to come home, not yet."

"Is it because of her? That woman?"

Ben shook his head. "No."

"But you like her."

"I do like her. A lot," Ben said.

His father sighed again, then straightened. He

squared his shoulders. "There's nothing I can say to make you change your mind?"

"No."

"You're breaking your mother's heart. I understand if you hate me, I've been hard on you. But your mother deserves better than this. Where did we go wrong?"

That was it, the last straw. "Enough. Okay? Just . . . enough. You don't have to like my choices. Honestly, I don't like all of them, either. But I'm trying to figure out where I fit, and that's my journey. Not yours. If you want to see where a road leads," Ben said after a moment, "you need to start walking it. And no matter what road I'm on, you should be able to love me anyway."

"I could never not love you." His father looked startled. "How could you even think that?"

"Then let me make my mistakes, whatever they are!" Ben shouted so loud his dad took a step back.

They stared at each other, both breathing hard. Both angry. Then his father nodded.

"You can stay here, if you want," Ben said after a moment. "You could come upstairs to the party. You could meet Amanda for real. You could spend some time with me, just . . . we could just spend some time together."

"No. I'm staying with Reuben Silver's son-in-law and daughter. They're *shomer* Shabbos. I'll be with them until Sunday, and then I have a train home. I won't ask you to be on it with me. But . . . Benyamin, the offer will always be there."

After that, they didn't have much to say. Ben thought about offering his hand to his father at the door, but didn't. His father hesitated, looking as though he might say something, but then to Ben's shock, he pulled him close for a hug.

"You can always come home. You know that. And if you don't want to come home, at least call us once in a while to let us know you're all right, okay? We're your family. We love you. Whatever road you're on."

Ben nodded, not trusting his voice. When he closed the door behind his father, he leaned against it, eyes closed, thinking very hard. Still uncertain about which path he wanted to take, only that he knew he was still trying to figure it out.

Chapter 10

Amanda hadn't seen Ben since the Chanukah party. Hadn't heard from him. She'd thought about at least sending him a text or leaving a note on his door, but in the end decided against it. He knew how to find her, if he wanted, and she wasn't sure he did.

This was the last night of Chanukah. Although she hadn't been scheduled to work at the home, Amanda decided to go in anyway, to light the candles with Norma. She'd brought the elderly woman a fuzzy blanket wrapped in festive dancing dreidels paper, because one of Amanda's favorite things about the holiday season was giving presents.

"So soft." Norma ran a hand along the fabric and beamed at Amanda. "Where's your young man?"

"Oh. He's . . . well, I don't think he's my young man."

Norma patted the blanket and settled it over her knees. "Are you sure? He looked very enamored of you."

Amanda smiled. "I think he has a lot going on in his life, and I don't think there's room in it for me right now."

"That sounds complicated."

"Yeah." Amanda paused, then let it all out. "His father showed up a couple days ago. They've had a falling out. Ben didn't really tell me why or what, but his dad wanted him to come home."

"Do you think he wants to go home?"

Amanda shrugged. "To be honest, Norma, I'm not sure what Ben wants. I thought he liked me . . ."

"He kissed you?"

"I kissed him."

"And he kissed you back?"

Amanda nodded.

Norma smiled. "Then does it matter who did what first?"

"I think it does. I can't explain why, except that I don't think he would have. I think he went along with it, but I definitely pushed the issue. And I get the feeling he's not into it. Or maybe not ready for it. Anyway, I haven't heard from him since then, and," Amanda lifted her chin, keeping her voice steady even though it felt like she might cry, "listen, I don't need to put up with some hot and cold guy who doesn't approve of me unless we're making out. Or whatever. And then judges me for it. And then blows me off."

"Or whatever," Norma said gently, with a tilt of her head to eye Amanda up and down. "He was raised differently than you, no?"

"Yeah. A lot."

Norma nodded. "It must be hard for him to break away from that."

"Well . . . it's not like I asked him to," Amanda said. "And it's not like I'm completely ignorant about what it means to be observant. It's just . . ."

Norma waited quietly for a moment or so, then prompted, "It's just what, dear?"

"Well, I've had a guy break it off with me because I was Jewish," Amanda said in a hard voice, hating the memory, which even now felt like a knife in the gut. "But I've never had one break it off with me because I wasn't Jewish enough!"

"And you think that's why Ben doesn't want to keep seeing you?"

"Maybe he didn't like the way I kissed. Would that be easier to handle? I don't know." She'd tried to make a joke, but it came out sounding flat and hurt.

"Men. Love. All this *meshugas*, no? Craziness," Norma added when Amanda looked confused. "All this craziness for the sake of love. It hurts, dolly. I know. I'm sorry."

Amanda drew in a breath. "It's fine. It's not like we had something, really. Just a few dates, some kisses. I'll be fine."

She didn't feel fine, though. That was a lie. She hadn't felt anything close to being okay since she watched Ben walk away with his father without so much as a look back over his shoulder at her.

She stayed awhile longer with Norma before heading home. Hating herself for it, she drove slowly past Morningstar Mocha, but she couldn't tell if Ben was working tonight or not. By the time she got to her parking spot, more snow had started falling. She stood on the street, looking at all the windows aglow with Christmas trees and a few menorahs here and there. The Festival of Lights, she thought. The time of miracles. Well, if she got herself inside and into a hot bath with a glass of white wine without letting herself burst into tears, that would be a miracle.

"Amanda."

Of course it was Ben. Of course. Looking handsome in a dark peacoat over jeans, his head bare and covered in melting snow. His dark eyes intense. He'd shoved his hands deep into his pockets, shoulders hunched, and looked cold, as though he'd been walking for a while.

She didn't answer him.

Not to play some sort of game, making him jump through hoops, but because she knew the moment she opened her mouth, she would either blurt out something embarrassing like "Why don't you like me?" or she'd simply start to sob. Pain was pain, no matter how little you wanted to feel it, no matter how stupid you told yourself the reason was for letting yourself hurt.

"I'm sorry," Ben said.

She could manage an answer to that. "For what?"

"For walking away from you like that, not telling you what was going on. For not calling you since."

He sounded sincere, and it was more of an apology than many men had given her in the past. She tipped her face to let some soft snow fall on her closed eyes while she thought how to answer. It wasn't okay, and saying so wouldn't make it.

"I thought we had the start of something," she said at last, still not looking at him. "I was willing to see where it went. I guess I was moving too fast."

His self-conscious laugh made her open her eyes. Ben was shaking his head, looking embarrassed. "I . . . it's just . . . Amanda, I have so many things to tell you, and I'm not sure where to start. But maybe we can talk about them inside? It's cold out here, and I just got off shift and walked home. My feet are soaked."

"I can make cocoa," she told him. "With marshmallows, even."

His grin warmed her, even though she was wary and didn't want to let it. Upstairs, she heated some soy milk and cocoa powder, added some sugar, and pulled out a bag of kosher marshmallows from the cupboard—kosher not because she kept the dietary laws, specifically, but because they were also vegan. Together, they sat across from each other at the dining room table, steaming mugs in their hands. She watched him blow to cool the cocoa; he looked up and caught her looking. She didn't care.

"I have some things to explain to you," Ben began, but stopped. She waited. He sighed. "It's a bunch of stuff."

"I'm not going anywhere."

"Her name was Galya," he said. "We'd known each other since we were kids. Her parents and mine were friends. They lived just a few houses down the street. They'd come over for Shabbos or we'd go there, and it just grew into something else over time. Everyone assumed we'd be together. They all wanted it. And I didn't think

I had another choice, really. It was what would've made everyone else happy. So, I asked her to marry me."

Amanda's stomach sank, but she tried not to let it show. Her fingers tightened on the mug, though. Ben noticed.

"I loved her, Amanda, but the truth was, I think it was because she was all I really knew. She was safe. My family loved her. She knew how to keep a kosher house, so she would've happily moved into the position of observant wife. She wanted me to work for my dad so she could stay home and raise our kids. She wanted to walk to synagogue and live in Brooklyn her entire life, blocks away from the house where she grew up."

"But . . . ?"

"Those were all the things *she* wanted," Ben said. "It confused her and hurt her feelings when I started talking about wanting to do more than that. I wanted to travel, see the world."

"And you wouldn't have been allowed?"

"Being *frum* doesn't restrict you from seeing the world or learning new things," Ben explained, "But it does make it complicated to travel, if you're trying to keep strictly kosher or observe the Sabbath and holidays. Living an observant Jewish life means a lot of rules, structure, guidelines. There are always times when you can bend the rules, I think, let's say by eating vegetarian in restaurants that aren't kosher. But there are a lot of observant people who won't do even that, because even if they're not eating meat, without a rabbi's approval they can't be sure that something unkosher had never touched their plate.

That sort of thing. I was willing to make compromises to the rules, and I didn't feel like it compromised who I was or what I believed. Galya wasn't. It didn't occur to her that you could love *Ha-Shem* and want to be a good Jew and still, every once in a while, watch some TV on a Saturday afternoon."

Amanda sipped her cocoa, not sure what to say. "So . . . what happened?"

"She fell in love with my best friend, Levi. He'd also grown up with us. He's really committed to being observant and Orthodox. He talks about making *aliyah* one day. He loves her. I think he always has. More than I did."

"And . . . she loves him?"

"Yes."

"When did that happen?"

"I don't know. Somewhere along the way she and I grew apart, and it became her and him. I never asked them, exactly. I just knew," Ben said. "And she'd have married me even though she loved another man, because she'd promised. Because our families and friends expected it. She'd have shackled herself to me and been miserable for the rest of her life. Both of us would've been. I couldn't do that to her. I made it like I broke it off with her, so nobody would blame her for anything, nobody would think she and Levi had done anything wrong. Then I moved here. And I met you."

"You met me," she agreed.

"And here we are."

The cocoa had gone cold, so she pushed it aside to link her fingers together. "I grew up Reform. I became Conservative when I left home to move here, because I liked the Conservative synagogue better. I hardly ever go to services except for the High Holidays, but there are times I'll go for a Friday night service because it's close enough that I can walk, and I like the fact they always have a really nice bunch of desserts for the kiddish. I've taken a few classes there, and sometimes in the summer I help out with the camp programs for kids, doing the crafts. I'm a vegetarian and have been for years, and you want to know something? One of the reasons *was* because being a vegetarian means I'm kosher by default. No worries about mixing meat and dairy if you don't eat meat. But do I worry about if the plate I'm eating off once had meat on it? Not unless it clearly hasn't been washed, and that's more of a yuck factor than anything religious."

When he didn't speak, she went on.

"I grew up Jewish but went to public school. We had a menorah but my mom really loved coloring eggs, so that's what we did for Passover. Being Jewish is a part of me, Ben. It's not everything I am, but it's a huge, important part, even if it's not as rules observant as you were raised."

"I can see that." He looked toward the menorah in her window. "You didn't light it tonight."

"I went to the home to do it with Norma. I didn't have a chance to do it here."

He stood and went to it, looking over his shoulder. "You want to do it now? With me? It's the last night."

Together, they lit the candles. The glow was bright enough to reflect from the window glass back into the room, especially after she turned off the lights to enjoy it more. Side by side, they watched the flames.

"I always liked to watch from the window outside," Amanda said after a few seconds. "Want to go out there with me?"

Ben smiled at her. "Amanda, I'm beginning to think that I'd like to go almost anyplace you'd like to take me."

Laughing, she knuckled his arm. "That might be the smoothest line a guy ever gave me."

"But it worked, right?" he asked her when they were downstairs on the sidewalk, looking up at the glow from her window. "My smooth line?"

Amanda wrapped her scarf closer around her throat and looked at him. "Yeah. It totally did."

"Good." His grin softened as he met her gaze.

Amanda didn't move, not even when Ben reached to snag her sleeve and tug her closer. The wariness must've shown in her face, because though he didn't let go, he didn't keep pulling. He let his hand slide down her sleeve to take hers, and squeezed her fingers.

"I have a lot of stuff I need to get worked out. Things I want to do and see, things about myself I'm not sure I understand, but I'm trying to," he said. "I'm a huge mess, if you want to know the truth."

She squeezed back. "Who's not?"

They both looked again up at the menorah, the candles burning low now but still casting out a strong yellow glow that made shadows on the snow.

"I mean . . . I'm not sure it would be fair of me to drag you into it, that's all. I like you a lot, Amanda."

"I like you, too," she told him. "I'm not sure why you think you'd be dragging me into anything. To be honest, Ben, as long as you're telling me what's going on in your head instead of hiding your thoughts, I can probably roll with it."

His brow furrowed. "I don't want you to feel like you have to take on my stuff. I don't know how long I want to stick around, what I want to do or go or where I want to live, or if I want to eat cheeseburgers or not, or anything like that. It's a lot to ask of someone."

"Not too much to ask of a friend."

He smiled. "And if I think of you as more than a friend?"

"Oh, well, in that case," she said, feigning a casual attitude she definitely didn't feel, "then I guess we'll have to have another sort of conversation."

"I just don't know what's going to happen, Amanda. That's all. And I'd hate for you to get pulled into something with me and then get hurt. Or disappointed."

"You know the miracle of the oil?" she asked him. "How they only had enough for one night but it lasted all the eight nights until they could get more?"

"Of course. Sure."

Still squeezing his hand, she faced him. "Well, I always figured that people were like that bottle of oil. You might think you only have enough for one night, but guess what. When it really comes down to it, you find you have enough to last eight. Hearts work that way. You might believe you can't open up to anything but one small thing, and the next thing you know . . ."

"You're burning?" he asked with a grin that lit his gaze, that intense gaze that sent shivers all through her.

She nodded. "Yes. Exactly."

"Well," he told her as he pulled her closer, and this time, she let him. "I'm hardly the guy to talk to about disproving miracles. Not when there's one right in front of me."

Her face had been tipping for his kiss, but that stopped her. "Huh?"

"Out of all the people I could've met here, I found you. And you're amazing, and wonderful and smart and kind and generous and understanding." Ben's mouth brushed hers. "And I'm crazy about you. If you ask me, that's a miracle right there."

Amanda pushed up on her toes to kiss him a little harder. Just a little. "Happy Chanukah, Ben."

"Happy Chanukah, Amanda."

And maybe that was all the miracle anyone ever needed, she thought as his fingers linked in hers. Meeting the right person at the right time. Whatever else happened after that, well . . . they'd have to keep walking on that road.

Together.

A Dose of Gelt

Jennifer Gracen

Acknowledgments

First and foremost, thank you Stacey Agdern for getting me involved in this wonderful anthology. I owe you one! Thank you very much, Tessa Woodward and Gabrielle Keck—it was a true pleasure to work with you. And thank you to my agent, Stephany Evans of FinePrint Literary.

For my grandparents, Grace and Irving Cohen, and Bert and Philip Kelman.

Holiday dinners with them and the rest of the family over the High Holidays or on Passover are some of my most cherished childhood memories. They all were proud to be Jewish, and passing on the traditions of Judaism was important to them. I think they'd be delighted that an anthology like this exists, and that I got to contribute to it.

Chapter 1

Evan Sonntag couldn't catch his breath, couldn't think, couldn't do anything but pant and smile. Which was fine, since his girlfriend seemed to be in exactly the same state. Gazing down at her beautiful, flushed face, he pushed back strands of her straight blond hair that stuck to her damp forehead. They were both coated in sweat. Shifting, he pressed his lips to hers for a long hot kiss before rolling off of her.

"Oh my God," Shari Cohen managed between gasps for air. "That was wild."

He nodded and his smile grew wider. "Sure sounded like you enjoyed it . . ."

She snorted and lightly smacked his shoulder. "Shut up."

"Aw, c'mon now," he teased. "You know I love making you sound like that."

She rolled her eyes, but grinned. "Well," she panted,

"there was my cardio workout for the day. Now I don't feel guilty about skipping the gym to come back here and let you have your wicked way with me instead. Not. At. All."

He laughed and leaned in to kiss her again. "Glad to hear it. Be right back." He got out of bed and went straight to the bathroom to clean up.

Shari lay in his bed in content satisfaction. As she finally caught her breath, she felt the adrenaline ebb and the sweet, relaxing afterglow flow through her and over her. Somewhere below on the Manhattan street, a car horn blared long and loud. Bluish light from the lamppost just outside streamed through the fourth floor window. She just smiled and curled into the blankets. Evan's apartment was small, his bedroom even smaller, but it felt cozy to her instead of claustrophobic. She shared her apartment in Brooklyn with a roommate, and had a decent-sized bedroom. His place was tiny, but it was all his, and they could be alone together without worrying about Gail overhearing or seeing anything she shouldn't. Besides, Shari loved spending time with him in his Chelsea neighborhood. Or maybe she loved it so much because she loved him.

Evan got back into bed, immediately pulling her into his arms. She tipped her face to his, an unspoken but unmistakable request for kisses. His fingers sifted through her hair as he sipped from her lips, slow and sweet, making warmth ripple through her. Ohh, what he did to her. She adored him.

"So," he said, pushing her hair back from her face. "You really ready to meet the whole clan tomorrow?"

"You really sure you're ready for me to meet them?" she teased back.

"I don't know . . ." He grinned playfully, and she saw the spark of mischief in his warm brown eyes. "Yeah, I guess so."

She ran her hand over the dark scruff on his jaw, so soft and long now it could almost be considered a beard. She loved to play with it. "What train are we catching?"

"Six-oh-seven out of Penn," he said. "We'll be a little late, but that's fine. It's a party, not a trial date." He pulled her closer so his free hand could sweep up and down her bare back in deliciously slow strokes. "Speaking of court, what time do you have to be at work tomorrow? I'll set the alarm now."

"I wanted to get in at eight-thirty," she said, letting her fingers drop from his jaw to caress the sparse dark hair on his chest. "The Carter case is killing me. You?"

"We'll go in together." Again his smile turned playful. "I always like to go in at eight-thirty, you know that. You're the one who straggles in at nine most days. Slacker."

"*Straggles?* I do not straggle, mister. In fact, I do not believe I have ever straggled in my life." She leaned up and her brilliant blue eyes narrowed at him. "Nor am I a slacker. You wound me, sir."

He chuckled and cupped his hand around the back of her neck, pulling her mouth to his for more tender kisses. "I love you."

Her smile bloomed against his lips. "I love you, too."

Evan hadn't thought bringing a woman home to meet his family would make him nervous . . . but his leg wouldn't stop bouncing. Sitting beside his girlfriend on the train, his damn leg wouldn't stop bouncing, as it always did when he was nervous or had adrenaline to burn.

"You okay?" Shari asked, her brows puckering slightly as she studied him.

"Fine," he lied. "Just thinking about work."

She glanced at his bobbling knee, then back up to his face. They'd been dating for seven months now; she knew his tells. Her pale blue eyes narrowed on him. But she said, "All right," and went back to her phone to continue playing Words With Friends.

Evan raked a hand through his hair and turned his gaze back to the window. He hated how early it got dark in December. The only things visible were lights from faraway buildings as they whirred by. The window served more as a mirror; he could see his reflection clearly and Shari's profile next to his. God, she was gorgeous. The corner of his mouth lifted, he couldn't help it. She was a beautiful woman, inside and out. To him, her sharp mind and quick wit were matched by her physical beauty. Her straight, shoulder-length blond hair fell forward, hiding half of her sweetheart-shaped face. Her pale skin was soft, always enticing him to touch her, like a siren's song. Her curvy, luscious body had the same effect. But it was her eyes that always captivated him, that clear sky blue, sparkling with intelligence and humor.

Her remarkable eyes and direct manner were what had

drawn him in the day they met, at the company picnic in May. It was a sunny day in Central Park, and strange not to see all his colleagues in their business attire. He played Frisbee with a few of the guys, then eventually went to grab a beer and a hamburger from the long table covered in food. As he was about to grab a paper plate, he noticed a short, curvy woman in front of him, scooping bean salad onto her plate. Her wheat-colored hair hung loosely, her attractive figure clad in a sleeveless blue top and tan capris . . . something about her compelled him. She was just . . . *damn*. His eyes skimmed over her and desire started to simmer in his veins.

Suddenly, she glanced over her shoulder, her bright blue eyes pinning his, catching him in the act. His mind went blank. Those eyes . . . he could stare into them for a week and never get bored. She grinned wickedly and quipped, "I can *feel* you staring at me, you know. Like what you see?"

Damn, she was direct. And brazen. She'd intended to embarrass him, he knew that. But he recovered quickly, his eyes not leaving hers as he said, "Yes, actually, I do. But with no disrespect intended. With what's left of my dignity, I assure you it was a genuinely appreciative ogle." He took a deep breath and added, "God, I hope you're not married. Or this could be a little awkward."

Her brows lifted, a dimple appeared as her grin blossomed into a smile, and a hint of color rose in her pale cheeks. How she could be sexy and adorable at the same time, he didn't know, but she was. Then she said, "It could be more than a little awkward. Or, it could be a little interesting." Then she turned to him fully and held out her hand. "Shari Cohen. I'm single. And you are . . . ?"

From that day on, they'd been together.

They dated discreetly, not wanting to become targets of office gossip. A few of their closer coworkers knew, but that was it. Luckily, the midtown firm was big; almost two hundred people worked for Goldberg, Stein, & Hanrahan LLP. They were both in Family Law, but their offices were on different floors, which was why they hadn't met before. Evan had worked there for five years, building a solid reputation as a matrimonial attorney. Shari had just joined the firm in January and was a Women's and Children advocate. They rarely saw each other at work, perhaps bumping into one another on the elevator or in the cafeteria once in a while.

After the first week of texting and flirting, when they ran into each other in the company gym one evening, he asked her to join him for dinner afterward. From then on they were an item, and quickly fell into a routine. They'd text to see if they were free for the night, then both go to the gym around seven for a short workout. After, they'd meet somewhere to grab some dinner. And after dinner, a few nights a week, they'd go back to either his tiny apartment in Chelsea or the apartment she shared with a roommate in Fort Greene . . . and ravage each other. He hadn't told her, but the truth was, he'd never had such great sex in his life. Shari blew up the myth he'd had in his head of the nice, prim Jewish girl; she was a lion in bed, passionate and wild. He couldn't get enough of her. Especially on the weekends. With the extra time to spend together, they'd go out and explore the city. They went to movies, restaurants, or on long walks with no destination in mind. Sometimes they'd catch up on work at home, never getting out of their pajamas. And always touching, cuddling, getting naked and enjoying each other . . .

The relationship worked. They were good together. They understood each other's heavy workloads and long hours, never begrudging the other for that, as past lovers had for both of them. The sizzling attraction and curious interest blossomed into true affection and caring . . . then went deeper, into love. They fit so well, it was almost seamless. Evan had never been in a relationship where it felt so natural, so easy . . . so *right*. It both thrilled him and terrified him at the same time.

Working as a matrimonial attorney, he'd seen the flip side of love and the worst in people. Their nasty sides, the dark hostile ugliness that came out as divorces went through the process was enough to make anyone shudder and cringe. The horrible things said, the tit-for-tat, the petty bullshit as former spouses attacked each other as a case dragged on . . . Evan was thick-skinned and always stayed pleasant but removed, even when he felt sympathetic for a client. He had to, and they were qualities that made him a damn good divorce lawyer. But over the years, it had soured him on the idea of romantic love. He'd gotten to the point where he didn't even think he would ever marry or find someone to make him consider changing his position on that.

Until he met Shari.

She was all he thought about. Her intellect and boldness turned him on as much as her body did, if not more so. She had quick, cutting humor and made him laugh.

And her kind heart, hidden behind walls he'd been willing to climb, only sealed it for him. Shari was a rare find, and he loved her. He'd told her so in the fall, as they held each other close one night, and was elated to hear she felt the same for him.

So why the hell was he so nervous about bringing her home to meet his family? It was their annual party, celebrating the first night of Chanukah. Always held at his parents' house, the house he'd grown up in on Long Island, it was a low-key but important gathering for the Sonntag family. His older brother Mitch and wife and three kids would be there, his older sister Alison and husband and two kids would be there, his aunts and uncles, maybe a cousin or two, and, of course, his Bubby. His sweet grandmother had turned ninety-one that summer, God bless her, and someone would bring her from her nearby assisted living facility to the house. He adored his Bubby with all his heart and looked forward to seeing her. He wondered what she'd think of Shari. She'd likely interrogate him about her while his mom, dad, sister, and sister-in-law would make latkes from scratch, a team effort, and he and his brother would entertain the kids in the living room with video games, card games, and wrestling matches . . .

"You're smiling. You look adorable."

Evan turned his head. Shari's voice had broken through his thoughts, and she was gazing at him with a cute grin. The dimple in her cheek was adorable, and he wanted to kiss it.

"What are you smiling about like that?" she asked.

"Thinking about my family, and the party," he said.

"Like I told you, it's such a tradition in my family, the big party on the first night every year. Ever since they had grandchildren to spoil, my parents go all out." He reached for her hand and interlaced his fingers with hers. "It's nice. I hope you'll enjoy it. I think you will."

"I'm sure I will," she said, leaning in to drop a light kiss on his lips. He raised his hand to cup the back of her neck and hold her there so he could steal a few more kisses. Her mouth was warm and tasted of the peppermints she usually kept in her bag. Her kisses made him burn, made him want more. If they weren't on the train, he could easily lose himself in her.

She drew back with a smile, leaned her forehead against his and murmured, "I'm looking forward to meeting your whole family. It's sweet that you asked me to come. It, um . . ." A spot of pink warmed her cheeks and her voice softened as she said, "It means a lot. It does, doesn't it?"

"I suppose so." He sifted his fingers through her hair, silky soft against his fingers. "But hey, it's not a total ambush. I mean, you've met my parents . . ."

"We've had dinner once," she said. "It's not like I know them well. And you said *everyone's* going to be there. So I . . ." She looked into his eyes. "You're presenting me."

He snorted out a laugh, but nodded. "Well, it's time. You know I love you. They're all going to love you, too." He took her mouth in another long kiss and felt her hand squeeze his in his lap. I'm being an idiot, he thought. Tonight's going to be great. Everyone will like her, she'll like them, we'll eat too much, and we'll go home. No big deal. Not a big deal at all.

Chapter 2

SHARI HELD HER glass of red wine and stood in the corner of the living room, taking it all in. The house was lovely, a split ranch decorated in warm earth tones, welcoming and comfortable. She knew that Brenda and Gary Sonntag had lived in Oceanside for almost forty years, raising their three children there—Evan had told her that, along with some other things. His older brother, Mitchell, was married to Leslie, and they had two girls and a boy, all under nine years old. His older sister, Alison, had married her college sweetheart, and they had twin boys who were already in their early teens. The family was a close-knit group, Shari could see that easily. They talked, laughed, and bantered, filling the house with vibrant sound and warmth. The smells floating from the kitchen were heavenly, and Shari couldn't wait to taste what hinted to be a delicious meal.

She'd offered her help in the kitchen, but Evan's

mother had refused to let her, insisting she was a guest. Then Evan's father had poured her a glass of merlot and asked a few innocent questions about work, her family, did she like where she lived, those kinds of things. Evan had his hands full playing Xbox with his nephews in the living room, but kept glancing her way and tossing her a smile or a wink.

Evan. She was head over in heels in love with him, but had been careful not to let him know just how much. Nothing drove men away faster than a clingy woman. She'd seen it in her line of work one too many times. So, even though she considered herself to be strong and had never been shy with showing her affection, something in her held back at times with him, and she knew it. Because . . . he was too important to her. Because he mattered, their relationship mattered, and she didn't want to open herself up one hundred percent in case it went wrong, which she knew would leave her devastated.

She loved him more than she'd loved any other man. Though they hadn't really discussed a future together, taking those steps, she could easily envision a future with him. It was almost too much to take, so she swallowed it. Until she was sure he wanted the same things, and sure it would work out. Maybe that was wrong, holding back just how much she loved him. But for the past few months, it'd felt like the only way to survive the astounding power of her feelings for him. It overwhelmed her sometimes, how much she loved having him in her life.

But when he'd asked her to come to his family's annual Chanukah party—where she'd meet everyone who mattered to him most—she'd been delightfully surprised, and hope had sparked. Maybe it was a way of showing her what she meant to him, and showing his family, too. Maybe it meant he was ready to commit to something more serious. Or maybe it meant nothing and she was reading into it. She'd tried to get some info out of him on the train, but of course once he started kissing her, her brain melted and she lost herself in the feel of his mouth and his hands and gone all gooey. No one had ever affected her the way Evan did, physically or emotionally.

Shari slipped into the bathroom at the end of the hall. When she came out, Evan was standing there waiting for her. He pulled her into his embrace and dropped a sweet kiss on her lips, his arms banding around her waist. "Hi."

"Hi yourself." With a smile, her head tipped back as he trailed a line of kisses along her jaw, then down her neck. "What's this for?"

"Missed you," he murmured into her skin. His head lifted. "Also, you've been summoned."

Shari blinked. "Excuse me?"

"My Bubby's here. Got here with my aunt and uncle while you were in the bathroom." Evan quirked a grin. "She wants to meet you."

Shari's stomach rolled. "Oh. Okay. Um . . ."

"She doesn't bite," Evan teased.

"That's good to know."

"C'mon." Evan took her by the hand and led her back down the hall. The noise grew louder as they approached. She took a deep breath, squeezed his fingers with hers, and set down her wineglass on the dining room table as they passed it. When they entered the living room, Mitch had taken over gaming with the boys, and a sweet-looking old woman sat in the corner armchair, where she could survey the whole scene.

"Bubela!" Evan cried, as if he were the grandparent. "You look fabulous!"

"Yeah, I don't look a day over a hundred, right?" she quipped.

"You're a goddess." He let go of Shari's hand to crouch down and hug his grandmother. Shari hadn't known what to expect, but Rose Sonntag looked fairly spry for ninety-one. Thin and bony, with soft wrinkly skin and her silver hair cropped short, her dark eyes were clear and her smile and voice were bright as she hugged Evan back.

She gripped his face between her hands and rubbed his scruffy jaw. "What is this?" she asked. "You need to shave. You look like a rabbi."

Shari pressed her lips together to suppress a laugh. She loved Evan's dark scruff, found it sexy as hell. Apparently, his grandmother disagreed, and it was adorable.

"Bubby, it's cold outside," Evan said, seriously charming as he continued to hold her hand and crouch at her feet. "It's winter now. I need it to help keep me warm."

"You grew it to impress your girlfriend, I'll bet," Rose said with a mischievous smirk. "All the young men with their beards nowadays. You're hiding that handsome face. So? Where is she?"

Evan straightened and held his hand out to Shari. Suddenly overcome with uncharacteristic shyness, she stepped forward and slipped her hand into his. "Bubby, this is Shari Cohen. Shari, my grandmother, Rose."

"It's such a pleasure to meet you." Shari smiled, reaching out to shake the old woman's hand.

Rose smiled back, taking Shari's hand between both of hers. Rose's skin was cool and soft as velvet. She peered up at Shari and said, "Nice to meet you. Shari? Or is it Sherri?"

"Like Sharon, but with an *i* at the end," Shari said. "People have gotten it wrong my whole life."

"I like it," Rose said. Her dark eyes raked over her from head to toe, and Shari couldn't remember the last time she'd been so openly scrutinized. "You're a beautiful girl."

"Thank you," Shari said demurely, flattered and a touch self-conscious. She saw Evan watching their exchange as he stood beside her, intent and curious. She felt like she'd been summoned to meet the queen or something.

"You're so fair," Rose said, still looking her over. "Where are your people from?"

"Excuse me?"

"Your people. Your family, ancestors, whatever."

"Oh! Poland and Germany," Shari said.

"I thought so." Rose gestured to her grandson. "We're Russian, the Sonntags. Evan's Russian and Romanian, with a little bit of Hungarian mixed in there. Between you and him, you've got half of Eastern Europe covered." She raised a hand to her short hair. "This silver was black as night when I was younger."

Shari just smiled. Evan's dark good looks had made her swoon from the moment she'd laid eyes on him. Her fingers often found their way into his thick wavy hair, such a dark brown it was almost black. His full sensual lips were wonderful to kiss, beat only by when they curved into a beautiful smile. He was five-foot-ten, which felt tall compared to her five-foot-three, and his lean, solid body appealed to her more than she cared to admit. But it was his warm brown eyes that she loved the most. His steady, intense gaze made her feel adored and special when it was fixed on her . . . like it was now. She lifted a brow at him, and he winked in response. Something in her relaxed; apparently she was passing the test so far, if he was at ease.

"Sit, both of you," Rose commanded gently, gesturing to the nearby love seat. "Talk to me. You met at work?"

"We met *through* work," Evan said as he sat next to Shari. "Company picnic."

"We work for the same firm," Shari chimed in, "but different departments."

"She's in Family Law also, Bubby," Evan said, taking Shari's hand in his. "But she's Family Court, an advocate for women and children."

Shari was surprised he hadn't let her speak for herself on that, but warmed to the note of pride in his voice and let it go.

"Admirable work," Rose said, nodding in slow approval. Her steady, focused stare reminded Shari of Evan. No doubt about it: her hands had a bit of a tremor, her skin so paper-thin you could see the blue veins beneath, and her soft wrinkled face was kind, but Rose was still as sharp as a tack. Shari liked her immediately.

She went on to answer all of Rose's questions. "I grew up in Philadelphia. Yes, my parents are still married, and I have one older sister. Yes, she's married, too, and she has a little girl . . . Tufts for undergrad, Columbia Law School . . . worked as a public advocate before switching to the private sector a year ago . . . I share an apartment in Fort Greene with a roommate, my friend Beth . . . no, it's had a renaissance, it's not a bad area of Brooklyn, it's nice now . . ."

But Shari couldn't help but gape at the old woman with the last question in her amiable but assertive interrogation. "Excuse me?"

"Do you want to get married?" Rose repeated. "Have kids, have a family?"

Shari felt her face heat, and couldn't look at her boyfriend sitting right next to her. *Awkward!* She recovered quickly. "Um . . . yes, of course I do. Eventually."

"How old are you?" Rose asked without missing a beat.

"Thirty-one," Shari answered. "I'll be thirty-two in February."

"Mm-hmm," was all Rose said, but it was loaded with a million unspoken words that Shari had heard over and over from the day she'd turned twenty-nine. *Time's ticking away, better find a man, don't you want to get married, if you want to have kids you better not wait too long. . .*

"My career is important to me," Shari said. "But I'm sure one day I'll find a way to balance both."

"You're a smart, beautiful girl," Rose said. "I'm sure you will."

"Dinner's ready!" Evan's mother's voice rang out through the house. "Come to the table, everyone!"

Grateful for the timely interruption, Shari got to her feet. Evan had already risen and was gently helping his grandmother up from her chair. Shari loved watching how he doted on her, how sweet he was with her. In their time together, she often saw his quick, sharp wit, his strength, his self-assurance that on occasion bordered on cocky—all of which had made him only more appealing to her. But this side of him, Evan being the tender, attentive, and loving grandson to this feisty older lady . . . Shari fell in love with him a little more, a little deeper. God help her, she loved him so much.

Chapter 3

ONCE EVERYONE WAS gathered at the long dining room table, before they began the meal, Evan's father brought the menorah to the table and gathered his five grandchildren around him to light the candles. It was a beautiful menorah, ornate and detailed, a seamless blend of gold and silver. Gary lit the *shamash*, then gave it to the youngest to light the one candle for the first night. Everyone said the short prayer in Hebrew, in unison. It made Shari feel more like she fit in.

Having that common bond, murmuring the simple prayer that she'd memorized as a child like all Jewish kids had, she watched Evan as he murmured the prayer beside her. She hadn't always dated Jewish guys—in fact, she hadn't in a few years—because that didn't matter to her. She dated whoever made her hormones wail or who made her laugh or who she could have intelligent conversations with. She didn't discriminate because of religion.

But now, looking at Evan, she had to admit that coming from the same background certainly made some things easier. Things that went unspoken, that were understood, just by virtue of the same heritage.

It was good that Evan's family had their big party on the first night of Chanukah; her family usually got together on the last night, and she'd be making the trip back to Philly in a week. She had invited him to come, and he'd agreed. It was a smaller gathering than this one—she had a smaller family—but this was definitely the kind of family shindig she liked. The Sonntags were a vibrant, vocal bunch, talking and laughing over one another as they passed plates of food around. And the food was fantastic. There were the homemade latkes, bowls of applesauce and sour cream, roasted chicken, brisket, steamed broccoli, carrots in honey, and sautéed mushrooms and onions . . .

"Everything is delicious," Shari said to Evan's mother, tipping her head to make sure she could make eye contact. "Really. Just wonderful."

Brenda beamed visibly. "I'm so glad you're enjoying."

"I like a woman who really eats," Gary commented.

"Dad!" Alison, Evan's sister, shot him an annoyed glance.

"What? What'd I say?" Gary looked around. "I hate women who just pick at salads and say they're not hungry." He nodded at Evan. "Real women eat. Glad you found one."

Shari couldn't hold back the grin. Evan simply kept eating, eyes on his plate as he cut into his slice of brisket with gusto.

After dinner, Shari was allowed to help with cleanup. While she was in the kitchen with the other women, Evan went back to the living room to hang out with his brother, brother-in-law, and the kids. They were caught up in a game of Apples to Apples, laughing and loud. Rose was back in the cushioned armchair, watching them all play with a besotted smile on her face.

"Hey, lady." Evan dragged over a chair from the dining room and sat next to his grandmother. She meant the world to him, but every time he saw her, he was starkly more aware of just how old she was, and it saddened him a bit. Every time he left her at a family gathering, he had that quick moment of wondering if it'd be the last time he'd see her. Now, he took her soft, delicate hand in his. "How are you?"

"Fine, just fine." She raised her eyebrows and her smile turned playful. "Nice girlfriend you've got there."

Evan nodded. "I'm glad you like her."

"I do. A lot. How about you?"

He snorted out a laugh. "Yeah, I like her a lot, too."

"You gonna marry her, then?"

He blinked and stammered, "Uh . . . we've only been together a few months, Bubby."

"How long?" Rose asked.

"About seven months."

"You're thirty-three. Seven months is long enough to know if she's the one or not." Rose pointed a crooked finger at him. "And you haven't brought a girl home since college. So that means something."

He rubbed the back of his neck. "The thing is, Bubby . . . I don't know that I want to get married."

Rose's eyes flew wide-open. "Ever?"

"Maybe." He shrugged. "Don't know."

She stared at him for a few seconds, then proclaimed, "Anyone can see that girl's crazy for you. She's a wonderful girl—smart, driven, and she's got a good heart."

"You can tell all of that, huh?" Evan said, trying to lighten the sudden tightness in his chest with banter.

"Of course I can." Rose shook her finger at him. "She's good for you. You're happy with her, I can tell. So what's the problem?"

"You're being a yenta, that's the problem," he said good-naturedly.

"And you're being stubborn." She narrowed her eyes as she gazed at him. "That job of yours, it's poisoning you if it makes you not want to get married. That's what I think."

Evan didn't say anything. He'd thought that more than a few times himself, but he wasn't going to admit it out loud.

"Don't you want kids?" Rose asked in horror, as if the idea of him not wanting children was the worst fate on earth.

He shrugged again. "Yeah, someday. But . . . Bubby, let it be."

She pinned him with her stare, then shook her head slowly. "I'm telling you. You let that woman go, you're a fool. I love you, boychik, but you'd be a fool."

"Who said I'm letting her go?" Evan asked. His grandmother's words bothered him, and they shouldn't have. "We're dating, we're good, everything's good."

"A woman like that . . . you think she'll wait forever?" Rose tsk-tsked. "Okay. I'm being a little pushy. I'll stop now. Good luck. I wish you luck, sweetheart."

Shari appeared in the arched doorway. Standing there in her wine-colored cashmere sweater, black slacks, and heeled black leather boots, she was a picture of urban sophistication. She shot Evan a quick smile before saying to everyone, "They asked me to tell you it's time for presents."

The five kids all jumped up, yelling happily as they rushed to the far corner of the living room. The stack of wrapped gifts was wide and high.

"The fun part," Shari said to Evan as she approached him, giving Rose a warm smile as well.

"Yup." He stood and shoved his hands in the pockets of his jeans.

"Hey." Rose tugged on the edge of his navy sweater. "You remember what I said, eh?"

Something like annoyance flittered through him, but it didn't settle and stay. He loved his grandmother too much for that, and he knew she meant well. With a nod, he bent to drop a light kiss on her forehead. "Yes ma'am."

WHILE THE ADULTS sat on the couch, the chairs, even the plushly carpeted floor, the kids tore off wrapping paper on gift after gift.

"We made a pact a few years ago," Evan said quietly to Shari, "that all the adults would stop getting each other gifts, and only get for the kids. That's why they have so many."

Shari nodded. "Makes sense. Family gets bigger, gift-giving holidays get more costly."

"Got that right." He rested his hand on her knee and leaned closer to whisper in her ear, "Am I coming home with you tonight?"

She kept a straight face, but the corners of her mouth curved up. "You inviting yourself over?"

"Absolutely."

"Oh, all right, if you insist," she said in mock resignation. She smiled as her eyes met his, sparkling with promise.

He leaned back to survey the chaos around them, then slipped his hand into his pocket and pulled out a small, flat square wrapped in silver paper. "I, uh . . . I got you something. Happy Chanukah."

The smile vanished. Her eyes flicked from the box in his palm to his face and back again. "You didn't have to—"

"I know. I wanted to."

"But I didn't—"

"So what?" He pushed the tiny square into her hand. "Go on, open it."

She did as he commanded. Inside the box was a pair of earrings, deep purple stones set in white gold. Her eyes searched his. "Are these amethysts?"

"Yup. Your birthstone." He grinned and added hopefully, "Do you like them?"

"Yes! They're gorgeous," Shari said. "Wow. Thank you, Evan." She leaned in and pressed a kiss to his mouth. "You didn't have to do this," she whispered.

"I told you. I wanted to." He reached up and tucked a lock of silky blond hair behind her ear.

"You two are so cute," came his brother's voice from across the room. "I can't take you!"

Shari blushed softly as Evan shot him a dirty look and said, "What are you, twelve?"

"I think they're adorable," Rose said with approval.

Evan felt all eyes on him and Shari, and it made him bristle. "You know—"

He jumped at a vibration against his leg. Shari quickly pulled her cell phone from her pocket and glanced at it. "Client. I have to take this, I'm sorry," she said, already on her feet and walking away. "Shari Cohen," she said into it as she left the room.

"I like her, Evan." His mother wasted no time. "I like her a lot."

"She's great," his father agreed.

"I like that she's smarter than you," his sister chimed in.

At that, he glared at Alison. "How do you know? Why would you say that?"

"Because I know *you*," she said, obviously teasing. Evan rolled his eyes at her.

"So . . . you two are serious, huh?" his father asked.

"Are you thinking of marrying her?" his mother asked.

"He would if he had a brain in his head," his brother said.

"It's about time he settled down," his aunt piped in. "Don't you think?"

"Oh my God!" Evan cried. He held up his hands in a gesture of surrender. "Would you all stop? Just stop!"

"He doesn't want to get married," Rose informed the group.

"What?" his mother asked, her eyes darting to her youngest son.

"Why not?" his father demanded to know. "Your mother and I have had a good marriage, it's not like you grew up with a bad marriage. Suddenly you're against marriage? Since when?"

Evan opened his mouth to speak.

"It's his job," his mother said sadly. "Dealing with divorce day in, day out . . . probably changed his mind. Made him never want to get married."

"Can you blame him?" his uncle said.

"But Shari's great," his sister said. "Ev, you have to think about it."

"Well, he brought her home to meet us all," his brother chimed in. "That's something in itself, don't you think?"

"STOP!" Evan shouted. The room fell silent, even the kids, and all eyes were on him. He raked his hands through his hair. "Shari and I are dating. That's all. Just calm down, all of you. And stop talking about me like I'm not here!"

"She's the one for you," Rose said. "That's why you're scared."

He turned to his grandmother and looked down at her. The serious, almost omniscient note in her voice made the hairs on the back of his neck stand on end. She smiled up at him, nodded slowly, and repeated, "She's the one for you."

He opened his mouth to speak but couldn't think of anything coherent to say. His mind had gone blank. The kids were all staring at him and the adults gazing at him with varying degrees of curiosity or expectation. He raked his hands through his hair and said, "I feel like I'm on a crappy reality show, and all of you forgot to tell me."

Shari walked back into the room, stopping short at the doorway. It was obvious she'd picked up on the different vibe immediately; she looked around at the faces of Evan's family, then back to him. "Um . . . everything okay in here?"

"Peachy," Evan ground out.

Chapter 4

SHARI KNEW SOMETHING was off, but had no idea what, or why.

From when she'd walked back into the living room after taking a call from a client, Evan's demeanor had changed. Drastically. The smiles he gave her, which were few, didn't reach his eyes. In fact, he seemed tense and withdrawn, and the only warm good-bye he had for anyone in the family was for his grandmother.

Boy, did she like Rose, who was a character. She liked all of his family, actually. They'd treated her kindly, had been warm and welcoming. She thought the evening had been lovely and gone well . . . but now, even though they were alone on the train, Evan was quiet. He hadn't reached for her hand or kissed her at all. His jaw was tight and the crease that appeared between his brows when he was stressed hadn't gone away.

Halfway through the ride back to Atlantic Terminal,

she finally asked, "Are you going to tell me what's wrong, or do you just want to go home alone tonight?"

"Nothing's wrong," he said.

"For a lawyer, you're a lousy liar."

He snorted at that. "I'm . . . I've just got a lot on my mind, that's all."

She stared at him, searching for a clue. "Did I do something wrong?"

"No," he said immediately. He shook his head to punctuate that. "No, not at all."

"Did something happen with a member of your family?" she asked tentatively.

"We're not on the clock," he said, looking away. "Stop the cross-exam."

Her eyes narrowed. "I left the room to take a call, you were fine. I came back a few minutes later, you weren't fine. I don't need to cross-examine you to connect the dots, Evan." She sat back in her seat and crossed her arms around her middle.

He didn't say anything.

They rode in silence for the next three stops. When her stop was announced as coming up next, she said tersely, "You're not coming home with me tonight."

He frowned at her. "Now you're mad at me?"

"Yeah, a little." She buttoned up her coat. "You pulled a total one-eighty on me tonight and you won't tell me why. For the first time since we've been together, you're totally shutting me out. And it stings." She wrapped her scarf around her neck, fighting to keep her voice calm and steady. "You obviously want to be alone right now. So go home, be alone. That's fine. Maybe you'll feel like talking tomorrow."

"I don't know what I want," he blurted.

She stilled. A cold prickle ran over her skin, even though her wool coat was buttoned to the top. "What does that mean, exactly?"

"I don't know . . ." He ran his hands through his hair. His discomfort was palpable, radiating off him in waves. "You're right, we shouldn't go home together tonight. I just . . . need a little space."

The chill was stronger this time, not only skimming over her, but through her. What the hell had happened? Her mind raced but she couldn't think of anything. Something had gone on in the few short minutes she was out of the room, that was obvious. But Evan wasn't giving her an inch. "Define 'a little space,' please?" she asked.

The muffled voice of the conductor announced her stop. Evan leaned in and kissed her cheek, not even her mouth. "We'll talk tomorrow."

Her stomach roiled. But she rose to her feet and said, "Happy Chanukah." Grabbing her tote bag, she walked away from him and didn't look back. She got off the train, managed to get up the stairs, through the terminal, and to the street. A cold wind whipped at her, sending her hair all around and bringing tears to her eyes. Sniffing them back, refusing to give in to them, she walked briskly down the street toward her building.

EVAN BARELY SLEPT that night. He tossed and turned, punching his pillow several times, staring at the ceiling as his brain kept going and going.

He'd gotten completely freaked out, is what had happened. Plain and simple.

The more his family talked about how perfect Shari was for him, the more they got pushy and in his business and talked about marriage and all that . . . the more he'd started to panic. He felt that panic blossom in his blood, his stomach, and his chest— that tightness and chill and rush all combined.

Part of it was his fault, of course. He'd brought a woman home to meet his family. That usually transmitted a clear message to both the woman and the family: *I'm serious about this one.* If he thought otherwise going in, he really was an idiot.

But it wasn't like he'd brought her home for the High Holidays, for Pete's sake. Chanukah wasn't a serious, highly religious holiday, it was one of the festive ones. Chanukah was just supposed to be fun, lighthearted, and it *had* been. Shari fit in seamlessly with his family, and it'd been good to see everyone. Until they all started harping at him like a bunch of old matchmakers. The only one who was allowed to say stuff like that, pull stuff like that, was Bubby. And boy, had she. She never held back, that was for sure. He was glad she liked Shari so much, but she'd gone on and on . . . Evan rolled to his other side, sighed for the hundredth time, and scrubbed his hands over his face.

Shari. He'd pulled away from her, lost in his confusion

and caught in a bit of panic, and he'd hurt her. He'd seen it in those expressive sky blue eyes of hers, the way they flashed before she got up and left the train. Damn. He felt awful about that. But . . . he just couldn't be with her right then. He felt weirded out by her, it was the strangest thing. He needed some time and space . . . but to what end, he wasn't exactly sure.

Evan had gone into Family Law, and specifically become a divorce attorney, because he knew, unfortunately, there would always be a need for one. Steady work was assured. People broke up all the time.

What he hadn't been fully prepared for was just how ugly divorce cases could get. He'd seen and heard vile, horrible, disgusting things come from the mouths of his clients and their spouses . . . the true darker side of human nature. The nastiness, the bitterness . . . of course he was wary of marriage as a result. Who wouldn't be?

He'd had girlfriends in high school and college. His relationship history wasn't anything crazy; he considered himself fairly average in that respect. Not a player, but not a monk. He dated. Because he liked women. He just hadn't had the time to get serious—between law school, then starting his career, he had very little free time. It wasn't fair to start a relationship when his life was that busy, and it was simply not feasible. Keeping it casual was how it'd been for him for a few years.

Until he'd met Shari. From their first date, he got one taste of her and couldn't get enough. It was easier that she was a lawyer, too; she understood the long hours, the need to decompress on the off hours, how the job could take over your life sometimes. She was equally driven, equally intelligent, and their chemistry was red hot. It was about more than lust or attraction, though. They genuinely liked each other. They had things in common, and never ran out of things to talk about. Spending time with Shari was always a pure pleasure. Great. Easy. That was what had sealed it for him: she was so easy to be with. It felt totally right.

But he still wasn't sure he ever wanted to get married. He didn't think Shari had been pushing him for a ring or anything like that. Or had she, and he'd missed the signs? Suddenly, he was unsure. But once marriage had been brought up by everyone and they pounced on him, he'd needed a breather. *Shit.* He punched the pillow into a new formation for what must've been the twentieth time. He had to figure out why he'd gotten so spooked. Why he suddenly didn't want to be with her.

The look on her gorgeous face when he'd given her the earrings came into his head. She'd been so delighted. The joy was unmistakable, and it had made him . . . well, plain happy. Happy that he'd surprised her, and that she'd been so obviously touched by his gesture. And he'd been proud, too. Because he'd made this fantastic woman smile like that. Because this incredible woman loved him. Since they'd told each other how they felt in the fall—that magic yet heavy L word—he usually glorified in that. And if he said he hadn't started to wonder if a future together with her was something he wanted to work toward, he'd be lying to himself. He had. Just recently.

Now, suddenly, he was running away from her, fast and hard. Like he couldn't get enough air, or space.

What the hell was wrong with him?

He grunted and rolled over again. The glowing numbers on his clock seemed to taunt him. Almost three A.M. He had to be at work at eight-thirty. Maybe he'd call in sick. All he knew was . . . he didn't know what the hell his problem was. He just needed to be left alone. By everyone. Even Shari.

Especially Shari.

SHARI WASN'T NECESSARILY avoiding Evan, but she wasn't seeking him out, either. She didn't get her coffee at the Starbucks on the corner by the office, where she often bumped into him in the morning. She didn't find an excuse to be on his floor, near his corner, as she sometimes did. He'd pull her into his small office, close the door, and kiss her senseless for a few hot minutes . . . stolen kisses that kept her satisfied and happy for hours afterward. And she hadn't tried to contact him, in any way. No phone call, e-mail, text, Facebook message, nothing.

She hadn't heard from him, either.

And with each passing half hour, the knot in her chest expanded a little. She buried herself in her work, grateful for the distraction.

Finally, at eleven-thirty, her phone pinged with a text from Evan. *Hi.*

She glared at the screen. *Hi?* That was it? She could already feel her blood pressure rising. Why, he . . . She took a deep breath, exhaled it hard, and typed back, *Hi.*

How are you? he texted.

Not so great, she typed, then quickly deleted it and wrote, *Fine. You?*

Off kilter. I got to work a little late today, he wrote. *Didn't sleep well last night. Then I overslept.*

She frowned at that. Evan was never late to work and never overslept. Not to mention that she'd slept horribly, thinking back on the evening over and over as she tried to figure out what had gone wrong. Finally she wrote back, *That's not like you.*

Well, I'm not feeling much like me right now, he texted.

Her stomach did a nauseous flip. *Are you okay?* she wrote. She couldn't help herself. She was concerned, and she loved him. Even if she was upset, if something was really wrong with him, she wanted to help. To support him.

Let's talk over dinner, Evan responded. *You free?*

She swallowed hard. Her whole body was already buzzing with adrenaline, a nauseating mixture of apprehension and dread. No way could she stay like this, wondering and speculating, until dinner time. *Actually, I'm not,* she texted back. *Working late. How about lunch instead?*

He didn't answer right away. Then he texted, *Okay. Meet me at Scarpelli's at one?*

Sure. See you there.

Shari sat back in her chair, staring at her phone where it lay on her desk. Why did she have a sinking feeling she was about to get dumped?

EVAN READJUSTED HIS tie again as he waited for Shari. She was always on time, but today she was ten minutes late. Was she punishing him somehow? It was possible. It's not like she didn't know the place; they'd shared many meals there, usually holding hands and staring into each other's eyes like moony kids.

He saw her enter the restaurant and immediately knew there'd be no moony-eyed looks today. Her whole body seemed rigid as she approached him. His eyes raked over her, taking in her black pantsuit, royal blue silk blouse—he liked when she wore blue, it set off her eyes—and those sexy heeled boots that always sent a little jolt of lust through him. Her hair was pulled back and up, which made her eyes seem bigger, even more compelling than usual, and they pinned him now. She wasn't glad to see him. It was in her eyes, her body language, her posture. Dammit, she was on edge, and he knew it was his fault. He'd missed her, just seeing her confirmed that. But he still felt . . . off.

"You look nice," he offered.

"Thanks." She draped her coat over the back of her chair, then took a sip from her water glass. "So? You wanted to talk? Talk. I'm listening."

Her cold tone and brusque words struck him like pelts of ice. He bristled. "Wow. That's not the nicest way to begin a conversation. With an attitude."

"Say whatever you need to say, Evan." Her gaze was stern and steady.

"Fine. I just . . ." The words evaporated on his tongue.

Did he really want to do this? "I didn't sleep well last night."

"Me, neither," she grumbled.

"Because of me?"

"Yup. Go on."

He sighed. "I don't know why, but I . . . I got a little spooked last night."

Her brows furrowed and she leaned in a bit. "About what?"

"You . . . us." He rubbed the back of his neck. "I love you. I do. But I . . . I think maybe I need some space. Just for a little while. Just until I figure out what the hell's going on in my head." He watched the color drain from her cheeks and felt like a total piece of shit. But he said quietly, "I'm sorry, Shari. I really am. But I think maybe we should stop seeing each other for a bit. I think that'd be best right now. For both of us."

Chapter 5

SHARI FELT HER heart sink to her stomach as a huge lump tightened her throat. Even though she'd suspected he might say something like that, actually hearing it was a hit to her heart. Calling on all her professionalism and training for appearing cool, calm, and collected on the job, she reached for her glass and took a few swallows of water. "Well. Before you make such a decision for both of us, do I get any explanation as to why?"

"Why what, exactly?" Evan asked.

"Why you're spooked. Why you need space. Why you suddenly want us to stop seeing each other." His silence set off the first spark of anger in her chest. "I don't know, anything. After what we've had, I think I deserve that much."

He nodded and let out a sigh. "Of course you do," he murmured. "That, and much more."

"Damn right," she said, trying to maintain her cool

front even though she felt sick to her stomach. "So tell me what's going on."

"I don't *know.* I just feel all freaked out and weird and—"

"What happened when I left the room last night?" Shari leaned in on her elbows and fixed him with one of her steeliest stares. "Tell me. Now."

A hint of color rose in his face, which stunned her. He rarely had physical tells like that. "They all loved you," he began quietly. "They really did."

That wasn't what she'd expected him to say. The tiny burst of pleased warmth that shot through her at his words made her both sad and even more frustrated. "That's nice. I liked them all, too. Go on."

He reached for his beer. "Then . . . they all got on me about getting married." He took a sip. "About you and me getting married. They all seem to think we should."

A chill skittered over Shari's skin. "I see."

They sat in uncomfortable silence for a few seconds that felt like minutes.

"You should be flattered." He tried to grin. "I mean, one short meeting, and they were so enamored with you they were ready to pick out china patterns."

She didn't move. "I take it you didn't agree with them. And felt pressured."

He nodded, his gaze sliding down to the table. "More than I realized. Once I started thinking about it . . ."

The more he hemmed and hawed, the more her annoyance turned into something sharper. "Have I ever even mentioned marriage?" she asked. "Pressured you in *any* way? Because as far as I know, I haven't. We haven't talked about it at all."

"You're right," he said. "I'm telling you, Shari, it's nothing you've done. As lame as it sounds, it's not you, it's totally me."

"Oh, I know that. Believe me." She stared as her mind worked, going over his words. Then it clicked. "Ahhh. I got it now. Your family freaked you out, and now . . . what?" Her eyes narrowed. "You suddenly think you have to ask me to marry you or something? And you don't want to, so you're running for the door?"

"No. I . . . I don't know." His voice had an edge this time. He took a longer swig of beer.

She continued to stare at him. His family, though likely well-meaning, had Evan twisted in knots. It was almost ludicrous . . . but for him to be this thrown off his axis, maybe this was only the surface issue of something more. "Evan. Do you think I expect that of you? You think I want a proposal or I'm leaving, posthaste?"

"No. Maybe. I don't know."

"I'm getting really sick of your saying 'I don't know,'" she ground out. "You're a smart guy, Evan. Smart, focused, and driven. You always know what you want."

"Maybe suddenly I don't." He scrubbed his hands over his face and huffed out a frustrated breath. "The thing is, Shari, I should tell you what I told them: I don't know if I ever want to get married. Not like I don't know if I want to marry *you*, but like I don't know if I want to marry *at all*."

With her heart suddenly pounding, she sat back in

her chair. "Well. Thanks for letting me know. After seven months."

"Shari—" he began.

"You know what?" she cut in. "I've never brought up marriage, and we've been together for seven months now. But yeah, I've thought about it. Who wouldn't?"

"Of course," he said. "Perfectly natural. I understand."

"No, Evan, I don't think you do." Her chest felt too tight, but she continued. "We've been involved in a serious, committed relationship. We spend all of our free time together, precious as it is for either of us. Usually, that makes people think it could lead to something even more serious. Especially if one takes the other to their childhood home to meet their entire family." She saw his eyes flash at that. "So if there was nowhere for this to go beyond a certain point, don't you think perhaps you could've clued me in sooner? Like, I don't know, at the *beginning*?"

His eyes flew wide. "What does that even mean? I should've promised you we'd end up married, or you wouldn't have dated me in the first place?"

"No!" She snorted and shook her head at him, even as she felt her blood race in her veins. "Of course not. But you know what? If I knew you never intended to get married, that there were definite limitations, maybe I wouldn't have let myself invest so deeply in a relationship that was doomed to leave me wanting. That I knew it would eventually have to end, because we weren't looking for the same things down the road." She realized her hands were shaking and folded them in her lap. "That was incredibly selfish of you, to wait all these months to tell me how you feel about marriage, that there were parameters. Do you even realize that?"

"Whoa." A muscle jumped in his clenched jaw as he stared. "That . . . wow."

She ignored the wounded look on his face and drew a shaky breath. "I love you, Evan," she said. "But you know what? After this conversation, I'm in agreement with you. A breather is a great idea. For both of us."

His lips flattened into a hard line and his dark eyes speared her.

"Don't look at me like that," she said. "That's what you wanted, right? Some space for a while? Well, guess what? Funny thing is, now I want that, too. Starting right now." She stood and reached for her coat.

"Wait. Don't leave like this," he said, bolting to his feet.

"You wanted space," she reminded him calmly as she pulled on her coat. He reached for her elbow but she backed away from his touch. "You asked for time to think. I'm sorry, Evan, but now I need that, too. Suddenly, you're not the only one who thinks maybe we should stop seeing each other." Shari grabbed her tote bag and walked away from him with quick, long strides, not looking back.

She burst out of the restaurant, knowing she'd need to cry and had nowhere private to do it. She'd be damned if she found a place in the office building she shared with him. So she walked farther up the sidewalk, turned into a McDonald's, went straight to the bathroom and locked herself in a stall.

The flood of emotions rose up and crashed down on her, and she sobbed hard. She felt stupid and ridiculous, for leaving herself so open and vulnerable to someone who'd never intended to commit to anything beyond what they presently had. She felt betrayed, and even a little used. She also felt mean, for not being more sympathetic to him. Maybe he'd just needed her to hear him out, and if she'd been there for him, he would have . . . no. No. She'd heard him just fine: he didn't want to ever get married. So where did that leave them? She wanted to get married and have a family one day. She wasn't willing to throw away that lifelong desire to stay with someone who didn't want the same thing.

Even if she was completely, helplessly in love with him. Dammit. She'd hoped for . . . well, she'd hoped. She cried harder. God, this hurt. Her heart felt like it was actually squeezing in her chest, trapped in a vise, and it was hard to catch her breath.

Ten minutes later she emerged from the stall, cleaned up her face, and headed back to the office. Work was going to be a blissful way to isolate herself tonight . . . and every night for the foreseeable future, apparently.

EVAN STARED AT the computer screen, seeing nothing. As he'd watched Shari walk stiffly away from him, his insides seized up, and he instantly knew he'd done the wrong thing. He'd hurt her, and the burn of that wouldn't go away no matter what he did. The look on her face . . . it made him shudder to think of it.

He was crazy in love with her. Why the hell had he pushed her away?

With a sigh, his head dropped into his hands.

His cell phone started ringing and he glanced at the caller ID. His mother. Wonderful. One of the last people on earth he wanted to talk to just then. He let it go to voice mail, along with the calls from his brother and sister from that morning. All of them calling to beam at him about how great Shari was, how nice a night it had been, yada yada. What should he say to them now? *Hi, guys. Well, I'm a grown man, but thanks to last night's grilling session, I flipped out like a scared kid and pushed away the best woman I've ever known?* Yeah, that'd go over big.

His office line buzzed. Seeing it was one of the assistants, he answered. "Hey Katie, what's up?"

"I have Meredith Andrews on line two. Are you available?"

"Sure, I'll take it." He cleared his throat before saying to his client, "Hi Meredith, how are you?"

"Not so great," she said glumly, which made a flicker of wonder spark in his head. For a woman in the midst of an ugly divorce, she was usually pretty calm, almost upbeat. He'd never heard her sound upset, like she did now. "He's giving me a hard time about the holidays. He wants the kids for Christmas *and* New Year's. I thought we'd agreed that he would have one holiday and I'd have the other. He's being . . . really difficult." She drew a shaky breath, and he could swear he could hear the tears forming in her eyes. "I'm just so tired of this."

"I'm sure you are. I'm sorry to hear you so down," Evan said, reaching for a pen and pad to scribble notes. Fifteen billable minutes later he ended the call and made a few more notes while they were fresh in his head. Meredith had predicted from the day she retained him that her ex would make everything as difficult as possible, and unfortunately for her, she'd been right. What should have been an open and shut case had dragged on for over a year and a half. The guy just wouldn't let it go smoothly, and his attorney had found ways to stall and throw up ridiculous roadblocks at every turn. When this case was eventually settled—and it would be—Evan intended to get Meredith everything she was entitled to, everything she deserved, and then some. It just all took time, and her patience and positive outlook were wearing thin. He didn't blame her.

Meredith's teary voice echoed in his head: *I just don't understand why he's being like this. I really don't understand.*

Something about the sadness in her voice and the words she'd said had caught like a hook in his gut. It was very likely the exact thing Shari was thinking about him right now, possibly including the tears, and it made his stomach clench.

Time and space. He thought he needed that, he'd asked for that, and she'd given it to him. And the truth was out about how he felt about marriage. He should be relieved. Grateful, even. So why did he just feel vaguely nauseous?

A group IM came up on his screen. From Jeff, one

of his coworkers whom he hung out with sometimes, to about ten of the other guys. *Anyone up for beers tonight?*

Hell yes, Evan typed in immediately.

SHARI'S CELL PHONE was ringing. Still half asleep, she rolled over in bed and looked at the screen. It was Evan, and it was one in the morning. She debated whether to answer it. Her heart tugged, wanting to hear his voice. But her brain answered sternly, *No way*. She let the call go to voice mail, then turned the phone off altogether. Her mind now filled with thoughts of him, missing him terribly, it took her almost half an hour to fall back to sleep.

When her alarm went off at six-thirty, she groaned herself awake. She didn't have to be at work until nine, but she'd planned to work out in the gym early. Now, she reset the alarm for seven-thirty and went back to sleep. The hour seemed to rush by in a blink; was that damn alarm going off already? She slammed her hand down on it to silence it and made herself wake up. The first thought in her head was of Evan, as usual. But today it brought a searing pang of sadness with it instead of her usual smile. They'd broken up. Kind of. She wasn't even exactly sure what they were at this point; but the one thing she was sure of was they weren't together like they had been.

Remembering how he'd called her in the middle of the night, she turned on her phone, intending to listen to whatever voice mail he may or may not have left. And it almost blew up in her hand with all the beeps. "What the hell . . . ?" she murmured, looking at her phone. There were about ten text messages. All from Evan. Her stomach roiled and her heart stuttered in her chest. With a mixture of wariness and hope, she started reading through them.

Hi, it's me. So . . . where are you at 1:07 a.m. that you're not answering your phone? Hope you're just sleeping. I just wanted to hear your voice.

I'm out with some of the guys from work. Beers at McCabe's Pub. I think you'd like this place. I didn't pick it, Jeff did. If I knew we'd be coming here, I wouldn't have come. Because this place reminds me of you. And now I really miss you.

Shari's throat thickened as she continued reading the texts.

Hi, me again. Getting pretty drunk now. Yes, drunk texting is poor form. But I haven't stopped thinking about you, and I wanted you to know that. In case you thought I wasn't thinking of you. I am. All the time.

Shari, I know I hurt you today, and I'm so sorry. Wish I could redo it. The whole thing. I'm really sorry. I don't blame you for being pissed at me. Maybe we can talk again soon?

Gotta remind you of something, Ms. Cohen. Just because I was a dumbass and thought I needed time and space doesn't mean I stopped loving you. I haven't. I do. And I'm sorry if I've made you doubt that.

Shari wanted to laugh and cry at the same time. Evan must've been drunk off his ass when he sent all the texts. But *now* he was making declarations of love? How about doing that sober? She could swear her heart rate had skyrocketed in under ten seconds.

Heeey. I just almost got into a fistfight with Alex because he said you were gorgeous. I told him not to go near you and kind of got in his face. It wasn't good. Plus, I just outed us to all the guys, and we're not even seeing each other anymore. Because I was stupid. This stupid guy loves you, Shari. Please don't go out with Alex. Don't go out with anyone. Give me time. Okay?

She wanted to laugh at that text, but tears stung her eyes as her heart squeezed with longing.

Drunk. So very drunk. Leaving now. Don't worry, taking a cab home. Want to take it right to your door, but I know you wouldn't let me in. Best for you, anyway, since I'd probably slobber all over you and beg forgiveness . . .

Just got home. Gonna fall into bed. I know I'm annoying you now, sorry. I just miss talking to you. I miss YOU, and it hasn't even been 24 hours. There's got to be a way we can work this out. Can we please talk tomorrow? I'll text you. I love you, Shari. I love you so much.

The tears spilled over and she wiped them away impatiently. She took a long, deep breath and expelled it, then another one. Evan had hurt her deeply. If he wanted to talk, she was willing to listen . . . but not yet. No way. She needed to get her armor in place first; she felt way too vulnerable.

How had everything gone so wrong so fast?

With a sigh, she got out of bed and headed for the shower.

Chapter 6

AT THE OFFICE, Shari went about her work wondering if and when Evan would really text her, or if that had been the blubbering of a drunken fool. By ten-thirty she was both annoyed and disappointed that she hadn't heard from him.

At eleven, while on the phone with a client, one of the assistants showed up at her door with a huge bouquet of multicolored flowers. Shari's stomach did a rolling flip as she gaped at them.

"These came for you," Tonya said, placing them on her desk. "Even in a vase already. Convenient."

Shari nodded, staring at the flowers.

"They're spectacular," Tonya said.

"They are, aren't they?" Shari said. "Thank you for bringing them." When Tonya left, she looked for a card, finding one on a plastic stick in the middle of the bouquet. It was blue and white, embossed with a silver Jewish star. Then she realized the ribbons wrapped around the glass vase were also blue and white. Were these Chanukah flowers?

> *Dear Shari,*
>
> *Too sick to come to work today. (hungover) (shocking, I know) But I realized I didn't get to give you your second present last night, for the second night of Chanukah. Hope these flowers are a decent substitute.*
>
> *I love you. Please forgive me for being stupid.*
>
> *Yours, Evan*

Shari stared at the colorful flowers— there were lavender roses, fuchsia gerbera daisies, orange spray roses, lavender carnations, and an assortment of greens to fill in the spaces. They were absolutely gorgeous. The card was cute, the thought sweet. But . . .

But she couldn't bring herself to talk to him. She was still too hurt.

Instead, she grabbed her phone and texted him. *Just got the flowers. They're beautiful. Thank you.*

Evan responded within a minute. *You're welcome. Hope it brightens up your office, and your day. Did you get the card with it?*

Yes. She hesitated, then added, *It was sweet.*

Sweet enough for you to meet me for dinner?

I thought you were hungover.

I am. Sick as hell. Pathetic. But I should be better by

then. And I really want to see you and talk to you. Have dinner with me.

Shari bit down on her lip, wavering. But she wrote, *Sorry, I have to work late.*

I'll meet you after, then.

No, Evan. I'm sorry. Not tonight. I'm not ready. She paused, wondering if she should go on, then did in a burst. *You really hurt me, you know. And gave me a lot to think about. You're not the only one reassessing our relationship now.*

He didn't answer. She held the phone and stared at it, waiting with breath held. Then it rang in her hand, making her gasp and jump. It was Evan. "Hi," she said.

"I'm not reassessing anything," he said without preamble. "I got scared, I admit it. My family got on my case, I felt pressured, I got jittery. I should have talked to you about it instead of pushing you away."

"Yes, you should have," she agreed. "But you didn't want to. You'd made up your mind, and that was it."

"I know," he groaned. "I was an idiot to let you walk out of that restaurant yesterday, and I know it."

"I don't know," she hedged. "During our short conversation you raised valid points. And if you recall, I did, too."

"We were fine before yesterday," he said, an edge to his voice.

"Funny, I thought we were, too. What did I know?"

"Shari, you're pissed at me, I get it. I don't blame you."

"I *am* pissed, and I'm entitled to be. But much more

than that, I'm disappointed," she revealed quietly. "I knew something was up. I tried to get you to talk to me. But you shut me out. Then you blindsided me. You all but dumped me, Evan."

"I didn't dump you," he insisted. "I just said I thought we should spend some time apart while I figured out what was going on in my head."

"Not much different," she said. "And what, you figured it all out in a few hours? Now everything's fine, it was a false alarm or a quick fix? That's bullshit."

"Shari," he said, "as I watched you walk away from me, everything was screaming in me not to let you leave. I know I did it all wrong, that I screwed up."

"Yeah, you did."

"I want to make it up to you."

"I don't know if you can," she whispered.

"Oh honey." He sighed deeply. "I'm so sorry I hurt you. I really am."

Her eyes stung. He sounded so remorseful. But how was she supposed to just go back to him and pick up where they'd left off? The issue was real, and it hadn't been addressed or solved. "Thank you for that. But I think I should get back to work now."

"Please meet me for dinner so we can talk more," he said.

"No." She reached over and started fidgeting with edges of the skinny blue and white ribbons.

"I want to fix this," he pressed.

"I'm sorry, but a bunch of drunk texts and pretty flowers isn't going to fix this."

"I know. We need to *talk*."

"Well, I'm not ready to talk. I . . . now I'm the one who wants time and space."

He swore under his breath.

"We both have a lot to think about, Evan." She sighed. "You don't think you ever want to get married. That's fine. But I do. Eventually I want to get married, have a family . . . if you don't want those things, we're at an impasse."

"I don't want to lose what we have," he said, almost pleading.

"Had." Her eyes slipped shut. "Please don't make this harder."

"Do you still love me?" he asked tersely.

"Of course I do," she sighed. "That doesn't just disappear overnight."

"Then I intend to make this *very* hard for you," he promised. "I was wrong. I admit that. And I handled it horribly. But I'm going to fix this. I'm not giving up. Because I love you, too."

Her breath felt stuck in her chest and her stomach felt woozy. She cleared her throat and whispered, "I have to go. Thanks for the flowers." She disconnected the call.

"HI, SWEETIE. ABOUT time you called me back," Brenda Sonntag said to her youngest child.

"Ma, don't guilt me," Evan warned. "I saw you two days ago. I have a bad headache and I'm in an even worse mood." With a sigh, he scrubbed his hand across his face. "Ma, I screwed up. I . . . I need your help."

"What's the matter?" she asked, immediately shifting into Mom Mode.

He paused. His head was still pounding, but at least he wasn't nauseous anymore. He had no idea how many beers he'd consumed the night before, but he'd paid for it all morning at the altar of the Porcelain God. The headache, however, wouldn't quit, and the rest of his body felt like he'd been hit by a truck. "I kind of . . . broke up with Shari. Sort of."

"You what?" his mother cried. "Why? When? What happened?"

"I . . . freaked out," he admitted. "You all got me so riled up about how she's so perfect, I should marry her, we have to get married . . . it gave me cold feet. And then, instead of discussing it with her, I said I needed time and space to think things over and pushed her away."

"Oh my God," Brenda moaned. He could picture her dropping her forehead onto her hand, as she usually did when she was upset.

"There's more," he admitted. "Thing is, I never told her that I don't want to get married. It was a surprise to her. So now she feels like I used her, like I lied to her."

"This gets better and better!" Brenda said, sarcasm dripping from her words.

"Needless to say, she won't see me. Now she's the one who wants space."

"I don't blame her! Wow, did you mess this up."

"Thanks, Ma," he ground out. He rolled over on the couch to a better position. "You know, what I didn't say to you, or Bubby, or that rabid crowd in the living room, and haven't even gotten to explain to Shari yet, is that I don't *think* I want to get married. Not one hundred percent definite on that. It's not carved in stone."

"So what's changed in two days?" his mother asked. "What, all of a sudden you changed your mind? That sounds like a load to me."

"I sent her flowers, asked her to dinner. Told her we need to talk. She said no."

"I don't blame her. She has every right to be mad at you, Evan. You led her on."

"No I didn't!" he almost shouted. It made his head ache more. "That's not true, and it's not fair."

"No? You two were serious. You've been together for a while now. You're thirty-three, she's what, thirty-one?"

"Yes."

"Okay. At some point in a relationship," Brenda said, "you have to make a decision: do we take this further, or do we end it here? If you never intended on taking it further, that feels like a lie, or a betrayal. Don't you understand that?"

"Yes," he admitted in a low tone. "I get it. I do. But . . . I wasn't lying, or meaning to betray her. I just . . . I love her. And yes, once in a while I had thoughts about us having a future together. If I ever did get married, I'd want it to be to her. But . . ."

Brenda sighed. "But your work has made you so afraid of marriage, you can't even consider it."

"Not afraid," he clarified, "but wary, absolutely. More than wary— downright cynical."

"That's very sad," his mother murmured. "Very, very sad."

Evan closed his eyes as his skull throbbed. Before, he thought he was being smart about it, staying away from marriage. Now, all of a sudden, he wasn't so sure. The damage he'd seen incurred by failed marriages wasn't something he could ignore. People could be horrible when they were angry and hurt. He didn't want that to happen to him someday. Then again, he'd never met a woman who made him want to take that leap of faith. Now that he had, the subject seemed to be coming up more and more. For the past two days, he'd thought about it so much his brain was exhausted.

"Why are you so against marriage?" Brenda asked. "Yes, sometimes it doesn't work out, like with your clients. But that's not everyone, honey. There are plenty of good marriages. Why aren't you remembering that? Look at your father and me. Think of Bubby and Pa, before he passed. They were married for sixty-two years."

"I don't know how they did it," he muttered.

"Because they liked each other!" his mother said, as if it were obvious. "Marriage is hard! If you don't like each other, if you're not friends, no, it probably won't last. Are you two friends, do you like each other? It's not just rainbows and lust and good sex clouding your brain?"

"Mom!" he said, almost a groan. "And rainbows? Seriously?"

"What, you don't have good sex?" Brenda tsk-tsked, enjoying teasing him.

"I am so not having this conversation with you," he said, cringing from the inside out.

She snorted. "Do you laugh together?" she asked, taking another tack.

"Yeah, I guess." He couldn't recall a specific thing that made them laugh together, but knew that they did often, over little things. Walking down the street, over a meal, in bed . . . yes, they did enjoy each other that way. And he loved Shari's laugh. It was full and throaty, and it always made his insides fill up with something like light.

"Your dad and I, we still laugh together," his mother said. "Sure, sometimes he drives me crazy. Show me a married couple that doesn't drive each other crazy once in a while! But I wouldn't give him up for the world. I'd never want to lose him. If you're okay with losing Shari, then stick to your plan of solitude and I wish you luck." Her voice softened as she added, "But I saw the way you looked at her. And how she looked at you. It made me so happy for you."

His stomach did a slow flip. "Ma, I have to go."

"Go on, then. I hope you fix things with her," Brenda said. "I think she is the best girl you've ever been with, by a mile. How happy you seemed together—it made your father and me happy. I had no idea I'd be hearing something like this."

"I know, Ma. I know. I'll call you soon, I promise."

"Call your grandmother, too. She's convinced you're going to die all alone and no one will find you until they trace the smell to your office."

Evan laughed for the first time in days. "Did she really say that?"

"Yup, she did. Bubby's very colorful."

"She is indeed."

"Good luck, sweetie. Love you."

"Love you, too."

He stretched out on the couch and closed his eyes. He wasn't going to fall asleep, but he just needed to rest. What a moron he'd been, drinking like that on a weeknight. Drinking like that at all. He wasn't twenty anymore, and the recovery time was worse and longer with each unfortunate hangover.

He'd just missed Shari so much it ached. And felt like shit for how he'd handled the whole thing. But drinking to numb the pain had only been a Band-Aid. Now, in his apartment, he felt the ache again, and the self-loathing was gnawing at him.

A groan escaped him as he recalled almost getting into a fight with Alex at the bar. First, Jeff had asked him why he seemed to be in a shit mood, and after three beers he'd told his friend the truth a little too loudly. Jeff and two other guys knew he'd been dating Shari, but the others hadn't. Then Alex, being a dick as usual, started in on him about it. But when Alex cracked, "Hey, she's hot. Maybe I'll take a shot with her if you're done," something had roared in Evan so fast and hard . . . the next thing he knew, he was right in Alex's face, gripping him by the shirt and warning him to stay away from her. Jeff and another guy had to tear him off and calm him down. He'd made an ass of himself. He didn't care.

All he cared about was Shari. He had to get her back. This was on him—he'd blown them up. His stomach rumbled, and for the first time that day it wasn't from nausea, but from hunger. Well, that was a good sign. He had to go back to work tomorrow. What he needed now was some soup, some bread, and some quiet time to plan how he'd get her to hear him out.

The sky was growing dark outside his window. He dragged himself from the couch, shuffled into his tiny excuse for a kitchen and grabbed a can of chicken noodle from the shelf. As he made his meal, he thought about her—as if he could think of anything else. He hated that he'd hurt her; that was the worst of it all. It actually hurt his heart, made him a little sick, to know he'd done that to her. He kept seeing her face at the restaurant, the way the color drained from it when he told her he thought they should take a breather . . .

Ugh. Dammit. Just thinking of it made his stomach clench again.

Somehow, he had to find a way to make it up to her. If she'd even spend five minutes alone with him, which right now, she wasn't giving him.

Chapter 7

WHEN SHARI ENTERED her office the next morning, there were two small gifts on her desk, wrapped in blue and white paper with silver bows. An envelope with her name on it leaned against them. She put her things down, took off her coat and hung it, then opened the envelope.

It was a Chanukah card, with a photo of a fully lit gold menorah on the front, the nine candles each a different vibrant color. Inside, the copy read, *May this Chanukah bring you miracles and light.* All the handwriting was Evan's messy scrawl, which she used to tease him about mercilessly. Now, the sight of it made her heart skip a beat. His words filled the entire card, both sides.

Dear Shari,

I know Chanukah isn't a big deal . . . but you are. You are a VERY big deal to me, and I'm so sorry I made you doubt that.

I'm sorry I hurt you, I'm sorry I didn't talk to you. And I understand that right now you may not be ready to talk to me.

In the meantime, I want you back so bad it aches, and I can't wait around for a Chanukah miracle. So I intend to give you a gift for every night of Chanukah to remind you of what we've meant to each other. Since last night was the third night, and you probably won't let me see you tonight, I'm giving you gifts #3 and #4 this morning. Then I'm caught up, and tomorrow will be #5, etc. Maybe some of them will put that "miracle of light" back into your heart when you think about us. As for me . . . you're all I think about.

We are great together. We were happy. I blew it up. Thinking we needed a break and brushing you off are the biggest mistakes I've made in a long time.

I'll do whatever it takes to make it up to you, and I'm not above bribing you with gifts. You know us lawyers, we can play dirty sometimes . . .

So, this is me groveling. Please can we talk soon? Let me know when you're ready.

I miss you. I love you.

Yours always, Evan

Shari felt a rush of adrenaline, a heady mixture of delight and disbelief, whoosh through her body. She read the card twice more in astonishment. Evan had really poured his heart out. He'd never gotten so raw and emotional like this before. In fact, no one had ever written her such a romantic card or letter in her life. As she put it carefully into her tote bag, she noticed her hands were trembling and she sank into her chair.

Yes, he'd screwed up. Yes, he'd hurt her deeply, for several reasons. Yes, she missed him and loved him, too. Yes, she'd also been thinking about him nonstop. But the bottom line was, if what they wanted for the future were different things, what was the point of continuing to be together? If they had to end it at some point, wouldn't it be easier now than later?

Unable to contain her curiosity any longer, she reached for the first gift and tore at the wrapping paper. A dry laugh escaped her lips and she shook her head as she pulled out a royal blue New York Mets T-shirt. During their first real date, over dinner, he'd asked her if she was a Mets fan or a Yankees fan. When she said Mets, he'd breathed a sigh of relief and said, "Knew you were awesome." They'd attended several games together at Citi Field over the summer. Those were some of her best memories with him; sitting in the sun on a Saturday or Sunday, eating junk food, watching the game, chatting about whatever, and just relaxing. He was always reaching for her hand, raising it to kiss her knuckles or just hold it in his lap. Remembering with a sweet sigh, she folded the shirt and put it into her tote, glad it was a tremendous bag.

The next gift was a little heavier. She tore away the wrapping paper and sucked in a breath. In the box was a pint glass from O'Reilly's Tavern, their favorite place to grab a drink after work. Only two blocks from the office, it was a warm, cozy Irish pub that always had good music playing, a welcoming atmosphere, and room to move. She loved that place. Shari couldn't even count how many drinks they'd shared there. Or how many laughs, or kisses . . . If they broke up for good, she didn't think she'd ever be able to walk into that pub again.

Setting the glass aside, she reached for her phone and called him.

"Evan Sonntag," he answered.

"You're playing dirty," she said.

"Yup, and I'm not sorry. Is it working?" he asked hopefully.

"Evan . . ." She sighed, the awkwardness creeping into her chest. "We do need to talk. But I'm not ready to see you."

"Why not?"

"Because I'm going to want to just fall back into your arms, back to how things were, and that's not going to solve anything."

"I don't know, it sounds good to me."

"We have issues to work out," she reminded him.

"I'm very aware of that," he said. "And I'm taking responsibility for my part. I'm just asking you to hear me out, Shari."

"I can't now," she said. She reached for one of the silver bows and fidgeted with it. "I have to be in court at ten-thirty. I need to do a bit of prep, then I'm gone all day."

"Have dinner with me, then."

"No, Evan. Just . . . not yet."

He was quiet on his end for a long beat. "You're punishing me."

She opened her mouth to dispute that, but realized maybe she was, a little. "I didn't intend to. I just . . . I still need some space."

"Shari—"

"Don't push me. I mean it."

He huffed out a frustrated sigh. "All right. But tell me . . . did you like the card?"

Her breath caught and she cleared her throat. "Yes. It was beautiful. Heartfelt. It meant a lot, really. And the gifts were perfect. But I have to go now."

"I'm glad you liked all of it," he said. "But . . . can I at least text you once in a while? I miss not talking to you. The little texts throughout the day, those used to keep me going. I miss that. I miss your voice. Dammit, Shari, I miss *you*."

"I miss you, too," she whispered. "And I love you, too. But that doesn't mean this is going to work out. You of all people know that sometimes love isn't enough if the two people want completely different things."

Tonya appeared at her doorway with a thick file bursting with papers.

"I have to go," Shari said quickly. "Have a good day." And she ended the call.

THE NEXT MORNING, Shari walked into her office to find Evan had gotten in before her— there was another present on her desk, a rectangle wrapped in the same blue and white Chanukah paper. A small netted bag of chocolate gold coins was taped to it instead of a bow. The note taped to them said, *Some Chanukah gelt to assuage the guilt. Ba dum dum.* She had to snort at that. Then she carefully ripped open the wrapping paper.

He'd given her a hardcover copy of the book *Outlander*, one of her favorites. He knew she'd read all the books in the series, and by the fall she'd convinced him to watch the television show with her. She'd talked about it a lot, the show and the books. Then she'd been so excited to get the second DVD when it came out that they had a marathon one rainy weekend in early October—the first eight episodes on Saturday, the second eight on Sunday. They'd cuddled in bed as they watched the show on her laptop, ordering dinner in both nights so they'd never have to get dressed.

He knows I have this, she thought as she looked at the book. Granted, her paperback copy was dog-eared from multiple readings, but . . . *wait*. She opened the cover and turned to the title page. It had been autographed by the famous author herself. Shari gasped like the fan girl she was.

She grabbed her phone and hit speed dial. As soon as Evan picked up, she demanded, "How on earth did you get an autographed copy of *Outlander*?"

"You like it?"

"It's—It's wonderful. It's a very thoughtful gift," she admitted. "But how?"

"I have my ways," he said.

"Tell me."

"Have dinner with me, and I will."

Her eyes narrowed and she hissed. "That's blackmail."

"That's right."

"I can't, Evan. I have plans."

"No you don't," he said. "You just still don't want to see me."

She hesitated, but finally said quietly, "You really hurt me."

"I know, honey. I'm so sorry." His gentle tone radiated remorse. "So, so sorry. I'll keep apologizing if you need to hear it."

"Maybe I do need to hear it," she said, a drop of defensiveness in her voice.

"Okay. Then I'll keep saying it. I'm sorry. I genuinely am. And I want to fix this. So have dinner with me, please."

"I told you, I have plans."

"That was the truth?" he said.

"Yes!" She snorted out a laugh. "It's Adrienne's birthday, a couple of us are taking her out tonight."

"Can I come along?"

"Ladies only, sorry."

Evan paused. She could almost feel him thinking. Then he said, "Okay. Have a great time."

"Thanks." Half of her was relieved she wouldn't see him, yet . . . half of her was disappointed. She was still so torn between whether she should go back to him or not. Until she knew for sure, it wasn't fair to get his hopes up with a dinner date, right? That's what she told herself.

"Tomorrow's Friday," he said. "The Chanukah Fairy will have to drop your last gifts off over the weekend to keep this going correctly. He wants to make sure you'll be home on Saturday?"

"Evan," she said as her stomach went wobbly. "I'm going to Philly for the weekend. Home to see my family, end of Chanukah and all that. You forgot?"

"I'm sorry, I did," he admitted. "Shit. Okay, right. When are you leaving?"

"Tomorrow afternoon, around one. I took a half day." She twisted back and forth in her chair in an edgy swaying motion. "Going to bring my suitcase to work, head right over to Penn, get to Amtrak, yada yada yada. I'll be home in time for dinner."

"When will you be back?"

"Sunday night. Probably take a late train, get back to the city around ten."

"I hate that I didn't know," he said.

"You did know," she reminded him. "I told you I was going to be gone for the weekend. I told you over a month ago."

"Yes, you did. It slipped my mind. My mind's been on other things this week," he said, a hint of frustration in his tone. "Like work, and my family, and most of all how I was a stupid pansy-ass and blew up the best relationship I've ever had."

"Evan . . . you're not a stupid pansy-ass if you meant everything you said." She reached up for a lock of her hair and twirled it around her finger. "If you don't want to be in a relationship that's long-term, I'm glad I know that now, instead of later."

"I didn't say I didn't want to be in a long-term relationship," he said tersely. "I said I didn't think I wanted to get married. I also said I didn't *think* I did, not one hundred percent definitely never."

"But what does that mean, exactly?" she asked. She could feel her cheeks get a little hot as the blood rushed to them. "I'm not asking you to commit to me right now, right here, for the rest of your life. That wouldn't be fair. But if you don't want to get married, that's something you should have told me from the start. And you didn't."

"You're not going to let that go, are you?"

"No, and I shouldn't."

"But I've apologized," he said.

"Yes, and I appreciate that. But it doesn't undo it, and even more importantly . . ." Her voice trailed off. Did she really want to say this? If she did, she couldn't take it back. It'd be out there. She swore under her breath.

"Whatever you were about to say, Shari," Evan demanded, "just say it. You're one of the boldest women I've ever met. Don't get shy on me now."

That made up her mind for her. "Okay. What I've been thinking these past few days is, if we now know you don't want to get married someday, and we know that I do, what's the point of continuing to see each other? It's going to have to come to an end at some point if we have this impasse. So before we both get in any deeper—"

"I'm already in deep!" he cried. "I'm crazy in love with you. I don't want to break up, I don't want to end this!"

"But it'll just hurt even worse later when it does end," she said sadly. "Don't you get that?"

"I—we—dammit!" She heard a loud sound, like maybe he'd kicked something. "Can we please get together and talk about this face-to-face?"

"Why?" she asked. "I have a valid point. You know I'm right."

"I *don't* know that you're right," he said. "And this suddenly sounds something like an ultimatum. I don't do ultimatums, Shari."

Her chest got tight and her blood simmered through her veins. "That's not what I was doing, Evan. Not at all."

"Really? Because it kind of sounds like it." His voice went low, the words tinged with anger. "Marry me or I'm leaving, that's what it sounds like on this end."

She huffed out air, the irritation morphing quickly into something darker. "That is *not* what I said, or even implied. What I said was, if we know this is going to end, why keep it up knowing that and knowing it'll hurt even more later? That is not an ultimatum. That's just common sense."

"According to whom?"

"According to me. And since I'm now royally pissed off, I'm hanging up."

"Shari, wait."

"Nope. I'm getting off before either of us say something we regret. 'Bye." She hit the button to end the call and had a fleeting vision of throwing the phone across the room, watching it shatter into pieces as it hit the wall. Her heart was racing and her face felt hot. She knew she was probably as red as a beet, as she always got when she was angry or upset. Thankfully, she had a great poker face when on the job. It was amazing how she managed to keep cool in her professional life but not in her personal life.

How had that conversation started off so nicely and ended in a blaze of fire? He wasn't hearing her. He was so desperate to win her back that he wasn't looking at the bigger picture. She bounded up from her chair and stalked out of her office, down the hall to the water cooler.

Evan had it wrong. She wasn't issuing an ultimatum. She was trying to protect both of them from getting hurt even worse down the line. Or, at this point, maybe just herself. Because every strained conversation this week, every disagreement, felt like another step away from each other instead of back to each other.

Chapter 8

ON FRIDAY MORNING Evan buried himself in his work, but the waiting was eating him up inside. He'd left another Chanukah gift on Shari's desk, but she hadn't called or texted to acknowledge it. They hadn't had any contact since their argument yesterday morning, and he'd burned over it for the rest of the day. This morning he hoped it'd be a clean slate, that she'd at least like the gift enough to contact him, and that he could apologize properly.

He'd gone on the offensive and jabbed at her, and she pushed right back. Hello, two fierce attorneys— of course the arguments were going to be like fireworks. But over the course of the day, he thought about the things she'd said. And had to admit . . . he saw her point. He understood what she was saying.

The thing was, he didn't want it to end. He wanted her for the long term. Possibly even something . . . yes, something as permanent as marriage, who knew? But they had to get back into a good groove and back into their relationship to get to that point. Being apart wasn't helping the situation. They had to be together to map out the landscape ahead.

Goddammit, he missed her so much.

At ten o'clock Evan's phone dinged and he looked at the text. *Just saying good-bye*, Shari had written. *Going back to Philly now.*

What? She'd left already? He typed quickly, *Wait, what?? I thought you weren't going down until later in the afternoon? I wanted to see you here at the office before you went.*

Changed my mind, she responded. *Took the whole day instead of a half day. On the train now.*

He swore under his breath and typed, *You already left??*

Yes. Should be at my parents' place by one. So . . . have a nice weekend. Added another day—won't be back til Monday night.

Evan stared at his phone, a wave of helplessness and angst washing over him. *I wish you weren't going*, he wrote. *Yesterday I thought about a lot of things, and I really wanted to talk to you about them.*

I'm already gone, she wrote back.

Her choice of words filled him with dread that prickled over his skin and a steely edge of frustration. *I'm already gone.* He'd blown it. That was it. The fight yesterday had pushed her even further away. He knew she was angry, but what if this was a way of putting more space between them so . . . so she could come back and end it for good? Didn't she know how much he wanted her, loved her? Had he pushed her that far? His stomach churned and his pulse raced. He felt like throwing his phone out the damn window. All he wrote was *I love you, Shari. With all my heart. Enjoy the weekend. See you when you get back.*

She didn't respond. After two minutes he set down the phone, raked his hands through his hair, and dropped his head into his hands.

A FEW HOURS later, at the end of a long, tiring day, Evan made a call and waited as the phone rang two, three times. Finally he heard his grandmother's voice. "Hello?"

"Hi Bubby, it's Evan."

"Ah! How nice." Rose sounded delighted. "How are you, boychik?"

He smiled, warming to her familiar greeting. "I'm fine, beautiful. How are you?"

"I'm fine, too," Rose said. "Just took a little nap. Going to go downstairs to play some mahjong with some of the other ladies in half an hour."

"Sounds like a party."

Rose let out a crackly cackle. "Not so much, but I like it. Anyway. Why'd you call, just to say hello?"

"Yup. That, and I heard you think I'm going to die all alone." Evan grabbed a nearby pen and started doodling circles on the edge of a legal pad. "Wanted to tell you not to worry about me."

"I can't help it, I'm a Jewish grandma," Rose said. "Worrying is in the DNA."

He snorted out a laugh at that.

"How's Shari?" she asked.

"She's . . . she's fine, Bubby," he lied.

"Oh good. I really like her, Evan."

"I know. You told me. Several times. And I'm glad."

Rose coughed lightly, then said, "You seemed a little cranky when you left the other night. I hoped it was just because everyone was nudging you, not because of her."

"You know me so well," he said. "You were right. I *was* annoyed that everyone was nudging me."

"I thought you were a hotshot attorney," his grandmother said. "Thought you had thicker skin than that!"

"Usually I do. But not about that," he admitted.

"What, getting married?" Rose let out a puff of air, a dismissive sound. "You don't wanna get married, don't get married. But you know what? I think you're just scared."

"You're not the first person to suggest that," Evan said.

"Well then, maybe we're all on to something." Rose coughed again. "Hold on, I need a drink of water." He heard her put the phone down, probably on her mattress. Less than a minute later she was back. "Why are you scared of marriage? Have you asked yourself that? I'm serious."

"I'm not . . ." He paused. He was going to say he wasn't scared of marriage, but maybe that wasn't true after all. "You should hear some of my clients, Bubby. The stories they tell me . . . they're horror shows. These people are so miserable, or angry, or bitter, or just heart-wrenchingly sad. They cry in front of me. They curse the person they used to love the most. It's not pretty."

"Life isn't pretty," Rose said without hesitation. "Real life is messy. And ugly sometimes, too. Pardon my French, but shit happens, boychik."

Evan barked out a laugh. "That's the Rose Sonntag I know and love."

"It's true!" she said. "But, as you go along in life, you hope the pretty things outweigh the ugly things. And you know what? Having someone to share the ugly times with, as well as the pretty ones? Is what makes it worth-while."

"Bubby, that's a beautiful statement. But I'm—"

"Scared!" she said. "You're scared. You love Shari?"

"Very much," he said soberly. "More than I realized."

"Think she'd be good marriage material?" Rose continued.

"I . . . yeah, probably."

"Stop beating around the bush!" his grandmother commanded. "Yes or no?"

Evan was glad she wasn't there to see the smile he couldn't hide. "Yes. Yes."

"Okay then. You think she wants to marry you?"

"I . . . I don't know."

"Well, maybe it's something you two should talk about," Rose suggested. "Don't you think? C'mon, smart guy. Use your head."

"Okay, okay," he said with a chuckle.

"Okay then." Rose cleared her throat. "It's so damn

dry in this place once they turn up the heat. I'm drinking water like I'm crossing the desert or something, it's ridiculous."

Evan smiled. "I love you, lady."

"I love you, too, boychik. So work is good? Everything else is good?"

"Yup. All is well. Just busy."

"Busy, huh? That's too bad," Rose quipped. "Hate when your business is booming. You coming home again anytime soon?"

"Maybe between Christmas and New Year's for a dinner. We'll see."

"Okay then."

Evan hesitated, about to say good-bye, but he changed his mind. "Bubby, can I ask you something?"

"Of course," she said.

"How . . ." He fumbled to get the words out. The soft, circular doodles turned into hard, choppy lines. "How did you know Pa was the right one? How did you know it would work out?"

"I didn't!" she proclaimed. "None of us know for sure if it'll work out! You think we're all psychic or something? You take a chance, you hope, you try. Because the alternative? Can lead to a pretty lonely life."

Her words settled into him like little balls of light, opening his eyes to something that seemed so obvious but was new to him.

"I'll tell you a secret." She cleared her throat again. "The night before our wedding, I could barely sleep. It was from excitement, sure, but it was also more like nerves. I got cold feet. I tossed and turned all night. I thought about calling it off."

Evan listened attentively. He'd never heard this story before.

"In the morning, I was so tired, and even more nervous. I was just a girl, you know. Nineteen years old! Could you imagine getting married when you were nineteen, Evan?"

"No flippin' way," he said.

"Right! Anyway . . . where was I . . ." Her voice trailed off. "Oh! Okay. The next morning, I was still jittery. Thinking about finding the nearest exit. Until I saw your grandfather." She sighed, almost dreamily. "He looked so handsome, and was smiling at me like I was the most beautiful, wonderful girl in the world. Like he'd never been happier to see anyone in his life." The tone of Rose's voice, so sentimental as she recalled the memory, made Evan's heart squeeze for her.

"And you got over the jitters and married him," he surmised gently.

"Well, yes, of course," she said. "But! I married him *without* the jitters. You know why?"

"Nope."

"Because I looked at him," Rose said, "and I thought, 'Okay, I'm scared of getting married. I'm scared of what if this doesn't work out? But the thought of *not* marrying him, *not* having him with me for the rest of my life, is a million times scarier.' Once I realized *that*, the cold feet were gone. Presto."

The words slammed Evan like punches to the gut. She was so right.

Yes, marriage scared him. Well, if he was being honest with himself, it wasn't the idea of marriage itself, but of a marriage *failing.* That scared him a lot. But losing Shari scared him more. The bottom line was, he didn't want a life without her by his side. He loved her that much. She was the best thing that had ever happened to him, and in a short time he'd hurt her enough to make her question everything. He had to make it right. He had to have her in his life, with him. In his arms, in his bed, in his home, in his travels, in every way that mattered. She was that important to him. That made taking a tremendous risk, a leap of faith, worth it. Love like theirs was worth that risk.

The realization hit him like an iron fist, and he sat up straighter in his chair. "Thanks for telling me that story, Bubby. Really. You're amazing. I have to go back to work now, though, okay?"

"Sure, okay," Rose said. "It was nice of you to call. You're a good grandson. I love you very much, boychik."

Even though he was a thirty-three-year-old man, her affection still warmed him. He figured you never outgrew hearing your loved ones remind you they loved you, especially from someone as special and wonderful as his grandmother. "I love you very much, too, Bubby. Happy Chanukah."

"Your mom and dad are taking me out tomorrow," she said. "We're going to the deli for lunch, and then we'll see a movie. Do you and Shari have a little something special planned this weekend?"

"Actually, I'm planning something *very* special. As we

speak." Movement from the corner of his eye made Evan turn to look out the window. It had started to snow. The white crystalline flakes were visible against the now navy sky, softly flurrying on the wind. An idea burst into his head. "Gotta go now. 'Bye, beautiful."

"Ha! Charmer." Rose's crackly laugh made him smile. "'Bye to you, too."

Evan ended the call, put his hands on the keyboard and started to search the Internet as a plan unfurled in his mind. Time for a grand gesture. Shari loved the sweeping romance of her favorite books and TV shows . . . he could pull off a little romantic something of his own. She was worth it, and desperate times called for desperate measures. Somehow, he had to make Shari see how much he loved her and wanted to be with her.

And if he couldn't make her see that, after all he'd done that week, and especially what he was about to do . . . then they probably really were done.

The drive and determination that had gotten him through his life kicked in with a vengeance. He couldn't lose her. He couldn't let that happen. He *wouldn't* let that happen. If it was ever time to pull out all the stops, this was it.

Chapter 9

Curled up on her parents' couch with her hands cradled around a warm mug of chamomile tea, Shari stared out the window to watch the snow fall. Caught by the beam of the security light outside, she could see snowflakes flutter through the air. She'd always found snowfall to be enchanting, since she was a little girl. It was peaceful and magical and beautiful, all at the same time.

She'd had a good childhood in this house, growing up in the East Falls neighborhood of Philadelphia. There were parks, play areas, and rec centers. Story time at the local library had been her favorite thing as a kid; her mom would take her and her older sister there every week. Her school had been a good one, and got her on the track to be able to get into top colleges. And the friends she'd made there, a lot of them were still her friends, even though they'd all scattered across the country and led busy lives. Shari loved New York, but this place would always be home to her. She hoped her parents never decided to move away.

"Hey lady," her father said. "Move over."

Looking up at him, Shari did so with a grin. "Plenty of room here."

"Oh good. Thought so." Bruce Cohen was short, a little rounder than in his younger days, and had gone bald back in his thirties. But the lines in his face only made him seem softer, as if the kindness within had etched into his features. Shari always loved the way his sense of humor made his blue eyes shine.

"Where's Mom?" she asked. "Stacey, Bill, the kids?"

"They're all in the den. The girls are watching *Frozen* for about the millionth time. I needed an escape and realized you'd already gotten out of Dodge."

Shari laughed. Her adorable nieces, at four and six, were obsessed with all things *Frozen*, and watched the movie almost every day, according to her mom. "I wasn't trying to escape, or be rude. I'm just tired," she said. "So I made some tea. I love watching the snow. And just sitting here feels nice."

"Okay," Bruce said. His eyes pinned her. "Now tell me what's really the matter. "Something's bothering you, I could see that as soon as I got home from work. It's all over your face."

She couldn't hold back a wry grin. "You know me too well."

"What, you forgot that?" He watched her take a sip of tea before asking, "Anything I can help with?"

"I don't think so . . ." Shari looked at her father. He was

a smart man, a loving man. As a young girl, she'd been a daddy's girl. As a teenager, when she fought with her older sister or she and her mom butted heads, he was always a safe port in the storm. He'd given her sage advice over the years. He'd always been sharply tuned into his girls. "Then again, maybe you could."

"Great. Try me."

Shari told him about what had transpired that week between her and Evan. Everything, from her going to Long Island with him and meeting his family, to the tense text exchange they'd had that morning. And that she hadn't heard from him since.

"I don't know, Dad . . ." Shari stole a sip from her mug. The tea was getting cool, so she leaned over to put the mug on the coffee table. "Am I being petulant? I thought my points were valid. He thinks I'm punishing him and giving him an ultimatum."

"Are you?" Bruce asked.

"I thought about that long and hard on the train ride here," she said. "And no, I'm not giving him an ultimatum. But . . . maybe I've been punishing him a little."

"A little, huh?" her father said. His bushy brows lifted. "I'd say more than a little. He gave you nice gifts, that he obviously put thought and effort into. You could have taken a walk down to his office and given him a few minutes. You chose not to."

She winced and fidgeted with the edge of the fleece blanket spread over her lap. "I know. You're right."

"As for the ultimatum part," Bruce continued, "I see

where you're coming from, and I don't think you were giving him an ultimatum."

"Thank you!" she said.

"But," he cut in with a knowing half grin. "Let me ask you something. And tell me the truth, because if you don't, you're not lying to me, you're lying to yourself. We're discussing this for *your* benefit."

She loved the way he always cut to the heart of a matter. "Okay. Shoot."

"Do you want to marry him?"

Shari drew a long breath and reached up to grasp a lock of her hair. "It wasn't really on my mind before all this happened. But since it has, I've been thinking about it a lot, of course. And yes." Her voice got small and soft. "Yes, I want to marry him. And I'd like him to want to marry me. And he doesn't."

"*Yet,*" Bruce said. "He said he's not totally sure that he never wants to get married. He's been pursuing you all week with the full court press. If deep down he didn't want to be with you, why would he bother doing all that?"

"I don't know," Shari mumbled. "Maybe because he likes to win?"

"Nah." Her father waved a hand in a dismissive gesture. "You've given him the out. You told him, 'Why stay together if we're going to have to end it.' That is a free ticket to Freedomville if he wanted it, right there. He could've said, 'You know what, you're right, it was nice knowing you,' and left. But he didn't."

Shari stared at her father. "Yeah. You're right. He could have left, and he hasn't."

"Honey," Bruce said soothingly, "sometimes it takes our heads a little longer to catch up with our hearts. Plus, he's a guy, and we can be a little dense sometimes."

Shari chuckled at that. "You've never been dense a day in your life."

"Sure I have! Go ask your mother, she'll tell you!" He laughed along with her. "But seriously, Shari. He's not letting go. His heart obviously doesn't want to let go of you. Maybe he's not ready for marriage right now, but he could be later. He might change his mind about that, because from where I'm sitting, the man obviously loves you. Maybe you need to give him a chance to get there, you know?"

Shari's heart stuttered in her chest. Her father, as almost always, was right. She thought about the conversations they'd had, the tense arguments . . . Evan kept trying to have a face-to-face meeting to talk, and she kept brushing him off. Because deep, deep down, he wasn't the only one who was scared. She was scared, too— of how much she loved him and wanted to be with him, and what if he didn't feel the same way? She couldn't bear having to look him in the eye as he told her that.

But he hadn't stopped trying. As he'd sworn, he didn't give up. He did everything he knew how to show her that he loved her. Those Chanukah gifts weren't just tokens to win her affections, like wine or chocolate or something general. Those gifts took forethought and effort. Each one had a special meaning. He'd thought about their best times together and made sure she remembered them.

He kept telling her how much he missed her, that he still loved her, that he wanted to make it work . . . and she was so afraid of further heartache, she'd kept him away. And the other truth was, she wasn't ready to get married right away, either. She'd just wanted to know it was an option for the future. Maybe she had to take a leap of faith and believe they'd work it out as they were meant to, as her dad suggested.

They. For her to say *they* could work it out—he had tried. She hadn't. She hadn't worked at a solution, or made any effort, like he had. In fact, thinking back on her behavior now, while it hadn't been done consciously, she'd acted like a child. She wouldn't even let him talk to her. All he'd asked for, every day, was a chance to see her in person so they could talk things out, and she'd denied him that at every turn. Her eyes slipped shut as she cringed inside. "Ohhh, I messed up," she whispered.

"You both did," her father said flatly. "Seems like he keeps trying to fix it. What are *you* going to do to fix it? Do you *want* to fix it?"

"Yes!" Her eyes opened to look at him. "But I don't know if I can. What if it's too late? He sounded so hurt this morning, even through texts, that I'd left without seeing him to say good-bye. What if he gets all huffy now, like I've been? Or pushes me away again?"

"Only one way to find out. Take that phone and call him, Lawyer Lady." Bruce rolled his eyes. "Sheesh. For a woman who went to Tufts and Columbia, you're being a real dope."

"You're so right." She laughed and moved in for a

hug. "Thank you for helping me see it differently. More clearly."

His arms wrapped around her and he dropped a kiss on her head. "Glad I could help. I'd wish you luck, but something tells me you won't need much."

She pulled back and asked, "You think so?"

He nodded. "Any man who goes all out like that? He loves you a lot. I'd bet the house on it."

"God, Dad, I hope you're right."

The doorbell pealed then, echoing through the house.

"Who the hell could that be?" Bruce wondered, rising from the couch. "I got it," he called back to the den as he headed for the front door.

Shari reached over to the coffee table for her phone and texted Evan.

Hi. I'd love to talk if you're available. Call me or text me when you can, please. I don't care how late. I need to hear your voice. I love you.

"Shari," her father said with a strange grin as he reentered the living room. "Someone's here to see you."

Evan stepped in from behind him. Snow was melting in his dark hair, clinging to his beard and his black wool coat. His warm brown eyes widened a bit as they focused on her. "I'm not being a stalker or anything . . . I just had to see you. If you'll just listen—"

She jumped up from the couch and threw herself into his arms, holding tight.

His arms immediately wrapped around her. He

buried his face in her hair and murmured, "Oh, thank God."

Bruce quietly walked out of the room.

"I thought you'd be mad at me," Evan said, not letting her go. "Just showing up here like this. But I couldn't wait all weekend for you to come back. I didn't want to lose any more time. I've been thinking, and I—"

"I've been thinking, too," she said. She pulled back enough to look into his eyes, but didn't release him. "Now I'm the one who owes you an apology. I was being kind of a brat."

"No, you weren't." His eyes sparked. "Well, maybe a little. But it's because I hurt you, and I—"

"You've apologized plenty," she said. "I just wasn't ready to accept it before. I have now. And I'm sorry, too." He looked so handsome. He was *there*. She ran her hands over his jaw. His beard was wet from where snowflakes had melted. "I was mad at you for shutting me out when you were upset . . . then I did exactly that to you. Which makes me a jackass."

He laughed. "I love that word. It's not used enough these days."

"Well, I just did, and it's true." She stared at him. "I can't believe you're here. I'm so glad you're here."

"You are?" His voice and eyes went soft. "You don't know how glad I am to hear you say that."

"I wasn't giving you an ultimatum," she said.

"I know that now," he said. "I thought about it, and I realized. But honey, I don't want to lose you. There's got to be some middle ground we can find."

"Yes, because I don't want to lose you, either," she said, looking into his eyes. "The truth is, I'm not ready to get married right now. But . . . I just wanted to know it was a possibility."

"Anything is possible," he said. His fingers lifted to caress her cheek. "I just know I want to be with you, and I'm in this for the long haul. Whatever happens in the future . . . it'll happen. But I know I want you to be the one there with me. I love you that much. You're the best thing that's ever happened to me, Shari. I mean it."

"I love you that much, too," she whispered. "Kiss me already."

He crushed his mouth to hers in a passionate kiss and sifted his fingers through her hair, holding her close. She kissed him back with all the love and adoration she felt soaring through her, relief and joy making her heart beat faster.

"God, I missed you," he whispered against her lips, nipping and kissing.

"I missed you, too," she whispered back.

They stood locked in an embrace, kissing and touching and whispering words of love and forgiveness, until her mother's voice cut in to their little romantic bubble. "Are you hungry, Evan? Take off your coat, stay a while. We still have latkes and some roasted chicken. I'll heat some up for you."

He pulled away from Shari with a broad smile to turn to her. "Mrs. Cohen, that would be fantastic. I'm starving, actually."

"All right, I'll go do that." She smiled back at him.

"Nice to meet you, by the way." She looked over to her daughter. "You want more, too?"

"Sure, why not?" Shari said. She watched her mother walk away, then smiled up at Evan with pure elation. "Happy Chanukah, huh?"

He chuckled and kissed her again. "Yup. Happy Chanukah. I think we just got our Chanukah miracle."

"The only oil in this house is in the latkes," she quipped.

"Close enough." He gazed down at her lovingly. "You're my miracle, Shari. You are. What we have together, and what we're going to have."

"I'm no miracle," she scoffed, but her insides felt like they'd filled with warm light from his heartfelt words.

"You are to me," he whispered.

A Home for Chanukah

Stacey Agdern

To the memory of Bernice Woller.

Who else would I dedicate a Chanukah story filled with music and memories to? I love you and miss you, Aunt Bernice.

Chapter 1

Jon

THERE WAS A loud, incessant knocking at the front door of Jon Adelman's apartment.

Unfortunately, he'd gotten home at an insane hour, he was tired, and all he wanted to do was sleep.

But the knocking wouldn't stop.

Sighing, he pulled off the cover, stretched and rolled off the futon, barely giving himself enough time to get his feet under him.

And then his feet met the cold, wooden floor. He recoiled, shuddering, trying to keep his balance as he adjusted to the job the winter had done.

"Coming," he managed, his voice sounding rough even to his own ears. He was living the dream, but dreams required sleep.

"Sorry," a small nervous voice proclaimed from the other side of the apartment door. "I . . . didn't realize."

He checked the clock on the microwave as he passed the kitchen. Twelve-thirty. "Fine," he shouted. His left hand gripped the doorknob and unlocked the locks.

Then he dropped the chain with his right. As he opened the door, he found himself staring back at a pair of bright green eyes.

He liked the freckles on her nose, the way her red hair hung down just below her ears. He wanted to run his fingers through it.

"Hi. I'm Molly Baker-Stein. I live in the apartment just above yours. We're having a . . ."

Jon rubbed his eyes and stared. Hard. He could barely manage to decipher the red-haired woman's rapid words. "Hi?"

"I'm sorry," she said. She looked embarrassed, nervous and he could see the flush rising up her cheeks. "You . . . I should let you go back to bed."

Thoughts of her in his bed ran through his head. He'd ask "Would you join me?"

"I'm sure you didn't mean that."

And apparently the necessary connection hadn't been made between his brain and his mouth, because he'd spoken instead of just thinking about having Molly join him in bed. "No filter," he said, by way of explanation. Then, because he really wasn't thinking, he gestured into his apartment. "Coffee?"

He wondered if she'd come into his apartment, and he also wondered what he'd do if she did.

All the same, he watched her as she stared into the hallway. He followed her changing expression as she seemed to debate whether she'd be better off coming into the apartment or having whatever conversation she'd want to have with him while standing in the hallway.

Not that he could actually read her thoughts, but he wasn't stupid. He'd been around the block; he also had sisters. He'd also already demonstrated his inability to think before he spoke, and the fact he was attracted to her. No wonder she was having doubts. She had common sense.

But she looked over his shoulder and he saw her mouth drop.

"You have no furniture! You have . . ."

She barreled past him into the apartment, which did, he'd admit, look bare and empty.

She looked like a biblical warrior with her green eyes blazing as she stood in the middle of his living room. "Why do you not have any furniture in this apartment?"

He wanted to point out his futon, or the bookcases, or his stereo; even the kitchen table and his collection of coffeemakers. But even he knew the pizza boxes he'd forgotten to bring down to recycling helped make his apartment look like the frat house he'd lived in during his last two years of college.

"You're living in this beautiful apartment and it looks like . . . empty, cold. Horrible."

"I have decorated," he said, grinning, "in the fraternal mode."

She raised an eyebrow and shook her head; his horrible joke had clearly fallen flat.

"As I said. Horrible. Why?"

"Are you one of those 'house should look like a museum' people?"

"I'm one of those 'house should look like a h

people. Your sanctuary. Your safe space. Not, I don't know, a . . ."

"A fraternity house. I get it." He shook his head. "So coffee?"

He watched as she looked at him, at the open doorway behind both of them, and sighed. Heavily.

"Yes."

Molly

MOLLY'D BARRELED INTO 6B with a sense of authority she didn't deserve, and had managed to act just like those horrible biddies that ran the building's coop board in the process. It was probably why instead of refusing his invitation for coffee, she took him up on it.

No. Not the guilt. Most likely she'd accepted because her sense of self-preservation had gone AWOL. Jon, 6B, had come to the door in only a pair of boxers, a ratty T-shirt, and early morning scruff. She couldn't stop staring.

"Any particular requirements on the coffee front?"

The words popped her thoughts like a balloon, forcing her to focus on his mouth, as opposed to his body. She came out of her daze, only to realize he stood in front of a long granite countertop that had been taken over by an elaborate array of coffee preparing machines. There was a grinder, a huge espresso machine, a drip pot, and then one of those machines that produced individual cups of coffee.

She couldn't help herself. "So that's what you focused on?"

He shrugged his shoulders. "I travel constantly and need a consistent supply of caffeine," he explained, before pausing. "I'm Jon, by the way."

"Molly," she said as he took her hand in hers, before realizing she'd introduced herself already. "That is . . ."

"I got it," he replied, smiling. "I'm tired but not hungover."

She laughed, wondering why he felt the need to clarify the reason for his semi-awake state.

Aaah. Yes.

She'd definitely made him think she was one of those horrible biddies. "Sorry," she said, attempting to fill her voice with as much sympathy and understanding as she could manage. "I'm energetic."

"Decaf?"

She glared at him this time. Only a fool would drink decaf. He was trying to be helpful; she could see the warmth in his brown eyes. Which meant he didn't deserve to have his head bitten off for what he obviously perceived as a helpful suggestion. "No. Not really. It doesn't taste the same, so I never drink the decaf."

"Good to know," he answered. "So what do you want?"

"Surprise me," she said. "Give me something good."

He nodded, and the smile on his face was a joy to behold. "Your wish is my command."

She found herself transfixed as he gracefully maneuvered around the coffee machines. He managed to work a coffee grinder, the espresso machine and a milk frother like musical instruments, in a crazy dance that had h- mixing her metaphors and getting the wildest tho in her head. Namely, she wondered what those hands and that agile body could do to her.

"See something you like?"

She couldn't be offended because he'd caught her staring. Especially considering she was thinking below the board thoughts about him, his coffee and his body. Embarrassment was apparently the emotional order of the day. "I . . ." she managed, despite the fact it felt like her tongue had inflated to twice its normal size. "I guess . . . I . . ."

"It's okay," he said in a voice that was genuinely charming. "I know I have a collection."

"And a *tuchus* . . ."

Now she could see the blush rising up on the back of his neck, just below the end of his coffee brown hair. But why?

Oh right. She'd actually spoken the words as opposed to just thinking about them. Again. "Apparently I have diarrhea of the mouth," she said, trying not to focus on him. At least, any more than she already had.

"You have a lot more than that," he replied.

Jon

JON FOUND IT weird to be sitting at the crappy card table he'd bought for twenty dollars in the middle of the architecturally awe-inspiring apartment he'd purchased for way too much money. Even weirder, the ancient specimen now served as his dining table. Yet there he sat, drinking the last of his cold brew in a mug that extolled the virtues of sarcasm while freezing his butt off despite the thin robe he'd managed to excavate from his closet.

But Molly? His cute upstairs neighbor? She, too, was sitting in a folding chair, in front of the horrid coffee table. Except she sat there like this was normal. At least she was drinking a latte he'd made out of his Ethiopian blend in his CHAI LIFE coffee mug. Of course she'd cupped the mug between her hands, as if she was trying to wrest as much heat out of it as she could.

Yep. His neighbor was trying to hide how cold she was. He'd better get this started and get her out of his apartment and back to, presumably, the warmth, of hers. "So?"

She looked from her mug back up to him, her bright green eyes punching him in the gut. He'd managed to startle her.

"Do you like it?" Her lack of response made him nervous before he remembered she was the nervous one. "I mean," he clarified, "The coffee."

She nodded. "The smell, at least." She blushed, and he couldn't help smiling. "I can't stop smelling it."

"It's comforting, at least to me," he confided in an attempt to make her feel better. "I'm glad." Which he actually was, but for different reasons. He enjoyed sitting with this cute girl who carried a sense of home on her shoulders. "So, aside from my good fortune and even better caffeine, what brought you to my doorstep this morning?"

Now she put the mug down and sat up a bit straighter. He found himself wondering if she was afraid.

"So the building," she began tentatively, as she grabbed the mug again, "has a party every year for the holidays, and I'm . . . organizing it this year."

"Okay,"

She swallowed, then took a healthy sip of the latte. "It's good," she managed. "Thank you . . ."

"You're welcome." He was glad she liked the latte he'd made her, but she was getting off track, and it became more obvious she was having trouble telling him about this party. "It's fine," he said. "Drink and be caffeinated."

She laughed. "Thank you. But anyway," she managed. "It's policy that we invite the new tenants personally."

He nodded. "If I'm in town for it, absolutely. Sure. When is it?"

She named a random date in December, a middle of the week date that seemed strangely familiar. "Sounds familiar, think I'm in town, and actually off that whole week, so that works."

"Good. Good."

The relief in her voice was mixed with a tinge of something else. It was a tone he recognized from conversations with his sisters, mother, grandmothers, and female cousins. Molly sounded exactly like a person who desperately wanted something but was afraid to ask him for it. He tried his best to be a mensch—a good guy—so he was going to smooth the waters and broach the subject.

"What's up?" He asked it casually, calmly, like it was nothing. 'Cause it needed to be. She had absolutely no reason whatsoever to confide in him, but he wanted her to.

"Do you have a car?"

He nodded. He did. It was the kind of car that made the uniformed guys who worked in the building's garage look at him sideways; it was old but functional. He'd promised his family that he'd replace it once he no longer felt like a fraud. But for now the ancient automobile still sat in his brand new, way too expensive but horribly convenient parking space, waiting to be used once again. "Yep."

"Oh fabulous! Because I need help."

Without even knowing what she needed, he nodded again. He wanted her to like him. "Sure."

She laughed, and he loved the sound of her laugh.

"Are you positive? Really?"

He raised an eyebrow, and the caffeine seemed to move his brain forward. "You're planning a party, a holiday party, in an apartment building, and you need a car. I'm thinking you need to go shopping?"

She nodded. "Yep. That's the gist of it. A few different stops, a few different places. I'm guessing your schedule is a mess . . . you mentioned you're out of town . . . a lot?"

He nodded, before getting up and grabbing his cell phone from the charger. He could access his calendar even if the phone hadn't fully charged. "I'm heading out tomorrow night for a few days but I'll be back on Thursday. Is that okay?"

She smiled, and the relief on her face made him want to pat himself on the back. That or kiss her.

"Yep," she said. "That works for the first trip."

"Good. Can I have your phone number, so we can figure it out?"

She nodded, then gave him the number, staring with the 917 area code he recognized as the cell phone number of someone who lived in Manhattan.

"So," she said once she finished giving him her number. "Thanks for the coffee and I'll see you on Thursday?"

"Thursday it is."

He stood up, followed her to the front door. Then he reached around her and unlocked it. In the moment before she left, she turned toward him and simply watched. The space between them crackled with excitement, tension, and something undefinable.

He watched her chest rise and fall beneath her sweater. He held his breath, waiting, wondering, knowing he could break the tension with one move. Except that was when he remembered he was still mostly half naked, and she was standing in his apartment. He wanted to kiss her; but here, now, it had to be her decision.

And as she wasn't making it, he put his arms around her. Drawing her close and hugging her like he'd hug his sister, or a friend. Slowly and carefully, making sure she wasn't pulling away. But there was no sign at all of that.

"Thursday," he said, kissing her cheek. She rested in his arms a while, letting her head fall on his shoulder.

"Thanks," she said before breaking his loose hold and stepping into the hallway. "Really."

"Not a problem," he said to her retreating back. "No problem whatever."

Chapter 2

Molly

THE FIRST THING Molly noticed about Jon's car was the exterior. It was . . . horrible. An old Toyota hatchback that had clearly seen better days. The second thing she noticed was the insanely expensive sound system. The third? The interior. It was spotless, well taken care of. It mattered to him.

"I'm sorry," he said, misinterpreting her awe as judgment. "I'll eventually replace it, but for now, it works. And that's what's important."

"That's what I see," she replied. "Remember, I'm not a museum gal. And the car's more home than your apartment." She covered her mouth, trying to keep any other words that might sound judgmental from coming out of it. "I mean . . ."

He laughed, his eyes twinkling back at her. "It's fine," he said. "But I get it, though. Actually," he grinned and settled back into the driver's seat, putting his seat belt on, "you've got me pegged at this point. Apartment's for sleeping, I spend way too much time in the car, on the road."

"So it has to feel like home. Or at least nice enough where you can stay in it for an extended period of time without wanting to take an axe to the interior?"

He nodded, checking his mirrors. "Pretty much. This gal's got a lot of miles on her. I need to be able to drive across the country. Which means nothing that can smell badly goes inside, and it contains a constant supply of music."

After his heartfelt speech, she wasn't surprised when shortly after he put the key into the ignition the car started up with a throaty roar.

"So where to?" he asked as they pulled smoothly out of the parking space, toward the parking attendants and the exit.

She wanted to jump up and snarl at the attendants as they rolled their eyes. They had no right to be judgy. If he was an idiot who treated them badly, absolutely. But Jon was a nice guy with a car they had no right to judge. No.

"Where to?"

She shook her head. "Sorry. I think there's a Bullseye store in the Bronx."

He nodded, his fingers tapping on the wheel. "Yep. I know that one. And do you want dinner?"

The question came out of nowhere, but she appreciated the thought and him for asking. "Yes," she replied. "Absolutely."

His smile reminded her of a menorah on the eighth day of Chanukah. Bright and beautiful. "Excellent," he said. "Onward and upward."

Jon

BEFORE PULLING OUT of the parking garage, Jon reached toward the sound system (the only part of the car he'd actually spent time upgrading). He put on some music, from a singer that mixed his favorite styles of Latin music and an old language he was trying to save from extinction.

"This is cool," she said, making him thrilled.

"Yeah. I like. He's my current project. Want to give him a bigger platform, but we'll see what happens. Not sure if my bosses will go for it. But I love listening to him nonetheless. He's got a great voice."

Her nonresponse made him wonder if he sounded like a jackass. "Sorry . . . I . . ."

She shook her head and smiled. "No. It's fine. You're passionate about what you do, which now I have to assume means you work in the music industry?"

He nodded again after they pulled into the Bullseye parking lot. "Living the dream," he said as he began searching for a parking space, and actually found one. As he pulled into it, he took a deep breath. "Miracles, they say, right?"

He could see the confusion in her bright green eyes, the slight tilt of her head and the cloudy lack of focus.

"Huh?"

"People who pay attention say that this is the season of light and miracles," he began, feeling like a piece of city-created propaganda, "which encompasses three of the major holidays that happen now. Diwali, Christmas, and my favorite of them all . . ."

"You mean the amazing holiday that makes my heart and stomach happy at the same time?"

"Are you a Chanukah fan, too?"

She nodded, and his heart beat a little faster in his chest. "My mom had a huge menorah collection; she made some—she was a huge crafter. But she also had this thing—whenever she found a cool one in a store—whether it was a Judaica store or not, she bought it. I guess she was inspired by all her friends who collected Christmas ornaments . . . My dad stored them every year and took them out for her."

"Mine's known for her latkes," he said, his mouth watering at the thought of his mother's crispy latkes. "The entire neighborhood gathers at my mom's house on the night she pulls out her Cuisinart. The neighborhood does an exchange; they started it years ago, actually turned it into a huge neighborhood block party after Hurricane Sandy. Someone makes eggnog, a few others make other dishes." He shook his head as the memories began to overwhelm him. "Wow."

"My great-aunt, now," Molly interjected, her voice soft, "she was the best at Chanukah time. She'd bring out the family recipes that she and my grandmother had saved over the years. She . . . she tried to make the holidays, all of them, special . . . oh God."

He wanted to hug her, just pull her into his arms as the tears started to fall. However, sitting in a car, leaning over a console and under the constraints of a seat belt, didn't allow him to. He reached for her hand instead.

When she took his hand in hers, he brushed her upper palm with the pad of his thumb and gently caressed her fingers in the poorest substitute ever for a hug. It was all he could manage without mentioning they needed to get out of the car.

Molly

THE SIMPLE GESTURE felt good; Jon's hand was comfortable in hers, and if Molly was being honest with herself, she would want more than just the feel of his hands on her. She'd stay with the hands for now. Besides, did she really want to leave the idyll of the car to deal with the craziness of the Bullseye store?

She looked out the window and saw the crowd of people in their winter coats on this Thursday afternoon. They filled the parking lot with their happy chatter, despite the cold.

"I think we have to go," she said. Then she realized what she might possibly have sounded like to Jon. "I mean," she clarified, "into the store."

She watched the disappointment and the relief chase each other off of his face, as if she'd managed to destroy his afternoon and then remake it all at the same time. It was a simple shopping trip, she told herself. She needed his car, and the only reason he was touching her was because memories of holidays she'd spent with Aunt Linda had come back to haunt her.

"Yes," he replied, making no move to let go of her hand. "We do. We should." She watched as he focused on their clasped hands. "I need this," he said softly. "You can have it back if you want, but I do need it."

She knew that, of course. She understood that he needed his hand back if he was eventually going to get out of the car; heck, she needed to be able to move herself, to get out of the passenger seat. She didn't want to lose the connection just yet, and that felt weird. She forced herself to let go of his hand, and he let go of hers.

Soon after, she was outside, standing in the parking lot, bracing herself against the cold.

MOLLY TOOK JON's hand as they stepped into the store, almost forgetting they needed a shopping cart.

"So what are we . . . ?"

She looked back at him, but he was still standing at the entrance, not far from the sliding doors. He wasn't moving, and he looked like he was focused on something else.

"Oh wow, so they did it. Niiice."

She couldn't mistake the awe on his face. How wide his chocolate brown eyes had gotten, and how bright. Even his mouth looked brighter for a reason she couldn't understand. She could only guess it had something to do with his work, which meant the music. But what? She wanted to know.

"What?"

"Listen."

Not just hear the music, he seemed to mean. She had to actually focus on it.

Okay.

The song playing on the in-store sound system was brash and loud, brilliant and wonderful. She'd heard it before, on one of the radio stations she'd been listening to; it had been the station's way of making sure the listening public knew that the word "holiday" was a word with actual meaning, and that "twenty-four hours of holiday music" heralded the addition of songs from other winter holidays into seasonal programming.

What was it called? "Modern Day Maccabees."

"I celebrate," David Streit sang over the loudspeakers of the store. "I celebrate. Cha-nu-kah. Oooh oh ohhhoh."

She also found herself remembering a recent Bullseye store campaign featuring that song (and a special edition of the album the song came from). Bull's-eye was among the stores across the country that adopted the song in advertising campaigns that finally acknowledged the power of the Chanukah dollar.

"I never thought," Jon continued, "that they'd agree to this one, but I guess they loved how accessible this message was. I'd actually expected them to use something not as confrontational, like 'Newly Fallen Snow' instead of this one." He shook his head, lost in a daze. "Wow. Wow. Wow."

"Living the dream?" she said, recalling his earlier words.

He nodded. There was awe and excitement in his eyes. She could deal with awe and excitement and disbelief. But she was still confused. So she asked.

"You . . . you did what?"

He blushed. "Sorry. Really. It's like . . ." he gestured toward the cluster of shopping carts in front of them. "Here," he said as he pulled one out.

She watched him test it, making sure the wheels weren't all crooked.

"It's like," he continued as he began to push the cart, "it's like you have this thing you love, and then it becomes important, and people start to ask you about it and take your advice? And then pay you for giving that advice, and so you're getting a *lot* of money to do the thing you never dreamed was possible?"

She still didn't understand him, but she figured he was talking about his life, and his profession. "I guess?"

They headed through the store, past the shelves of red and green, of pine needles, small trees, past the wooden candelabras that reminded her of a special gift her mother had once made for a friend. There was also the remains of a Diwali display; paraffin wax, gorgeous pots, wicks, and tea lights sat in disarray on elaborate velvet draped shelves because someone probably couldn't bear to dismantle it after the Hindu festival had ended. Finally, they arrived at an oasis of blue and gold, a section at least twice the size it had been in years past.

There were menorahs of all sizes, packaged candles, latke mix and boxes of sufganiyot—special Israeli Chanukah doughnuts, imported from Israel. There were cookbooks and cookware, including the new "Kate Feldman for Bullseye" line. There were books by people like Rabbi Elijah Cohen talking about finding the "Mitzvah in Chanukah" and of course the brand new Bullseye edition of David Streit's Chanukah album. All of it would have brought Aunt Linda to tears.

"We need plates, napkins, and cups," she said, bringing the subject back to their mission. "And silverware. Maybe two different colors?"

She liked how he nodded. "You think there are going to be people who keep kosher at the party?"

"I know," she replied. "I know for sure there are. My upstairs neighbors, at least. There are a few others. And a few Hindus who would probably appreciate the nonmeat silverware. So we're going to try to have at least something for everybody."

"Because we know what it's like to be a stranger."

She wondered whether he'd used that line before. It sounded like something Aunt Linda would have said, and maybe that's what she needed to hear.

Jon

Two hours, a horribly long line at the checkout, and an überfilled carload later, he was behind the wheel again.

"So are you kosher?"

She shrugged. "I don't eat anything obviously unkosher, but I'm not . . . I don't cook well enough myself to be pure about it. You?"

"I have a bacon weakness. Other than that, I'm in a situation where most of the food I have access to is kosher, so I try to keep to that. But if someone tells me that my life isn't complete unless I try this particularly amazing traditional dish from somewhere that isn't kosher, then I will." He nodded, and his stomach growled in anticipation. "So let's do this."

He drove along the streets, glad that Seaman Avenue was not a parking lot for once. The music was influenced by Sephardi culture, another singer's Sephardi/Latin fusion. She was dancing in her seat but trying not to be too obvious. He liked seeing her take as much pleasure in music as he did.

"It's okay," he said as he tried to find a parking space. "I'd be doing it, too, if I wasn't strapped in. So much of why this music works so well is that it comes with the goal of making its listeners want to dance, you know? That's what makes part of it good."

"Wow," she replied, surprise and excitement in her voice. "I wish I was as passionate . . . consistently passionate, about what I do for a living. I'm not . . . well I like it, but I don't work hard at it. At least I haven't."

"What do you do?" he asked, though part of him had a feeling he knew already.

"Interior design," she said. "I'm also considering starting a party planning business."

He laughed, but tried not to laugh too hard. It figured, though, as he pulled into the miracle of a parking space he'd found across one of his other favorite restaurants in the area. He knew all too well how impossible finding another space in this area was.

"Okay," he said. "We're not far from the place."

"Parking spaces are at a premium?"

He nodded, glad he didn't have to explain himself. "Yep."

When they got out, he took her gloved hand in his, not hesitating, and began to walk the short distance to the place that served the best mofongo in Washington Heights.

Molly

THE WAITERS AND the maître d' all seemed to know Jon; they greeted him like a member of the family. Which was a good sign, considering this was the first time Molly had eaten mofongo. The restaurant smelled amazing, which made her drool even before they sat down to eat.

"We'll have the cheese, vegetable, and the salmon mofongo."

"To drink?"

"Just water, I think, at least for me. Molly?"

"A mango juice, please, and some water."

As the waiter headed off to bring their order to the kitchen, Molly settled back into the comfortable leather bench.

"Wow," she murmured. "How . . . how did I manage to live so close to this place and not try it before?"

"People live within their own experiences, I guess," he replied. "I mean I'd never been here before I was dragged by my ears. The guy I was meeting for lunch practically demanded it when he realized I hadn't tried it. So we came and my stomach was hooked. It was about . . . a year ago?" He grinned. "Now I come regularly because I need my fix."

"I could understand. I can't even imagine how good the food is, if my mouth is watering even waiting for it to arrive." She grinned and then sat back, remembering there was something she'd wanted to ask him. "Anyway, you were talking, remotely, about what you do, and now that you know my embarrassing run into your apartment was an occupational hazard, what do you do?"

He laughed and grabbed a sip of his water. She wondered what he thought of the craziness that had come out of her mouth, then decided the shake of his head meant that he was thinking about answering her. At least she hoped so.

"Okay, so you really want to know how my craziness started?"

She nodded. "I asked, didn't I?"

This time she could see resignation in his eyes. "Okay. So my favorite music has always been CJM—contemporary Jewish music. I remember hearing it for the first time when I was in college, and it changed my life. The music was bright and wonderful and full of faith that I couldn't find anywhere else. I started to follow all the amazing artists that perform it, went to their guest cantorial spots, saw them in concerts. Graduated from college, you know. Then I got a paid internship with a record label, doing exactly what you'd expect to do as an intern. Of course, I listened to my music, too."

He shook his head, and she nodded back at him, already picturing the scenario in his internship.

"You know how it goes," he said. "People asked what I was doing whatever weekend, and I'd tell them. Going to see this show, with this guy. Going to that Shabbat service because this person was going to be the guest cantor. As I said, it's how I . . . connected with Judaism, but to them I was the intern with the crazy music obsession."

She nodded, watched him take a sip of his water, fascinated.

"Anyway," he continued, tapping his fingers on the table in front of them, "all of a sudden, people started asking me really pointed questions. Like whether they should sign this guy who's on the verge of a Music Award nomination and whether I'd seen a consistent crowd, or one that got larger around him and his musical colleagues."

"So what did you do?"

"At first I wasn't sure. I mean, I'd like to think I understood what they were asking, and I figured at the least, they'd see if I'd paid attention while working at this job. So I told them something. I talked to them about his series of concerts, and his sales and how he's got this huge fandom, and how he was personally responsible for the growth of this huge Jewish music online site. It was everything they'd mentioned they were looking for when signing an artist. The very things they stressed when telling me what to look for."

"So what happened?" she asked, but she knew already. At least, she had a feeling.

"So, they offered him a deal, not only a deal, but created a brand new label for him. Then they hired me to bring more artists to the label, and asked me how to sell the kind of music he and other artists like him were creating. It was like . . . wow. Wow."

Then it hit her hard, like a lightning bolt. She was sitting with the guy who was famous for telling one of her favorite musicians that he needed to write the song that won him his second Music Award. "You're . . . you're the Jon that told David Streit he had to write 'Day of Peace'?"

She could see the blush rise up his cheeks, and at that moment she knew she hadn't misjudged him. It was excitement that drove him, not a sense of entitlement. He was a *fan*, not a glory hound.

"Well," he finally said, after he seemed to compose himself, "I didn't exactly say that. I told him he needed a song that would explain the Jewish concept of Shabbat to those who didn't understand it. Otherwise the collection of songs he'd written and put together would make no sense on the mainstream level, and as those in charge of the label put it, he wouldn't have a first single. 'Day of Peace' was how he responded to what I said."

She nodded, smiled, saved from any other silly words by the arrival of their food.

Jon

A FEW HOURS, full stomachs, and a check he insisted on paying later, they'd arrived back at the building. "So," he asked as they stood in front of the open hatchback, "where do you want these?"

The look in her eyes reminded him of expressions he'd seen on his mother's face, the last thought he wanted to have at this point. But Molly's expression spoke to the fact of how seldom she'd expected, asked for, and gotten help. Her eyes were wary, her mouth wide.

"What?"

He gestured to the bags and the ridiculously full trunk, the way the plates were threatening to jump off of the tailgate, and how the bags of napkins showed signs of wanting to fly through the breeze. "These. You need help carrying them."

He said it like it was a foregone conclusion, making it clear she wasn't going to have to worry about carrying all of the bags from his car. Then to soften the bite of his harsh tone, he shrugged his shoulders and grinned. "It comes with the chauffeur service."

That made her laugh, and then it was okay. He let her take a bunch of the bags, then he took what was left before following her to the elevator.

"I think I have space in my apartment," she said offhandedly as they waited for the elevator.

"We can put the bags in mine if you don't."

The words came out of his mouth, but he didn't expect to say them. And once he had, he didn't mind. "It's okay. I have the space."

She shook her head and smiled back at him. But the smile was . . . small, shy. "I have space. Besides. I want you to see my place."

There were many reasons she could want to show him her apartment, some of which were okay to think about in the confines of the small elevator. Others were not as okay, and he desperately tried to think of the good ones. "So," he managed, "you . . . I mean how did you get into interior design?"

She smiled. "I was lucky that my family gave me a sense of home. Not stuff everywhere, but the entire house felt lived in, loved. Our drawings weren't just put on the fridge, they were everywhere. My mom, my dad."

She paused, adjusting the bags as the elevator door opened. "It was also my great-aunt—Aunt Linda—she was . . . amazing. She taught me how to craft—to sew and knit—and enjoy it. She made the house, and her apartment, smell amazing. She taught me how to keep just enough . . . stuff around and how to place candles. I didn't want to be anything else."

The excitement in her eyes made him believe in her and her ability. There was a difference between liking someone, caring for someone, having chemistry with someone, and believing in them. Without believing, there was really nothing else. And he believed in her. "I can't wait to see," he said.

She blushed, just that little bit. That blush, and the bright color it placed on her cheeks, made him smile.

Molly

SHE HEARD HIS footsteps behind hers, and her heart sped up. She wanted him to see the inside of her apartment for many reasons, some of which she felt more comfortable with than others. But she went with it and walked him to her front door. "Here," she said as she dropped some of the bags so she could reach her keys. Once free of the burden, she reached into the pocket of her coat and removed the key chain she'd made at Aunt Linda's knee.

Carefully, easily, as she'd done a million times before, she unlocked the door, both locks, and shouldered it open.

"Here we are," she said as they walked into the space. "Home sweet home."

It actually was, if she could say so herself. The light touch of cinnamon from the air freshener struck the perfect note, the kitchen and the pillows on the couch were organized just so. "Put the bags on the floor by the couch," she told him. "The rug can take it."

He laughed, wiped his feet on the mat before heading into the living room and dropping the plastic bags he carried next to the couch. He was conscientious, and she loved that (and the sound of his laugh).

But then he stopped about halfway through, saw her coat on the kitchen chair she put it on without thinking, and gestured to his own coat. "May I?"

She nodded, because clearly she wanted him to stay maybe for a little while. "Sure. Do you want anything? Coffee? Water?"

"Water's fine," he said, grinning back at her. "I'm a bit of a coffee snob."

She laughed and headed to the kitchen. Yes. The guy who had an array of coffee machines in his barely furnished apartment had to be a bit of a coffee snob. "A glass of cold brew water coming up."

She pulled down two glasses and reached into her fridge and pulled out the pitcher. Yes, she sighed to herself, she drank filtered water in a city where tap water was amazing. But she was paranoid, proud, and poured two glasses of the filtered water before heading back to her living room.

"I'd give you tea," she said as she passed him a glass, "but I suspect you'd consider it a sacrilege."

Once again he laughed. It was comfortable, and made her insides melt just that much more. His glass looked comfortable in his hands; heck, he looked comfortable in her apartment. Maybe she wanted him to stay longer . . .

But instead he took a long drink of the water and took a breath. "Wow. That was good," he said. "I needed that."

"You're welcome," she replied. "So . . ."

He sighed, and she knew what was coming. From the reluctance and shock she saw on his face after he looked away from his watch. She didn't want him to leave just yet.

"I have to go," he said softly. "I really have to go. I leave early tomorrow morning for a few days. But I'll be back next Tuesday night, so Wednesday?"

She nodded. He stood, slowly, as if he was waiting for her. Which, considering it was her apartment, he probably was. So she stood, took his outstretched hand and led him to the door.

But as they stood on her welcome mat, she couldn't resist the look in his eyes and the open, welcoming expression on his face. She'd held herself back before, but not this time. So she leaned up, put her lips to his.

Soft, sweet, his tongue tentative in her mouth. His five o'clock stubble scratched above her mouth, but she didn't care. It felt good. His hands cupped her cheeks, holding her close and carefully. She was in control, but all she could think of was him, and how it felt to kiss him.

But he pulled back, took a deep breath and looked at her, regret in his eyes. "I really have to go," he said softly. "I'll call you?"

She nodded, well aware that whatever this was could end here and now. It would be easy for him to forget her and his obligations. But as he stood there, expecting an answer, she gave him one. And nodded back.

"Sure."

He ran his fingers down her cheekbones one more time, as if he was savoring the feel of her skin against his. She didn't mind. In fact, she liked it. But then she opened the door and let him go like he said he'd wanted to. "Good night," she said softly as he walked away.

Chapter 3

Jon

THIS TIME, JON met Molly at her door, a bouquet of flowers hidden behind his back. "Hi," he said as she opened it. "I got you something."

Her green eyes widened, and he could feel the sweat pouring down his palms. "What?"

Excitement and uncertainty seemed to war in her eyes. "Well," he began, not wanting to seem like a complete idiot. "I remembered you had some really cool vases in your apartment, and I figured that they might want filling. So . . ."

He carefully brought the flowers out from behind his back. He stepped back a little, so that if she was allergic, it wouldn't be a problem. Unlike the asshole who'd once given his sister a concussion by shoving flowers in her face.

"I wasn't sure," he said, shrugging as she seemed to stand like a statue.

Suddenly, her excited grabby hands snatched the bouquet from his fingers. He watched, transfixed, as she grasped the bouquet in between her palms and smelled the flowers with her entire body.

Which meant he was completely caught off balance as she grabbed his elbow, coat and all, and pulled him into her apartment. He stood on the mat, watching her as she went to the nearest vase and proceeded to put the flowers in it.

"Wow," she said softly once the flowers were on display.

He was going to say something silly like he was glad she liked them, but she stole the words from his mouth with a sudden kiss. He let himself get lost in the feel of her mouth on his, the taste of her on his tongue, the way her hair felt under his fingertips, silky and soft.

"Well," she said as she broke the kiss. "We're never going to be able to make dinner at this rate, and sadly, we need to." She blushed. "I made a reservation."

He nodded, smiled. He was usually the one who took care of messy details like reservations, or at least was the one who knew who to call to take care of it, but he liked that she did this time. "Okay," he replied before offering his hand. "So off we go?"

She nodded, took his hand in hers and smiled back at him. "Off we go."

Molly

MOLLY STOOD IN front of her apartment door, Jon's hand in hers as they waited for the elevator. And she liked that. A lot. "How was your trip?" she asked.

"Not bad, not bad," he said, smiling. "Wonderful scenery, great services, and just an amazing atmosphere in Chicago. They've got a festival they organize every other year, and we wanted to know . . . well anyway, the people I met were so nice and so excited. How have you been since I've seen you?"

She shrugged her shoulders. "A few clients were being prickly, but I reminded them that we're working on their house, their space, not mine, you know, and that, well . . . anyway, they got a bit clearer about what they wanted and we're now on the right track. Which is good."

He nodded, like what she said mattered to him. And she liked that, maybe more than the fact he was a very good kisser. "Design must be tricky like that, where you're doing something for someone else and yet there are times you want to put your personal style into what you're doing."

The elevator doors opened and she led him in, her hand still firmly in his. As the doors closed, she turned toward the front of the elevator, back against the wall. He did the same, and they were standing next to each other, filling the small space.

"And you do," she said, smiling, hoping she'd remembered the point she'd been trying to make. "But design's about the person whose place it is. Just like you with that festival. You came down to help them make *their* space better."

He shrugged. "It's hard, because people have been putting on Jewish music festivals for so long by themselves, without support from the mainstream music industry.

So there are moments where they think I want to co-opt what they've done, you know? But I'd like to think the label I'm working for is very much about community, and filling spaces. Not taking over where we weren't wanted or needed."

She leaned into him, her eyes meeting his as she put her head on his jacket clad shoulder. "Oh, I can see," she said, feeling the giddiness come out of her. "I can totally see that you did it. You absolutely convinced the festival organizers that you'd bring them help, not a coup d'état."

He blushed, then looked down at his shoes. "I guess," he said, slow to answer even as the blush spread across his cheeks. "I guess so?"

"I know so," she said,

He nodded. "I guess we did."

In that moment, he looked almost too perfect. His mouth was too close, too bright. She leaned up a little bit, trying to meet his mouth with hers. Thankfully he realized what she was doing and met her halfway. She felt his arm coming around her back to steady her against his body.

"Mmm," she murmured as his lips met hers again, as his tongue teased the roof of her mouth. She wanted more, as her hands went down the sides of his parka, trying to find an opening, or maybe a zipper. All she wanted was to feel him against her . . .

But the elevator came to a halt with a sudden movement, and she pulled her mouth away from his, even as she grabbed tighter onto him.

"You okay?" he whispered, or at least it sounded like

he'd whispered, considering his voice was obscured by the sound of the elevator bell.

"Fine," she said as she untangled herself from him, one mass of humanity becoming two people again. Except as she pulled away, she realized that she didn't like the feel of standing on her own. Maybe that was wrong, but she didn't care.

"Fine?" he asked, his voice sounding unaffected. But the fact that he hadn't moved an inch from the corner of the elevator said the words she wished to hear even if he hadn't spoken them aloud.

"You?" she wondered. "You okay?"

"Fine," he said. "Just fine."

That didn't sound right. But he stood there, not in pain, but . . . confused. Because when she finally really *looked at him*, she saw that he was holding his hand out to her.

Fixing the problem immediately, she took his hand. "Stuck?"

He laughed as he pushed himself away from the wall with his free hand. "In some ways," he said, laughing before gesturing toward the open elevator doors. "However, madam, I would like to remind you that our chariot awaits."

She nodded, grinned and followed him through the doors, her hand still holding his. "As you wish, good sir. Lead on."

Jon

JON LED MOLLY to the car, hand in hand. He was still smiling after the kiss in the elevator. The kind of indelible smile that came from feeling the promise of so much more. So he unlocked her door before opening it and helping her inside. Once she was settled, he closed the door and walked around to the other side.

"So where to?" he asked as he settled into his seat, checked the mirrors, and put his seat belt on. This was her show, and she'd even made dinner reservations. All he needed was a direction.

"Not sure," she said, smiling. "Hold on a sec, okay?"

He nodded, then watched as she put her own seat belt on. Once she'd settled in, he watched as she reached into the bag she'd placed on the floor and pulled out her phone.

"Sure," he said. "So we're going to a deli?"

She was bent over in her seat, her hair swaying back and forth. She was focused on the phone in a way that he couldn't fathom. It was as if her life depended on that phone; the sighs, the snarling, the growls. She was annoyed, worried . . . he wasn't sure.

"Can I help?" he asked

"I'm trying to find the address," she confessed.

He nodded. Hence the adorable intensity of her search and the embarrassment in her voice. If he'd waited till he pulled out into the street to ask her where they were going, he'd probably be annoyed. Now, he was just grateful for the investigation and her thoroughness. Because the last thing he wanted was to navigate his way through Manhattan, in horrible stop and go traffic, looking for a place that might not still exist.

"The problem," she said as he watched her tuck a

strand of hair behind her ear, "is that this place keeps moving. People discover it, a larger space opens up and it moves to accommodate. You'd think this cycle couldn't continue, but it does. Anyway, the whole thing is enabled by the fact that the chef's grandson is in real estate, so . . ."

She trailed off, and because he'd started listening to the sound of her voice as opposed to what she was saying, he wasn't sure whether he was supposed to answer or let her continue. He decided to stay quiet and let her go back to searching for the missing address. Yet as she continued to type furiously at her phone, he wondered why he didn't drive a car that had a GPS.

Because, he reminded himself, he'd had the option of adding a top-of-the-line stereo system or a GPS to his horribly out-of-date car. And because he was unable to think past his next moment, he bought the sound system. Which made him a jackass.

She went back to typing on her phone, and his focus turned toward the strands of her red hair that he really wanted to tuck behind her ear. But because of the degree to which she'd been focusing, she probably wouldn't be able to handle an unexpected, unwanted touch from him.

"Anyway," she interjected, the sound of her voice busting into his thoughts and grabbing his focus again, "it's moved like three times over the past two years, and I haven't actually been there in a while, you know? Just called."

For some reason, he wanted to know why she hadn't been to this place in over two years, why she hadn't been able to walk in the door yet knew it well enough to order takeout. But instead of asking what he had a feeling would be an unwelcome question, or touch her, or act in any way impatient, he nodded his head and took a deep breath.

"Okay," she finally said amidst a sigh "it's on Thirty-Eighth Street.

Which meant he couldn't take the West Side Highway to get there (it would be a parking lot), so he had to do some street driving through midtown, the kind of midtown horrible that existed between Madison Square Garden and Times Square. His least favorite thing. But he'd drive through that mess for her, of course. "Thirty-eighth and what?" he asked.

"Seventh? Eighth? Sixth?"

She looked adorably confused, so it would probably be a horrible idea to ask her if the place had parking. So he didn't. Instead, he nodded, smiled, and put the keys into the ignition. "Let's do this."

Molly

MOLLY FELT LIKE an idiot. She wondered what had possessed her to get into Jon's car without a clear idea of their destination. Unfortunately, until she sat beside him in that car, fear had paralyzed her. Even contemplating going into that space without Aunt Linda was turning her into a scared little rabbit.

Fear was also destroying her chances with the cute boy who had volunteered out of the goodness of his heart to drive her. A chauffeur who kissed better than she'd ever been kissed before, and that was before the amazing, wonderful moment that had ended too quickly in the elevator. But now she was screwed. Big-time.

She sighed, sitting back in her seat. And then discovered the car wasn't silent anymore. There was music, a song she recognized.

"I love this song!"

She hummed along, then began to sing, horribly, off key, to the story of a singer who was unexpectedly drawn into a deeper connection with a woman he'd just met by the music they were dancing to. And caught Jon's slowly growing smile out of the corner of her eye.

"Me, too," he said.

As she was discovering, Jon was deliberate about what he listened to; there were reasons for every song he played, every note that came out of his very *very* expensive sound system. He loved music, and was unapologetic about it.

"I'd be dancing, too," he continued, "but well." He gestured, unnecessarily, at the wheel in front of him.

She grinned back at him and began to move her hips and shoulders. Swaying back and forth as much as the seat belt would let her, following the rhythm until the song, and their red light, ended.

She also realized she knew the next song he'd put on, about a guy who really enjoyed doing the things that made his gal happy. She even liked watching him attempt to dance behind the wheel the next time they stopped. And how he altered the lyrics to fit his purposes, well, rather . . . her.

"You like watermelon candles?" he wondered.

"And kisses sweeter than Moscato wine," she replied, earnestly.

"And my fingers through your short hair?"

The last made her laugh; she wondered what he was thinking. Glad she hadn't messed up. Which meant he deserved an explanation. "I'm sorry," she said softly. "This was my aunt's favorite place. The chef and my aunt were . . . involved as much as she'd let him. We were there every Friday and every Saturday night. She wasn't well for a while, and I just . . ."

She felt the tears come, even though she didn't want to break down in his car. But she was.

"I'm honored," he said softly, and she felt his hand on hers. "I'm honored that you're taking me to a place that means so much."

She managed a smile, a watery one at best. She knew it, but she didn't care "Thanks for driving, but, maybe we should have taken the subway or something. So much traffic . . . it's making me crazy, and I'm not even driving! I have to wonder what it's doing to you."

He shook his head and hit the gas again "Nah," he said. "It's fine. And, to be honest, I'd actually rather drive than have to wait for the subway. Yes, we have to find parking, and deal with the traffic, but I do it so often that it doesn't really matter. It'd be weird not to have a car with me."

And yet another of her idiocies came to light as they stopped once more. "I didn't even think of that . . . of parking. I'm so sorry . . ."

Once again he shook his head. Whether out of kindness or habit or whatever, she wasn't sure. "It's fine," he replied. "As I said, I drive everywhere. Mostly. So I know of different places to park. Here." And she watched, completely spellbound as he made a left turn out of nowhere and pulled into a garage. "This is one of my favorites, and it's nice to be able to use it when I need to."

The song switched, from English to Hebrew, to a woman's clear voice singing over a guitar. She listened closer, starting to recognize that it was a bright, fast paced version of a song speaking about the goodness of G-d. She'd sung a version of that song at Saturday morning services with Aunt Linda. "This is beautiful," she whispered.

"And apt," he replied, grinning. "Because it is good."

She watched him navigate the space of the parking lot and pull into a space with the ease of someone who did know exactly what they were doing. "I'm impressed," she said.

"No need," he answered, and she saw the flush that began to color his cheeks. "I come here a lot. It's kinda like my unofficial office garage."

"You still managed to pull a parking garage out of nowhere, and . . . well," she smiled, "I think that's a victory. And fabulous."

He laughed. "Victory I'll take. Fabulous," he continued as he put on the parking brake and shut off the car, "not so much. But thank you."

Then he unbuckled his seat belt and got out of the car, running around to the other side. "Here," he said when he opened her door. "My lady?"

She took his hand, and his lead, getting out of the car,

moving to stand at his side. She watched as he closed the door behind her, locked it, and once again offered his hand. She wasted no time in taking it.

"Shall we?" he asked.

She nodded, feeling lighter and maybe a bit hungry. "We shall. Onward and upward to food."

He laughed, and in that moment she felt comfortable and prepared to do something she hadn't been able to do in over a year. With Jon's quiet confidence and support, she took a step forward, toward the piece of her great-aunt's heart she'd left behind. And maybe toward the future.

Jon

THE PLACE WAS huge; that's all Jon could really think of after they'd gotten past the entrance. It was gigantic, and it smelled amazing. Like home in a way but not.

Yet because Molly refused to move more than a step away from the entrance, there they stood. Even as the clientele seemed to move like a mighty ocean, backward and forward, in and out, to a table or to the counter, Molly—and as a result Jon himself—stood silently, merely steps away from the door.

He put his arm around her, drew her closer. He hoped that the contact would remind her that she wasn't alone. But he didn't want to do anything that was going to make her feel rushed, like speak or move.

He also expected a reaction. The squeeze of a hand;

something that let him know what she was thinking or feeling. But what he got was something else entirely. He felt her turn toward him and put her head on his shoulder. He felt her shudder beneath his touch before he heard the gasping breath and a short plaintive wail that usually heralded tears.

"I can't do this," she whispered, anguish in her voice. "I can't . . ."

He nodded. "Okay," he said as he stroked her hair, then her back. "You don't have to if you're not ready."

But she showed no signs of moving, and he wasn't going to move her until she was ready to do that, either. So they stayed where they were.

Except at some point he became aware of how accommodating the crowd was, how they weren't being asked to move, or bumped into or yelled at. The New York that Jon knew wasn't as rude as what people thought, but had its edge. People needed to get places, do things in the short time they had during their daily lives. But this? This reminded Jon of the suburbs of his childhood, and he didn't know how to explain it.

"Molleleh . . ."

The deep rasp of a voice broke into the sudden silence. He looked up to see an older man, with a bit of a white scraggly beard, sweat pouring from his brow even if it was the dead of winter, standing between them and the crowd, his eyes blinking.

"Oy, Molleleh," he said again.

He felt Molly's grip on his sides tighten, heard her gasp a breath. "I . . ."

Then she was out of his arms, heading toward the older man and letting him pull her into an embrace. He didn't want to watch; this was a private moment, and they deserved not to have his ears (or eyes) focusing in on every word. So like usual, he listened to the music.

A Chanukah song played in the background. Jon recognized it as something an a cappella group had released a few years before. He tried to remember the crazy video that the group released along with the song.

"Jon?"

He focused on the voice he'd started to think he'd recognize anywhere. Molly was beckoning him toward where she stood, the older man's beefy arm around her shoulder.

And so he walked over to her.

When he'd managed to cross through the ocean of people and arrived in front of her, she beamed at him. "This," she said, gesturing to the older man, "is my Uncle Abe."

Molly

The food smelled amazing, but it always did when Uncle Abe was involved. She didn't even order; she let him work his magic as they sat at the small table just off the kitchen. And he'd produced latkes, kugel, and brisket that made the cold winter air disappear.

Uncle Abe also seemed impressed with Jon, which boded well. Jon was the perfect gentleman to boot; he treated Uncle Abe with respect, which was important. He also ate well, and made complimentary noises about the food when his mouth wasn't full.

"So what do you do, Jon?"

Uncle Abe's question came as Jon's mouth was full of brisket.

"Uncle Abe," she said, maybe in his defense, maybe buying him time. "Give him a chance to eat."

Abe nodded, his eyes focused on Jon's. "Yes . . ."

"So," Jon answered, wiping his mouth with a napkin, "I work with musicians, and I like to think that I'm creating an all-star team of the best and the brightest. But I really like the fact that it's a job I enjoy, something that I never in my wildest dreams thought I'd do."

"When you were a kid, this is what you thought you'd do?"

"When I was a kid, Mr. Lefkowitz," he said as he shook his head, "if you'd told me I'd be doing this, I'd have thought you were lying or altered by some chemical substance. Because when I was young, it wasn't possible."

"So what happened? And please, Jon, call me Uncle Abe."

Jon smiled, and she loved what that smile did to his face. "A miracle happened, Uncle Abe," he said formally, "and I was ready."

She watched the solemn expression as Uncle Abe nodded.

"You see it, too, hmm?"

Uncle Abe smiled. "I know a few things about miracles. Thank you for bringing me another one."

She watched as Jon raised an eyebrow. "What? How did I . . . what?"

"Well the first one is that good song about Shabbat. You're that Jon, hmm?"

She saw the blush make its way across his face, the bright red color that matched her freckles and her hair.

"I . . ."

"Oy. You didn't write the song, *tateleh,* but you made sure that boy knew he had to write it. Which was your first miracle. The second? Well, that you brought my Molleleh, my little Molly, back to me."

Jon

JON REALLY ENJOYED sitting with Molly and her uncle as they shared stories and reconnected. The food was amazing, and the fact that Molly had allowed him a bit deeper into her life and heart was a priceless gift he'd have to figure out how to reciprocate. Unfortunately, the evening seemed to wear on Molly. She was tired. And she was crying. She tried to hide the tears, but he watched her fail. Watched as her green eyes turned brighter, as the drops of water trailed down her cheeks.

He was too far away to give her his napkin, a tissue or dry her tears himself. It was the only moment he regretted giving Abe the only chair adjoining hers, and the only reason he'd ever be annoyed at himself for gallantry.

Now they were leaving, having gone through the routine of placing the order for the party after they'd eaten their fill. Abe had even offered to come to the party, and he could see the brightness in Molly's eyes as she told him he should come, but not with the food. As her guest.

Another embrace followed. Then Jon led Molly out of the restaurant; his coat clad arm around her, her hat-covered head on his puffy shoulder.

"Thank you," she said softly.

"You're welcome," he replied. "Anything."

"Really?"

He smiled as he continued toward the car. "Yes."

They walked enveloped in cold and silence, and maybe a bit of something else. He hoped so, because the silence wasn't bad. It was just there. He pulled her in closer and kissed her cheek. He felt her squeeze his glove covered hand with her own.

When they reached the car, he could barely let her go, but he did, settled her in, put her seat belt on, and closed the door.

He drove fast, the heater barely working, but he didn't care. He needed to get her home, to her apartment and the safety of her own space.

"I don't want to be alone tonight," she said softly as they pulled into the garage. "I just . . . I can't."

He nodded. "I'm here," he said. "I'm here."

Molly

MOLLY TOOK JON's hand as they headed into the elevator. As the doors closed behind them, she let him hold her and put her head on his shoulder. But she wasn't going to cry; not in that elevator and not on his coat. She forced herself to be strong and fought the tears.

"It's okay," he said.

The tone of his voice held neither pressure nor expectations. It was soft and gentle and promised he'd help fill the space that had opened in her heart.

"Hold me," she whispered.

This was grief, and she knew it well. It tasted foul, destroying the sweetness of Uncle Abe's hours in the kitchen and the sweet stories he shared. Dammit. She hated this. It made her weak and she wasn't.

But Jon didn't ask any questions, didn't say anything stupid. He didn't even pressure her to answer some dumb question. He just let her hide in his arms, and let her cry on his shoulder.

"I miss her," she said. "I still . . ."

"You always will," he replied. "And it's okay. Trust me."

"Don't leave me alone tonight," she whispered. "Please. Don't."

"Not going to," he replied as she buried herself deeper into his hold. "No chance. Your place or mine?"

"Yours," she said softly. "I'll meet you?"

She felt him nod against her. "That's fine." She felt his fingers running through her hair. "Get comfortable, and come down . . . I'll be waiting."

Jon

When the elevator arrived at her floor, she showed no signs of letting go of him. He didn't force the issue, even as the bell rang and the doors opened.

"I should . . ."

"Nah," he said. "I'll walk you home."

She laughed, and it was a sound he treasured. He knew how difficult it could be to laugh sometimes.

"I guess chivalry isn't dead?"

He shook his head as they walked out of the elevator, smiled at her and led her to her apartment door. She showed no signs of letting him go even then, so he smiled. "Yours is fine."

She put her head on his shoulder again. "I feel so silly," she said softly.

He simply held her. "It's okay," he whispered once he decided it would be okay to talk. "I understand."

She sniffed, though her eyes were bright with tears she clearly didn't want to shed. But aside from the tears, he saw doubt, which was okay, too.

"Come on," he continued, holding out his hand. "Together?"

She nodded tentatively as she let him go, taking his hand instead. "Together."

Molly

SHE REACHED INTO her pocket, pulling out her keys. Both locks, she reminded herself as she unlocked the door. She could barely think clearly enough, yet somewhere in the back of her mind she found herself wondering whether she'd managed to clean her apartment, maybe it was still a mess . . .

"It's okay," he said.

She wondered what had clued him into the fact that something was wrong. Well, the tears and the fact that they were still standing in front of her door with the keys in the lock. He was also holding her, and could probably feel the tension in her muscles.

"I'm sorry," she managed once she was capable of moving her fingers enough to open the door. "I—"

"It's fine," he said softly as the lock clicked open. "It's okay. Memories can do that."

She nodded, wondered how he understood so much. Then realized he probably had memories of his own. She wondered if he'd tell her his story, his memories, because she wanted to learn about the man he was when he wasn't working.

"I'll tell you," he whispered. "I'll tell you everything you want to know."

His hand reached out, covering hers on the doorknob. It was warm, slightly callused, and it felt like home already. He twisted his wrist and the doorknob opened beneath their hands.

And with him behind her, supporting her, she felt like she could step over the threshold.

Jon

Jon expected her to breathe or relax in some way once she'd stepped into her apartment. She didn't. She barely seemed capable of stepping beyond her welcome mat.

He held her, whispered into her ear. "It's okay."

"I need to be strong," she said, her voice barely louder than a breath. "I . . . I just can't,"

"That's okay, too," he said. "There will always be days like this."

"Why can't they stop? Why—"

"Shhh," he murmured. "It's normal. I promise . . ."

He watched as she pulled herself together, took a breath, wiped her face with the back of her hand.

"I'm all right," she said, her voice a bit stronger than it had been.

It might have been a trick, probably it was her attempt to convince herself. But he wasn't going to break down a wall she'd built. "Sure," he whispered, but he didn't move. He'd let her pull away from him on her own.

And she did, stepping two inches away from him.

"Take off your coat and stay awhile," she said, a sniffle behind the words. "I'd like that."

He nodded, reached for his zipper as she started separating the buttons on her coat from the hooks. Then he put his coat on top of hers, his scarf on top of her hat, his gloves on top of hers. As she removed her winter layers, he searched her face for signs of life, of something that wasn't the sorrow that seemed to drown her.

"It's okay," she said.

He nodded, not sure whether she was trying to reassure herself or him. He didn't have words for either. So he just let the silence speak for him; he hoped she'd be able to find the right answer.

"You're good?"

He nodded. "Absolutely," he replied. "I'm splendid."

She gave a short, quick nod. "I'm going to change, okay? You can stay . . . leave . . . or . . ."

"I'll stay," he said quietly. "You get comfortable." He couldn't miss the relief in her eyes; he wondered what she'd expected him to do. Maybe someone else would have been disappointed or annoyed. But not him.

"You sure?"

He nodded. "I'll make myself useful somehow." Then he thought of his sisters and what they'd want in a moment like this. Not just from him, but from . . . a guy they might like, or feel something for that was more than friendship. They'd want chocolate, they'd want affection. They'd want something special. "Cocoa?"

She nodded. "Yes. Please. Maybe? Of course."

He laughed, but tried to keep it calm, cool and relaxed. "I'll be here with cocoa when you're ready for me. Okay?"

Once again she nodded, but there was something else in that nod. Maybe a little bit of strength. Possibly some self-assurance. He hoped. Either way, as she walked away and headed toward her bedroom, he knew he'd be there for her when she came back into the living room.

Molly

Only a fool would leave the guy she might be starting to fall in love with in her kitchen alone as she went to change into comfy clothing. Yep, Molly confirmed, she must have lost her mind. But there she was, in her bedroom, taking off the rest of the winter layers, and changing into comfortable clothing; a shirt that reflected the name of her favorite candy, a pair of gray sweats she'd worn since her first year of college. It was horrible. But it's what she needed, and maybe Jon understood that. At least she hoped he did. It was important to her, and perhaps to *them*, that he did.

She needed to be held, to cry, and she needed him to get that she was grieving and not be terrified by her emotions. Though he seemed like he understood. As she walked back into her living room, she couldn't mistake the smell of chocolate coming from her kitchen.

"Whoa," she managed, the words slowly coming out of her mouth. "How?"

He had a bunch of different ingredients laid out on the counter, and both the teakettle and a pot were going on the stove. The pot had a plate on top of it, almost like the improvised double boiler she'd seen on a cooking show. And the smell . . .

"Sisters," he began. "I have two of them. Both of them

like hot cocoa." He paused to stir what had to be the remains of the baker's chocolate she'd bought ages ago.

"One is lactose intolerant, the other is not. Two different recipes, taught to me by two different sisters, and a mother who had a third recipe. This," he continued as he waved a hand over the counter, "is a . . . hybrid mix of all three. You didn't have milk in the fridge, but you didn't have any other dairyless things, which meant . . ."

He shook his head as the blush rose through his cheeks. "Sorry."

"You're adorable," she managed. "I'd hug you, but you're busy. It's a tricky thing you're doing. I'd never touch a double boiler . . . or whatever it is you're doing. I'll kiss you after you've finished making the cocoa. Maybe I'll supply a special treat to go along with your concoction."

She tried to remember where she'd managed to put her secret stash of fluffy, white, gooey kosher marshmallows. She always overbought during Passover and slowly doled the results of her treat hoarding out over the year, only to continue overbuying the next Passover. It was a cycle she enjoyed, which paid off during moments like this one.

"Here," she said, holding the package of marshmallowy goodness out to him. It was closed, wrapped well with the treats inside.

"Thanks," he said, surprise in his voice. "Wow. You are amazing."

She blushed. "Thank you," she said. "I'm addicted and obsessed. Not amazing."

He smiled, then turned back to the complicated maneuverings that making his hot cocoa required. Stirring, pouring, and then topping the mugs with the marshmallows she provided.

"Voilà," he said with a flourish as he placed the mugs in front of her.

And then, without pausing for a second, she kissed him. She let her fingers fly through his hair, her tongue brush his, and her mouth press against his own.

"Thank you," she murmured against his mouth. "Thank you"

Jon

Jon wasn't sure how they ended up on her couch, her holding him like he was her own personal security blanket, but he wasn't going to complain. She needed this, she needed him, and he was comfortable.

"Talk to me," she said. "Please."

"About?"

"Your childhood? Your parents?"

He sighed, taking a breath as he managed to pull a piece of her hair off her face. "Mom was special. Took my sisters and me everywhere. We had the best road trips, the best food. We went crazy places each summer; my mother had family everywhere, and so we'd visit them on the way to some weird great American landmark. It was wonderful. The rest of the year, she took me to practices, debate, Sunday school, music lessons, and bar mitzvah lessons, and didn't even complain once. "

He held his breath, waiting for the question he knew she'd ask, the question everybody asked him. And when it didn't come, he smiled. "I had four sets of grandparents who doted on me regularly, and if they didn't like my mother, I never knew it. As far as I knew, they loved her as much as they loved my sisters and me. Childhood was . . . amazing, actually. I was lucky to have the relatives I did on both sides of the family."

"I loved my parents," she said, settling her head on his chest, "but they live on the other side of the country. I didn't grew up in New York, but I went to college here and never looked back. I had Aunt Linda, and that was all I needed here, really. I mean I went back for certain things, but I mostly made my family come here. My grandmother didn't need much of an excuse until she died, and my father indulged my grandmother, and my mother indulged my father. I was an only child," she said, "so they all, I guess, indulged me."

"Mom still lives in Westchester," he said. "One of my sisters lives in Queens—the one who's lactose intolerant. The other lives in a Prospect Heights shoe box, as she sinks most of her money into her crazy Manhattan bakery."

The question still hung between them; at least he could hear it.

"I lost my father when I was about ten," he said, because she needed to know and wasn't going to ask.

"Nobody expected it; he'd gone out for a jog on an early morning, and . . . he never came home. It was hard. My mom figured it out, but it was hard. She focused on us instead of herself. She wanted to make life better for us, easier for us. I know, now, my grandparents all chipped in and helped her, but there it was."

"So that's how," she said softly.

He wondered what she meant, what she was talking about. Then decided that it didn't matter so much.

"It's how you understand," she said, her voice barely louder than a whisper. "It's how you get why I'm such a mess right now and how you know it will eventually be easier even though it won't ever go away, or that you don't ever want it to go away."

"It won't. It doesn't. I mean, yeah. I wish he was here to be part of the craziness that my life has been, and I wish I could have asked his advice for so many things, but my grandfather . . . both of my grandfathers stepped up in in a way that never would have happened otherwise."

"So you got to know them better than you would have?"

He nodded. "Yeah. I did. I definitely did."

She sniffed, and he pulled her closer. "I guess I did, too. I mean . . . . . . coming here, staying here, living here . . . I got to know Aunt Linda better than I ever would have if I'd stayed back home. I got to see the world through her eyes. And yet . . ."

"You lost her."

And that was when she burst into tears on his chest. All he could do, all he wanted to do, was to hold her like she needed. This time he let her cry on his stomach, held her in the warmth of her apartment, filled with love and memories.

"This was her place," she said, her voice scratchy with tears. "It's hard . . . I've made it mine in most ways but I just . . ."

"You need a bit of her to still be here," he answered. "I know. My mom left his study the way it was for years. Longer, I think, than she needed it to be there. Mostly because she realized that I went in there a lot. I did homework in there, went in there to study and to maybe try and smell like him for a little bit. It made me feel like he was still there for just a little bit."

"Your sisters?"

"They're older than I am so they got more of him. They didn't really . . . act like they'd lost him in front of me all that much, because I think they focused on me, and making sure I was okay. I didn't notice when I was younger, but I'm guessing they did a lot of crying with my mother after I'd gone to bed." He paused and remembered late nights where one of his sisters needed hot chocolate. "It's also when I learned how to make hot cocoa, and why I started to obsess over coffee."

She put her head on his shoulder, settled in against him like she'd needed a pillow.

"Mom was busy on certain days," he continued. "Saturday was an early morning. Breakfast was my mom's favorite meal of the day, so she taught me how to make coffee. Every Saturday morning she'd make breakfast and I'd make her coffee, and we'd talk. We'd have time to chat. My sisters both liked cocoa, and they were always trying new recipes, you know? They always had a willing guinea pig in their little brother, so I drank a lot of cocoa and paid attention to the recipes."

But he trailed off, feeling her breath rise and fall on his chest. He smiled, lay back against the armrest and closed his eyes, dreaming of her.

Chapter 4

Jon

JON LOOKED AT the clock and wondered when Molly was going to arrive. He was looking forward to seeing her, even though he wasn't sure how he'd react. The parting hadn't been bad, just confusing.

He also still hadn't gotten over the mess of emotions from the trip he'd just gotten back from. He hadn't put away the laundry and CD's he brought back, and they sat in his living room, almost like an open wound. That, plus the awkward parting, left a huge weight on his shoulders.

But when he opened the door, Molly's bright, happy expression chased most of that away. He thanked God, the city streets, and the winter dusk for all of it. She kissed him, the cherry taste of her lip gloss chasing away the awkwardness of a two A.M. departure.

"Hi," he said, finding something in her eyes to be excited about. "Missed you."

He did. He hadn't brought her a gift this time; they'd exchanged a series of e-mails and text messages in the darkness of his lonely Austin night. He did, however, send her his hybrid hot cocoa recipe. He hoped she appreciated it as much as he appreciated having her on the other end of his texts and e-mails.

"Glad you're back," she said as she broke the kiss. "So happy to see you."

He wasn't going to focus on the fact she hadn't said she missed him. She'd said she was "happy" to see him, and he'd try to be okay with that. Instead of focusing on the hard parts, he ushered her into his apartment. "Glad to be back. " Then he stepped away, turning toward the pair of boots he'd left by his mat. "Any other client issues?"

"It's been fine," she replied. "A few clients did have issues, but they were small and fixable. Thankfully."

"I'm glad," he said and smiled. Didn't mention how horrible the trip to Austin had been, tried not to think about it. But it was easy to look at the bright smile on her face, fall under the spell of her green eyes and maybe shove Austin out of his mind for a while. Again.

"Do you have an agenda?" he asked as he tied his boots and headed toward the front closet. "Or are we open?"

"I have a general agenda," she replied. "Nothing specific. Things we need and a question about where to get them." She paused as he pulled his parka out of the closet. "I'm pretty open."

He nodded. "Sounds good," he replied. "I like that." Then he put on his parka and checked his pocket for gloves. "You ready?"

She nodded. "Absolutely."

So he grabbed his wallet and his keys and ushered both of them out the door, locking it behind them.

Molly

MOLLY HADN'T DECIDED what bakery she wanted to order the cake and the pastries from. There were so many different bakeries in Manhattan that she'd always been confused when looking at her options. Jon said that his sister had owned a bakery, so she figured he'd have some insight into which one they should use.

"So," she said as they headed out into the garage. "Any ideas?"

He smiled slightly, shook his head and sighed. "About?"

She wondered if she'd managed to tell him what they were up to today, then realized she probably hadn't. "Sorry. Dessert is on the agenda for today, so I wanted to know your feelings about cakes."

She didn't expect him to be anything but honest, even if it meant he had no idea.

He shrugged; apparently today was a day where gestures trumped words.

Yet as she thought about it, there was something about Jon's mood and the way he spoke that she hadn't seen before. He'd always been upbeat, and even as he smiled today, she could see something was different. So she had to ask. "Are you okay?"

"I guess. This trip was hard."

Which if she actually had been paying attention to anything other than a rapid beating of her own heart upon seeing him, she probably would have noticed. But she didn't. "I'm sorry."

"It's not your fault," he said. His tone was breezy, but she could hear the . . . pain? Anguish? No. But something.

"I've gotten so used to these trips being easy, fun, and generally amazing, so when something like what happened comes up, I'm not prepared."

She wanted to ask him what happened but didn't want to pry. He seemed like he was a private person, hiding his feelings behind the shield of his job. "I'm sorry," she said before realizing she was repeating herself, despite the fact that he said she shouldn't apologize. "I feel bad. Call it the empathetic sorry. I wish it were better."

The genuine smile he gave her was reward enough. "Thanks," he said, his voice sounding a bit clearer. "I needed that. Now, what were you asking me?"

She laughed, recognizing a change of subject when she heard one. "Cakes, desserts," she said. "What are your opinions?"

Another bright, genuine smile from Jon was his response. Now, they were getting somewhere.

"There can be only one," he said as he took her hand. "But I have to warn you, my sister takes no prisoners."

She laughed. "Okay." She smiled back at him. "I think I'm ready." At least she hoped so. She wondered what his sister's bakery would be like. Then she decided that if his sister was as focused on baking as he was on music, it would be amazing indeed.

Jon

THE DRIVE DOWN to Stars and Icing Forever was quick and easy; there was even a good space in the parking lot near the store. Jon hoped that going into the shop would be easy; he wasn't really sure what to expect. His sister Naomi had her moods, but also had her best friend and co-owner Serena to even them out. He even wondered if either his sister or Serena would be in the shop this afternoon, then decided it didn't matter.

"Okay," he said as he and Molly stopped just outside the shop. "This is it. They make everything, I think."

"You think?" she wondered. "She owns this place? Wow."

He turned toward Molly and saw her standing as still as a statue, wide eyes focused up at the sign, her mouth in the shape of the perfect O.

He knew what the sign looked like, of course. Silly cupcakes that were painted red, white, and blue. The blue and white six-pointed stars on the corner, and the dash of Hebrew certifying the place was kosher, by no fewer than ten different organizations. He knew all of those little details as if they resided on the back of his hand.

He also had to remind himself that Molly didn't. She hadn't seen Stars from the beginning and couldn't really know it was his sister's passion project come to life. To Molly, everybody else in the city, and possibly the entire country, Stars was the holy grail of baked goods. Especially after the cake Naomi had made for the press conference/party announcing the creation of the label he worked for.

He smiled at her, and when she didn't really, he squeezed her hand. "You still with me?"

"Give me a minute," she said as she took a deep breath.

He nodded, then told her, "It's going to be okay."

"I know," she replied, a small smile moving across her face. "That's what scares me."

He laughed, then herded her toward the entrance of the shop. "Here we go," he said as they walked in. The smell of the place always hit him hard, no matter how much he braced himself. It hit him now, the smell of pastry, as he made his way into the loud and busy bakeshop.

"Do we need to take a number?" she asked, her voice soft and full of awe.

He thought about it, then decided it would probably be better if they went to see if Naomi was there; she usually yelled at him if he didn't. So he shook his head. "No," he said. "Not tonight."

She gasped. "Wow. We . . . don't need a number. Wow."

He gripped her shaking hand, grinned, and headed up to the front counter.

"You need a number, dude," the young woman behind the counter said.

Jon didn't recognize her, but that was okay; he didn't keep track of the people his sister hired. More importantly, as far as he was concerned it was awesome that she needed to hire more people in order to handle her still growing business. He was extraordinarily proud of what his sister had accomplished. "Is Naomi here?" he asked nonchalantly.

"Who's asking?"

"Her brother," he replied, smiling. "I know she'll kill me for not letting her know in advance that I was coming, but tell her I have a surprise for her."

"She has a brother?" The young woman turned to the person standing next to her.

He didn't recognize her either.

"Naomi Adelman has a brother?"

As if the confirmation from her coworker wasn't enough, Jon himself nodded. Then he reached into his pocket and pulled out his driver's license, before putting it away and taking out his card case. He passed a card each to them. "Here you are. Confirmation." he said, smiling, then said to the first counter woman, "It's fine if she's not here or she doesn't want to see me because I'm an idiot. Tell her I said she was right about Austin."

The woman nodded and walked, leaving the counter, and someone else moved up and took her place.

Jon brought Molly to a chair near a door at the back of the shop.

"Well," a very familiar voice said moments later. "I still love you, you big dork."

He got up, and grinned as he hugged Naomi. "Love you, big sister." He took a step back and looked at her, trying to place the shade of blue she'd dyed her hair. "Blueberry muffin?"

Naomi rolled her eyes, as he expected she would. "Muffins? What?" she said indignantly.

He raised an eyebrow; his sister's inability to choose a shade that wasn't food related never surprised him.

"It's crumble," she said, "but yeah, I could see it as a muffin." And then she turned, met Molly's startled eyes. "You, I presume, are the surprise?"

"Molly," she said softly. "I'm Molly and I'm—"

"Overwhelmed by my brother's inability to act like a human being when other people are involved?"

Jon rolled his eyes as Molly laughed. "Yes," he said, throwing as much sarcasm into the tone as he could. "My loving sister."

"Yep. The bitch lives in Forest Hills."

The expression on Molly's face made him wonder if he'd get out of the bakery alive. And maybe made him think he might not want to.

Molly

Jon's sister Naomi was a hoot. She was sweet, wonderful, and did not bat an eyelash when she sat down to discuss the wide variety of pastries Molly wanted for the party.

"You want both sufganiyot and gulab jamun?"

Molly nodded. "Is that possible?"

Naomi's smile made Molly grin with excitement. "Serena—my partner in pastry—has been dying to play with those lovely doughnut variations, so you'll get them. Which means," she said as she turned to Jon, "Mom's finally going to get her teigelach for Rosh Hashanah next year."

Jon's eyes suddenly shone as bright as his sister's; it was obvious the two of them loved their mother. "Oooh. So we all get to benefit from Serena's pastry experimentation. Excellent."

Finally, despite Jon's desperate and consistent attempts to interrupt, Molly had finished her order. "So that's the list," she said, checking it a second time before taking a deep breath. She felt good, but now wasn't quite sure what to do. Dinner, maybe? Except she didn't want dinner; she just wanted more pastries.

"So," Naomi said, breaking into her thoughts. "Do you guys want to sample or did you just come in to order? 'Cause I need guinea pigs."

She wasn't sure how to answer Naomi; there were many words that wanted to come out of her mouth, most of them wrapped up in awe and praise. And maybe a concern as to whether she was being serious or not so much.

"Feed us," Jon interjected, his hand sliding into place around hers.

Cute boy with suddenly perfect timing? She would have declared her adoration then and there if she wasn't so terrified. His hand in hers was a calming physical reminder of his presence, and she was more than grateful.

"Please."

Naomi looked between her and Jon, the expression on her face hopefully veering on the protective side as opposed to the angry sister side. "You're translating for her already, hmm? Very interesting, Jonny boy. I like that."

"Thanks," he managed.

Molly couldn't help but giggle, and yet as she saw the blush fill his cheeks, she wondered.

"Um . . ."

"Oh don't worry, you boring silly pants loser," his sister teased, "this is how things happen when it goes well. At least I think. I hope."

Molly found it interesting that the implication that they were dating didn't scare her. In fact, it made her excited.

Jon

AFTER SHE'D STEPPED away from her weird combination of mama bear and giggling Gertie, Jon was pleased that Naomi fed them. A lot. New pastries, old favorites, savory experiments, and sweet classics. She plied them with enough hot cocoa (including one batch Jon was sure she'd spiked), lemonade, water, and tea that he felt he was going to float away. He was sated.

More important to his sanity than the food was watching the effect Naomi had on Molly. She giggled, smiled, and relaxed. His sister plied her with sugar, of course. But Molly's happiness made him gleeful, and he needed that. Even if some of big sister's stories came at his expense.

Now, as Molly sat close enough to him to touch beneath the table, it felt more than comfortable. It felt perfect.

"You're lucky I didn't bring out the cute baby Jon stories," Naomi noted, her baker's hands barely affected by her steaming cup of tea. "But that will happen later if my brother doesn't screw it up."

Jon rolled his eyes as Molly looked at him, a bright light in her eyes.

"Really? There are baby Jon stories?"

"Of course there are baby Jon stories," his sister said, her tone indignant. "There are always stories of baby siblings doing something cute or adorable or pouring flour all over themselves in an attempt to look like frosty the snowman."

On any other night, in any other situation, he probably would have yelled at his sister. Yet tonight her insistence at bringing up old and embarrassing stories didn't bother him at all. And he was smart enough to see the difference instantly. It was Molly. Seeing her upset had hurt him, and he wanted to give her things to laugh at, and things to smile about. He also figured that after the crazy, horrible trip he'd taken, he needed some life-affirming silliness that only situations like this could give him

But the expression on his sister's face deserved some kind of answer. So he shrugged his shoulders and took another swallow of tea. "Fine, whatever," he said half-heartedly. "Sticks and stones and all that nonsense."

He saw his sister's eyes go back and forth between him and Molly. Then Naomi rubbed her hands together and stood up. "Well," she said. "That was lovely, but it is late now and I need to either get back to work or close the place down for the night. And you two need to get home."

He looked at his watch, not entirely surprised that it was later than he'd expected. "Thank you, Naomi," he said as he got up to hug her.

"Love you, too, you little brat," she returned gleefully.

"Thank you so much," Molly said. "This was amazing."

"Welcome to the family," his sister, the ogre, replied. "Well, at least thank you for letting me meet her first, even though it's probably not what or when you intended. She paused. "Wait. Is this for the swanky building you moved into after Mom threw a hissy fit?"

He nodded. "Um . . ."

Molly laughed. "Yes," she replied. "And, for what it's worth, you'll fit right in."

"Excellent," Naomi returned gleefully. "See you guys at this party?"

Jon, out of words, nodded. "Absolutely."

Molly

MOLLY WAS THRILLED. Despite the cold, she felt like she could fly. "Oh my God," she gushed, her voice almost a delirious rasp.

Thankfully, Jon seemed level-headed. The adorable man wasn't acting like the best thing in the world had just happened. That was probably because to him it hadn't. After all, it was meeting his sister that had her so star struck. And the fact that he seemed comfortable with her euphoria made her even happier.

"Oh my God," she said again as she squeezed his hand. As if she'd forgotten the rest of her vocabulary, and every single tone that didn't reflect awe.

Once again, if it were possible to eat Jon's expression

with a spoon, she would. It was patient, sweet, and happy in its own way. It made her want to kiss him. Then she realized she could. So as the door of Stars and Icing Forever closed behind them, she did. Her back to the door, she stood up on her toes and put her lips on top of his, letting her tongue explore his mouth. All she could think about was how he tasted, how he felt against her. She felt warm, happy, and light.

Until he broke the kiss, reminding her of the winter cold, her heavy jacket, and the dark night.

Yet she couldn't be angry about it; he looked so sad, she couldn't do anything but brush the errant strand of hair out of his face and smile back up at him. "We should head back," he said, his voice full of regret.

Except heading back didn't have to be bad. In an effort to capture the happiness bubbling up inside of her, she grabbed his hand and began to skip. Which was difficult, because he was laughing, and taller, and it was icy, but they managed to skip together. She did not ask him how (or why) he'd learned to skip; the smile on his face was answer enough. By his side the winter wind didn't seem as chilly. Like experts, they managed to avoid the patches of ice that turned the sidewalks of midtown into a death trap.

Jon was also smiling again. It turned his face into a work of art. She wanted to explore it, sketch it, something, so she could reproduce the moment anytime she wanted to. It was a glorious smile, the kind you couldn't make without being genuinely happy. She hadn't put it there, but she wanted to keep it there. She wanted to make him feel as reckless as she did, and desperately wanted to continue giving him something to smile that way about.

So right in the middle of the street, mere steps away from the parking lot, she kissed him. She ignored the whistles from bystanders and the snarls from people who had to move around them. She focused on the way he tasted and how comfortable he felt against her. Her hands rested on his scarf, then his cheeks. It felt amazing.

She wanted to . . .

He squeezed her hand as he broke the kiss.

"I heart you like this," he said. "I really—"

"Heart, hmm?" She grinned, tried not to laugh as she squeezed his hand. "Think I could light you up like a menorah." His blush was adorable, yet it made her wonder whether she'd gone too far.

"Let's put it this way," he said. "I don't think finding afikomen is going to be difficult . . ."

And immediately, as playfully as she'd been, he was able to mix his metaphors and follow where she'd taken him. Which made her kiss him again, this time damning her gloves to the other side of the planet, wishing she was standing on a beach instead of the cold city sidewalk, dreaming of pulling her fingers through his hair, not her gloves just above his hat.

"Mmm," he replied. "My place is closer."

"One floor?" she wailed against his cheek.

"Come on," he said, before dropping an unexpected kiss on her lips. "Let's get to the car."

His intentions were clear and she nodded, taking his offered hand in hers

"On three?"

She nodded, and then, on his signal, as fast as they dared, hand in hand, they raced across the icy streets to the car. They stopped at the passenger side and he kissed her quickly before he opened the door for her. Now, she felt his hands cupping her butt above her coat. She felt the urgency in the kiss, but knew he was desperately trying not to pin her against the car or anything that she couldn't get out of.

But then he let her go, his mouth separating from hers, the loss a bitter taste on her tongue.

"Do we?"

"Upstairs," he said, sighing even as he rubbed his face with his hands in what had to be defeat. "Otherwise I won't be able to drive."

"Fair point," she returned, knowing full well what he meant even if he hadn't been clear about it. She was also glad he felt the loss of their physical parting as keenly as she did. The last thing she wanted was to feel like this and not have it reciprocated.

But she discovered that she wasn't alone in her agony as she watched him take the long way toward the driver's seat, behind the car and not in front of it. She watched each careful step he took till he got around to the driver's side. Then she watched him open his door and get in.

Then it was her turn, and as she settled in and closed the door, she took a deep breath, rubbing her arms even as she found it colder inside his car than she'd been outside it. She found herself hoping, even praying, that they wouldn't hit traffic, a fuller than normal parking lot, or any other obstacles that would obscure the path between this car ride and his apartment. The faster they got there the better, she decided, as he pulled out of the space.

Jon

THIS WAS THE kind of night Jon hated having brought his car. He wanted to hold her on the subway, kiss her as it sped along the tracks and through midtown then up to their stop. He wished he could have held her hand and ran with her up the stairs and along the street, through the bitter cold and into the building, kissed her again as the doorman looked on, scandalized.

Instead, he had to drive, and focus on the crazy midtown traffic. He had to steal glimpses as she sat in the passenger seat, too close and yet too far away. He had to let the music he chose set the tone and the mood, let the lyrics save the place for his words and his hands.

She smiled. He liked the look of that smile, the focus in her eyes.

"Hmm."

He held his breath and tried not to drive too quickly through the streets of the city; there were lights, cars, crazy pedestrians with a death wish, and buses that had to get where they were going, drivers of horrible looking cars be damned. All of them were an obstacle to him touching her. He hated it. Wished there was some kind of transporter or something that would save him the effort.

Yet when he finally pulled into the parking garage, he was grateful. Except he had to remind himself that the journey wasn't finished. He still had to get to his space and park in a way that didn't destroy his car. So he forced himself to breathe, to steady his hands and drive safely. Ten and two on the wheel, inhaling as he turned into his space, hoping he didn't have to adjust too much. He needed to find the lines and not cross them.

He set the parking break and pulled off his seat belt.

Then he felt her hands on his arm and turned toward her. He put his lips on hers. Her fingertips finding purchase beneath his scarf, on the nape of his neck, pulling him closer. He leaned in over the emergency brake and the console, his fingers questing under her hat.

She tasted of the herbal tea his sister had given them and the sugary pastries she'd eaten afterward. He'd regretted not being able to lick the powdered sugar off her nose, but this . . . this kiss, this powerful moment, was no time for regrets.

"Mmm?"

He tried not to focus on the sound but on the moment and the feel of it.

She pulled him closer. "You with me?"

She sounded out of breath, which was a good thing, but it took time (and her tongue) away from his mouth. "Yeah," he murmured against her lips. But then he realized . . .

She pulled back even farther. "Upstairs?"

He nodded. "Yes."

Molly

THIS TIME WHEN she kissed him in the elevator, she didn't give a damn who was watching. She could barely force her fingers away from the zipper of his coat before he began to move it down the track. His hat fell away easily, and she let her fingers luxuriate in the silken perfection that was his hair.

His mouth felt strong and powerful against hers; he didn't hide from the kiss this time, didn't seem to take a moment to remember himself or his surroundings, like he had in the car. She liked him like this, liked the way his mouth felt against hers. Almost as if by their own accord, her hands found the zipper of his coat, then buried themselves beneath it, wrapping themselves around the waist of his pants, brushing against the softness of his flannel shirt.

He let her push him against the elevator wall, and it took almost a Herculean effort on her part not to jump up, grab his shoulders, and put her legs where her hands had been.

But she didn't. And when the elevator bell sounded, he kissed her cheek.

"Your place?"

"My floor," he murmured into her ear.

Then he lifted her, easily and calmly, into his arms.

She grinned up at him as he carried her out of the elevator and into the hallway. She also tried to remember the last time someone had lifted her, held her in this way, then realized this was a first.

"I like the way this feels," she said, luxuriating in his unexpected strength.

"You like it?" he asked, his eyes as excited as the smile on his face.

"I heart it," she returned as they reached his apartment.

Jon

"NOW WE'RE GETTING somewhere," he said as he attempted to reach for his keys. "Heart, hmm?"

She nodded. "Heart."

"I think this is one of those moments where I wish I'd paid the money for the security system that lets you open your door with the touch of a button."

"One of those moments?"

He found himself laughing, although he understood the reason for the tease. "One of those, yeah. You know. When your arms are full, from grocery shopping or something like that."

"Something like that?"

He laughed, but then, with the expression on her face, he realized he had to clarify. "You know, this is the first time I've done this. I mean carried a girl that I might—"

"A girl?"

"A girl . . . a woman that I might heart."

She laughed, and he loved the sound of that laugh. "Might heart?"

"Might."

And then she kissed him against the doorway, and the force of her lips on his felt like fire. It was perfect.

"I'd have to heart someone who I was bringing in here, you know," he said. "To my own private mess."

After punctuating his words with kisses, he proceeded to carry her across the threshold, laying her across the horrible futon that sat, like the eyesore it was, in the middle of his living room.

"I'd have to heart someone who was bringing me here," she replied, her voice holding a hint of wickedness, of excitement.

He watched as she took off her coat, letting it join the one he'd managed to remove. Then she kneeled and reached up, grabbing his scarf and using it to pull him down toward her. Their lips met in the middle, the feel of them so powerful and strong.

His shirt was flannel, buttoned, and came off easily. Her dress and tights joined it shortly as her hands made short work of his pants, his questing fingers meeting the wet silk of her panties.

"Oh God," she moaned in a voice that made him reckless.

Molly

He explored her beneath her panties, searching for her clit. His fingers were agile and gentle, and she wanted more of them on her. But the touch of his fingers deep inside of her made her want to scream. His fingers knew what they were doing, and she grabbed at his shoulder and cried out against him.

He kissed her shoulder, then she watched him stand. She had no choice but to marvel at the sight of him; his body was beautiful. Like a runner's; tight in all the right places, muscular but not the overly huge muscles of someone who lifted weights. He was perfect, and much stronger than she'd expected beneath the heavy clothing they had to wear.

"Be right back," he whispered.

She nodded, and wondered where he was going. Then she remembered that their apartments had the same floor pattern, so he was either headed to the bathroom or his bedroom. She grinned, anticipating what would happen when he came back. She wanted more of him.

She watched the halls, the walls, and then her mind started to wander toward the apartment and what it would look like with just a little love. It was a blank canvas; maybe she'd suggest some darker colors on the walls, put some comfortable furniture in the living room that he could fall into if he was too tired to make it to his bedroom . . .

The sound of footsteps against the wooden floor of the hallway echoed across the apartment. She sat up, trying to see who it was, then smiled, remembered that it was only the two of them before relaxing at the prospect of his return. Reality, she decided, was much sweeter than her daydreams.

"Welcome back," she said as he slowly got back onto the mattress, brandishing the condom he'd gotten like a flag.

"Miss me?" he murmured as he settled back in to join her, ripping the condom open and putting it on.

"Yes," she replied, grinning. "I definitely did."

Now that she knew what he could do with his hands, she didn't want preamble. She was already wet and ready. That meant there was no obstacle between her and her desire to have his dick inside of her, making her come in the same way his fingers did.

"I need you," she murmured.

Thankfully, he understood what she meant. There was no more foreplay, just entry. She was ready for him. He wasted no time; he was big, ready, and she knew he'd fit inside of her like a glove. And he entered her slowly, pushing past her resistance, before she felt him settle, her body moving to fit around him.

She felt his hands grip her shoulders, and found herself drawn to the graceful curve of his hips. She looked up at him, put her hands around his waist and moved with him as he rocked back and forth. The wave, the feel and the motion and the . . .

"Oh . . ."

"Right with you," he grated, his words a gasp. "I . . ."

And then she felt it, the tightening and the sudden loosening. Magic, perfection, and the best kind of exhaustion. The grip of his hands tightened on her shoulders, and she heard the moan that came from deep inside his throat. And then, as they both lay exhausted on the mattress, she smiled at him and kissed his sweaty cheek.

Molly

SOMEWHERE IN THE darkness, Molly heard Jon's voice

"Tea?" he murmured.

"Mmm . . ."

He kissed her forehead, got up and headed out of the living room. She, watched, transfixed, as he maneuvered around his kitchen, using a hot water thermos she hadn't noticed before to fill two cups. He was so comfortable in his kitchen, moved around it so well. She wished she could move half as well around her entire apartment.

But there he was, and when he returned with two cups of tea, she took hers carefully in both of her hands and sat with her back against his chest, one of his arms wrapped around her.

"I like this," she said.

She heard the rumbling of his chest before she heard him speak. "I do, too. Think I could get used to this."

She smiled, feeling the slight heat of blush on her cheeks. "Yeah."

"Wish I didn't have to go," he said. "But I have a few more hours in this mess."

"Where to this time?"

He put his cup down and carefully pulled her closer. "Nashville. They're thinking about opening another office down there, and they've got a really good Jewish music scene."

"You been?"

"No. Not yet. They tell me it's great, though."

"Mm. Mess?"

He laughed, and he turned, so she could see the look in his eyes. "Yeah. Mess. I'm starting to think I should, at some point soon, start to put some effort into making this place seem more like a home than a frat house."

His face was all contemplation, dreaming of the future. The model she'd been playing with earlier popped back into her mind unbidden. Like she needed any help to start playing with spaces. There was a reason she did what she did, after all.

"I see the wheels turning," he said, kissing her forehead. "I absolutely see those wheels turning. And maybe, at some point soon, when I'm home for a bit longer than twelve hours, we can discuss it."

"It's not my fault I see furniture and colors when you see music," she quipped. "So come on, you know I'm going to ask."

He nodded. "Yeah. I do know you're dying to ask."

She looked up at him, and she could see the wheels turning in his eyes.

"And it probably might help to talk it out with you before I actually go ahead and do something."

He'd said the last grudgingly, as if he really didn't want to.

"It's fine," she said. "We don't have to do this now."

He laughed and kissed her forehead, snuggling closer in to her. "You said the magic words, you know. You said this for you is like music for me. So come on. Ask me."

She shook her head and sighed. "So what would you do?"

He shrugged, sighed. She could see his words weren't going to come easy. Finally, he smiled. "I guess the first thing would be to make this an actual living room, you know? Get a sofa that matched the vibe of coming in here, with people or myself. Something that I could listen to some tunes on. A bookcase or something."

Her mental model got a bit more detailed. Dark colors, comfortable couches, like she'd thought of, a stereo and a cabinet with space for CDs or whatever sound system he wanted. Maybe a TV on the wall.

"Then I'd turn my bedroom into an actual bedroom instead of storage. A nice bed, place to put stuff. Not picky. A desk for the second bedroom. Really turn it into an office."

The mental model expanded from a room to the whole apartment. She allowed his words to shape it; a smaller stereo system, desk space, folder space in the second bedroom. Comfortable carpeting, maybe space for a fridge. And then a bed, dresser, and a table for the bedroom. Another TV on the wall in the bedroom?

She thought a bit more, then opened her eyes to see the look on his face. "I'm sorry?"

"It's fine," he replied, smiling back at her. "I opened the door for a reason." He pressed a kiss to her temple, smiling back at her. "Go on, where are we now?"

She had more ideas in mind, but this was going to be *his* place when he got around to it, *his* idea. Which meant she had one more question to ask him. "Any colors?"

This was the one that seemed to catch him off guard. He shrugged his shoulders, then settled back in. "Don't know," he finally said, trailing off as he looked around the room. "Maybe blue, white. I'm an Empires fan."

"Empires?"

"New York Empires. Semenov, Emerson, that new guy, they call him lucky seven?"

She tried to look interested, tried to muster a degree of understanding, at least.

"Hockey?"

She shook her head. "No . . ."

He raised an eyebrow, as if to say that of everything they'd talked about, this was the thing he was most surprised about. "You're not interested at all?"

She shook her head. "Sorry. Not really."

He nodded, squeezed her shoulder then closed his eyes again. "Colors, right? Um . . . blue, white, red? Maybe?"

Her fingers itched for paper, pen; some way to transcribe the model from her head onto paper. Maybe a sketch?

But instead of giving her a pad, he took her hand in his. "I like this."

"Me, too," she said, kissing his cheek. "A lot."

He took her teacup, and she watched as he brought it toward the kitchen, leaving it on the table. She watched as he walked back to where she lay on the bed, all long legs and hips that swayed. She watched in happy anticipation as he climbed back onto the futon, curling up next to her. She put her head on his chest.

"I leave in a few hours," he whispered. "But for now, we're perfect."

Chapter 5

Jon

JON HATED THE way the winter sun didn't rise until later in the morning. Because leaving Molly in the dark took much more out of him than he'd expected. He knew it was going to be hard; getting up out of bed in general was difficult for him, but this was different. She was sleeping, sprawled out across his mattress, her hair brighter against the white of his pillow. He loved the way she looked there; so much that he wanted to join her again.

But he forced himself away to pack; grabbed the laundry he'd retrieved before he'd gone to get her, his plastic bag of shower stuff and his suitcase. He shoved the clothes in his suitcase, his shower stuff in his backpack, along with the files he needed and the chargers he'd left lined up on his card table.

Once again he passed the middle of his living room, and the futon he'd placed there for all the word to see. His eyes, of course, drifted toward Molly. He couldn't help but stare; she was like a siren, calling him back to bed with her. He wanted to take a picture; he'd never been happier than he was at that moment.

Yet instead of taking a picture, which would remind him of how horrible his place looked, he headed into the kitchen. It would be cruel to wake her when she looked that comfortable; he figured at least one of them should get some use out of his horrible futon.

He moved as quietly as possible, reaching for a piece of paper from the pad where he wrote his to-do list. He needed to write her a note, explaining why he'd left her and what she should do now that he had. Then, after drawing a diagram to show where his nondairy creamer was (in the one cabinet with the annoyingly squeaky door), he set up the coffee.

Once that was done, he watched her again, waiting until the phone in his pocket buzzed, heralding the arrival of his town car. And as the seconds passed, he realized that he didn't want to leave. The realization surprised him. Until this moment his relatively short career had been amazing. It regularly reminded him of the wonderful music that existed in Jewish communities across the country, and made him feel even better that he got to help bring some great voices to a much wider audience. But this time?

He wasn't sure what was at the root of it. Could it be concern that the sour experience he'd had on his last trip was going to carry over into this one? This was Nashville. This was looking at a second set of offices, not convincing someone who'd been an independent artist for years to sign to a label they didn't trust. Nashville wasn't going to be a situation where he'd be called a traitor for working with a label. He'd be going to services at a beautiful temple and listening to musicians who lived in a town where major label interest in Jewish music meant something. This would be good, a fun trip, with good food, great company, and better music.

So if he were being honest with himself, he would admit the lack of desire to travel had more to do with the redhead sleeping on his futon than any actual travel anxiety. No, he wouldn't damn his dreams. And as he finished packing his suitcase, closing it, he realized that he'd give almost anything to have another ticket and a seat on the plane beside him.

Molly

MOLLY STRETCHED, ROLLED over, and realized she was alone. She sat up with a start and looked around the almost empty apartment. There was no sign that anybody else was there. Looking closer, she didn't see either the suitcase that had been left by the hall closet or the pile of clothing she'd seen on one of the folding chairs. That could only mean one thing.

Jon had left her alone in his apartment

She took a deep breath.

Even though she lived only a floor away, Jon let her sleep as he went off to catch his early morning flight. She could barely believe it; but it was true. A guy who hadn't yet adjusted to living in the building had left her in his apartment alone.

She took another deep breath.

Holy crap.

She stretched again, wrapped the sheet around herself and rolled out of the bed. Then she held the sheet with one arm and grabbed her clothing with the other. Thankfully, the futon hadn't done that much damage to her back.

Now that she'd managed to gather her belongings, she headed down the hall toward the bathroom, so she could at least splash some cold water on her face. The hall itself was clear, and she could see color and design and change.

No. He said he'd do it in the future. She was *not* going to turn his apartment into a home while he was gone.

She finished washing her face, dressed, and headed back into the kitchen. On the counter by his "coffee bar" was a note and a mug.

Molly-

Make your way upstairs when you want to. You were too beautiful to disturb.

I left you a mug, and I prepared the single cup coffeemaker. I think there's nondairy creamer in one of the cupboards, but the door is squeaky so I didn't check. Use as you will. . .

Looking forward to seeing you when I get back.

Heart,

Jon

It was, she decided, the cutest note anybody had ever left for her, especially considering the fact that he'd gone ahead and drawn the insides of his cupboard. *Drawn the inside of his cupboard instead of opening it because the door was squeaky.* He hearted her. And she was comfortable enough to say she hearted him back.

She set up the coffee, removed the creamer and the sweetener from the cupboard, and went to wait for it to brew. As the smell of coffee permeated the apartment, she tried to think of how she could do something as nice and as wonderful for him as he did for her.

Chapter 6

Jon

WHEN THE PLANE touched down at JFK, he sighed in relief. Home.

He'd had a wonderful trip; great food, amazing music, and great people. He'd even liked the office space that the Nashville group had found for the fledgling label. But Nashville wasn't New York, and he was tired.

He barely made it through the car ride awake.

"Mr. Adelman," the driver said. "You're here."

He shook himself partly awake, shoved the door open and stepped out of the car. For once in his life he was grateful for the winter chill. "Thanks."

He hefted his bag, signed the driver's sheet, and took his suitcase from the open trunk.

"Mr. Adelman," the doorman greeted. "Welcome back."

"Thanks, Rocky," he replied

"Hope you like it."

He raised an eyebrow as he headed toward the open elevator door, somewhat surprised at the reaction. "What?"

"You'll see," Rocky said, shaking his head. "You'll see."

But the list of things he wanted to see was small. Two different items on it.

The first was his bed. No matter how well he slept when he was away, it was almost like he *had* to sleep on that horrible futon. He knew he needed a new one, but part of the reason he kept that thing was because he knew where he was when he got up with a crick in his neck and a slight backache. Those pains meant he'd made it back to New York, whether his trip was successful or not.

The second was Molly, he reflected as the elevator door opened. He'd bought her presents when he was away; a hockey jersey, some kind of food delicacy that he was told he wasn't allowed to leave without, and her Chanukah present. He'd had it shipped, very well aware that it wouldn't have survived his suitcase (or even his carry-on). They'd talked a few times, texted and e-mailed. He'd even called her from the airport that morning and made plans to see her that evening, once he got up from his desperately needed nap.

Something he saw out of the corner of his eye broke through his thoughts and brought him back down to earth. It was a bow, in the red, white, and blue of many things he loved. He liked the colors, of course, but the bow and the tiny Jewish star he saw hanging from the bow confused him. It wasn't yet Chanukah or a birthday, so why would someone put a bow his door?

He shook his head, deciding he was too tired to think about the bow on his door. He'd deal with it later. He reached into his pocket, took out his keys and unlocked the door. He opened it and discovered he couldn't breathe.

He'd left a bare, unfinished, neutral smelling apartment with a futon he'd had since his second year of college and a coffee table he'd purchased with one of his best friends for his very first New York apartment. He saw neither of those things, and . . . this space smelled.

He didn't have the words to describe the colors, the mess, the furniture, and the apple-scented assault on his senses. This was horribly, unquestionably wrong. It might possibly be what would happen if his dream of making this apartment a home turned into a nightmare.

Jon tried to breathe and failed. He desperately wanted comfort, ease, relaxation, familiarity. He wanted his own possessions, his own space after traveling.

This wasn't it.

He tried to think of who might have done this, who might have invaded his privacy this way. And then his heart clenched. Because the only person who had this kind of access, the only person he'd told about his desire to do something with the place at some point, was Molly. Molly also had the resources to do *this*. Molly had the contacts. Molly was good at her job; he'd Googled her at one point.

But it felt like a betrayal. He'd given her his keys, and she'd taken over his apartment. Without his permission. She'd made his safe space unrecognizable.

He put his bags down, and closed his eyes. Tried to find some degree of calm and failed. He was angry and disappointed and upset and all of those horrible things at the same time. So he left the apartment, closed the door and locked it. Then he went upstairs.

Molly

MOLLY HAD BOUGHT a few candles from her favorite candle shop, and couldn't wait to light the first one. So she'd chosen a custom scent meant to symbolize Chanukah, and lit it before lying down on her couch with a cup of tea. As the candle's strong cinnamon scent filled the air, she began to contemplate when she'd make latkes. The party was in less than a week, on the first night of Chanukah. Life had been going well; she had decorated a few spaces and finally finished as much as she could do with Jon's place without his involvement. She lay back against her couch, closed her eyes

She couldn't believe she'd been able to do it. He hadn't given her much, but she did her best with the material he'd given her. Designing and organizing a space for him had been a way of giving him the sense of home that he clearly seemed to miss. He was homesick for something he'd never had, or at least that was what it seemed like. And that made decorating and designing his space, in his apartment, the perfect first Chanukah present.

She couldn't wait to see him.

Yet she had started to drift off when she heard the knock on the door.

Stretching, she got up off the couch and put her teacup on a coaster. "Coming," she said as she headed toward the door. She wondered who it could be. After opening it wide enough to see who it was, she was startled.

"Jon?"

"I need you to come with me. Now."

She swallowed. There was no expression on his face, no hint of emotion. She wanted to say something, anything . . . but there was nothing she could say in the face of the blizzard in his eyes.

"Just come with me."

He didn't offer his hand, just waited with the barest hint of patience.

The tears began to gather inside of her, and she did her best to focus. She blew out her candle, grabbed her keys, closed and locked the door. Then she followed him down the hall toward the hidden staircase that separated their floors. Along the way, she hoped he would soften, maybe even speak to her, but nothing.

He yanked open the metal door to the stairway, still silent, and she followed. His posture made him look like he'd been cut from winter's ice.

"I—"

"No."

She sniffed, and wiped her eyes sloppily with the back of her sleeve. Her heart pounded with every step she took. She tried to keep up with him but knew it wasn't going to be easy. Especially when they arrived at his apartment.

It was as if he was about to place her head in the guillotine. She held her breath as he opened the door, not even pausing to see if she'd follow him. He stormed inside and gestured wildly, angrily.

"What is this?"

The tone of his voice made her shiver. She couldn't think. The words were stuck. "I—"

"No."

He stepped farther into the apartment and she followed him.

"This," he gestured widely, "is an invasion of my privacy. I realize that I discussed things with you and said that I'd work on getting this done, but this . . ."

She watched the expression on his face go from frozen to hurt.

"I trusted you," he said, as the sadness crept into his voice. "I left you in my apartment with my keys. And this is what you did."

"I—"

He put his hand up to keep her from speaking, and the words that wanted to jump off her tongue stopped. Completely.

"Yes," he said, sounding tired now. "Your intentions were good. I understand that. But . . . no. It was an invasion of my privacy. My trust. I want all of it gone. By the time I get back next week, I don't want any evidence this ever happened. We're done. I can't deal with this. You didn't have any right whatsoever to decorate my apartment without my help or approval."

She couldn't say anything, still didn't have any words she could use to make this okay. "I—"

"No. You did it. You get it undone."

Then he gestured toward the door, and even though he didn't say a word, she knew with every fiber of her being that he meant her to leave. Only when she got to her own apartment one floor above did she let herself break down.

Chapter 7

Jon

Jon couldn't stay in the "renovated" apartment. Not at all. His skin crawled, his heart was beating too quickly. The only alternative was that he had to go. So he headed downstairs, bags in hand. His hands were shaking too much to drive, so he needed a taxi.

The elevator came quickly after he'd stabbed the button, and Rocky looked at him as if he'd lost his mind.

"What's wrong Mr. Adelman?"

"I need a cab. And it's Jon."

Mercifully, Rocky was good at sniffing out cabs, that or able to call one at a moment's notice. Either way, it was a huge relief when the bright yellow cab came up to the front door.

"Where are you going?" the driver asked.

"Brooklyn. St. Marks between Franklin and Classon," he answered almost reflexively. Then he closed his eyes and sat back in the cab, letting the rhythm of the city put him to sleep. Or at least tried. Because he couldn't shut off his brain. He was upset, annoyed, out of his own head. So he looked through the window, watching the cars, listening to the noise.

He hoped his sister was home, on one of her few days off. He needed family. And as the cab drove through the traffic filled streets of the city, he realized how desperately he needed it. It didn't matter that the Brooklyn Bridge was so clogged that it reminded him of a parking lot. All he cared about was that his sister was going to be on the other end.

Finally, they pulled over in front of his sister's apartment building. He paid the driver, tipping him extra, knowing how much of a pain it had been to drive through horrible traffic created by the two boroughs at rush hour. And then he got out of the car, closed the door, and headed to the building.

"You up there?" he asked as he pressed on his sister's buzzer.

"Yep."

The buzzer rang into the darkness, the door opened easily, and the elevator waited. His sister opened her door quickly and wasted no time in dragging him inside.

The surprised expression on her face shocked him more than the annoyed/impatient one he'd expected. "What the hell?" he said.

"What the heck are you doing here now?"

The answer wasn't an easy one, so he chose an easy question. "You have bourbon?"

He knew his sister all too well and was absolutely certain that she couldn't exist without a few different varieties of bourbon in her liquor cabinet; if he was being honest with himself, it was part of the reason he came to her instead of anybody else. So he expected her to roll her eyes. "Obviously," she replied, boredom in her voice. But then she focused on him, widened her eyes and stared. "What's it to you?"

Wanting some bourbon from his sister's stash was different from knowing it existed. And when he felt like his world was falling apart, asking for some was difficult. But bourbon was soothing, especially when he was drinking it and spending some quality time with her. So he took a deep breath, ran a hand through his hair and looked straight at her. "I would like some."

His sister sighed, staring at him. He wondered if she could tell his heart was breaking.

"Yep. I'll give you the good stuff. But you have to tell me what happened."

Over two glasses of strong Kentucky bourbon and some freshly made pecan pie, Jon poured out his story. He finished, and sat back against Naomi's couch.

"You asshole," Naomi said, rolling her eyes. "You unbelievable asshole. "

"She—"

"Surprised you?"

"Invaded my privacy."

"You can't invade privacy that you didn't have, Jonny boy. She didn't steal anything you didn't *give* her. She took care of something that was on your to-do list. Did you even *look* at the place?"

He shook his head. "No. I didn't."

She put her glass down and ruffled his hair under her fingers. "You stay here tonight, you go away tomorrow?"

He nodded. "Tomorrow."

"So you go away tomorrow, go back to your apartment and then see it. Then you decide what you need to do. Okay?"

"But she—"

"No. This is a professional woman, not an idiot. You need to see whether she actually stole your privacy or she listened to you."

And deep down, with the help of the bourbon and the pie, he could admit to himself that his sister was right.

Molly

MOLLY WOULD ADMIT that she was a wreck. Her clients were well-mannered and didn't mention if they noticed her eyes were a bit redder than they should have been, or if there were tracks of tears along her face or moments where her voice was raspy when it otherwise should have been clear.

She was able to dodge her phone calls. She managed to hide in her apartment until Friday, when Uncle Abe's booming voice came out of the ancient answering machine she refused to replace.

"Molleleh," he said. "I need to see you tonight. You come to me and I will make you some good Shabbos dinner."

She couldn't refuse a voice like that, not ever, not him. Especially now that she'd taken the time to bring him back into her life again. So she pulled herself together, threw some makeup over the tear tracks, and headed downstairs.

Rocky was on duty in the lobby, and she waved to him.

He smiled at her. "You look beautiful tonight, Miss Baker-Stein. Where are you going?"

Where was she going? Then she remembered; an address that would never change, one that remained fixed in her memory. "To Queens," she replied. "I need—"

Rocky shook his head, as if he found the idea of a taxi absurd "I'll call my friend—he has a car. Better, more comfortable than a taxi for tonight. He'll give you a card, you call him and he'll pick you up when you're ready to come back, okay?"

She nodded, but then she saw the sad smile on Rocky's face. The ever perceptive doorman probably saw beneath her horrible patch job of foundation. "Okay."

She got into the town car when it arrived, and after she told the driver her destination, relaxed. There was something about the craziness of New York on a Friday night that made her feel at home. Everybody was going places, and tonight so was she.

When she arrived at Uncle Abe's building, she took the driver's card, paid, and got out of the car.

"I'm here," she said after pressing the buzzer.

"Come on up," Uncle Abe said, his booming voice carrying across the night.

When she got upstairs, the smell of fresh challah overwhelmed her.

"Come, come," Uncle Abe said as he opened the door. And then he hugged her. "Oy, Molleleh. You are a sight for these sore eyes."

She sniffed. "Thanks," she said. "Your invitation came at the perfect time."

He laughed, a booming laugh that split the room in a way that filled her heart. "Invitation? You don't need an invitation, my little Molly." He kissed her forehead. "We will have Shabbos, then we will have dinner, and then you will tell me why you are so upset, *kapesh*?"

She nodded. "Okay."

ONCE HER STOMACH was full of challah and kugel and brisket (!!!!) and all of the wonderful things that Uncle Abe had spent hours making, she sat with a cup of coffee and spilled the whole story. She was surprised she managed to make it through the whole thing without sobbing.

"Bah," Uncle Abe said. "He doesn't understand your gift, he doesn't get you."

And then she lost it. She lost it all over his shirt, sobbing like she was a little girl all over again, crying on her father's lap. She sniffed and hugged him. "I just . . . he . . . I wish . . ."

The words tried to come, and she tried to explain, but she only had the capacity for tears.

"There, there, Molleleh. It's okay, Shhh."

Her uncle let her cry for hours, it seemed, not really doing anything but patting her head, letting his fingers run down her back.

"The only good thing he did, Molleleh," he said after a while, "was he brought you back to me. That was *it*. He doesn't deserve you." He kissed her on the forehead. "You deserve a prince, Molleleh. You do. You deserve someone who loves you with everything he has and doesn't let go. Who understands when you give them something more precious than life."

"But," she managed, trying not to start crying all over again, "he trusted me, and I—"

"You gave him something he needed, and he was too blind to see it." He smiled. "If that boy is smart, he'll realize how stupid he was. The question is what you're going to do when he tries to get you back."

Chapter 8

Molly

EARLY ON THE Sunday before the party, Molly got a call from Stars and Icing Forever.

"Hello??'

"Hey. It's Naomi. I've got some new things I'd like you to try, I kinda want to test them at the party but I won't do that until you taste them first. Can you come down?"

"I . . ."

"It's okay. I promise. For what it's worth, I'm on your side."

It took a bit for her to realize what Naomi was talking about, then she decided that she didn't want to discuss it further.

"I have chocolate," Naomi said.

"I'll be right down!"

She pulled herself together, threw on a sweater, sweats, her lovely, fuzzy winter boots, then a scarf and her heavy winter parka. Finally, she shook her head and went to the elevator. It was quiet. She couldn't deal with any people this early on a Sunday. Heading out, she waved to Rocky and jumped into a waiting cab.

When she got to Stars and Icing she felt overwhelmed, as before. This time, Naomi herself came out from behind the counter and gave her a hug. "Oooh," she said. "My brother is an asshole, and I'm going to feed you sugar. Come on."

She wasn't sure how to answer that, but she figured she'd be all right.

IN FACT, SHE was more than all right. Pastries and coffee and what seemed like the beginning of a friendship awaited. And yet once they moved on to the spiked hot chocolate portion of the brunch, Naomi turned to her with a clear and frank expression on her face.

"My brother's an idiot," she said without preamble, in a way that made Molly want to sob again. "And I think it's because we babied him after Dad died. My sister, Mom, and I. It's like we all felt we had to keep him in some kind of cocoon, you know, which helped and hurt. We let him have more space than he deserved, let him be . . . more focused on things than he should have been. Not material things, mind, but . . . the genuine sentimental stuff."

"Huh?"

Naomi shook her head. "You must have noticed his insistence on keeping that horrible car? And how that go-dawful card table looks like it should be burned, and all?"

Molly nodded. "Yeah?"

"To him, they're not just things, they're memories.

Which you get, of course. But they're . . . when my mother got rid of the disgusting, old couch we'd had—after one of the springs got loose? He went out and took a picture when we'd finally taken it outside."

Naomi's words made Molly want to cry all over again. "Oh my God, I—"

"Oh for God sakes. The idiot told me what happened. All you have to do is hold on and wait until next week to call in your people to fix the apartment. You didn't randomly walk in there and put your style in there, I'm assuming. If you're anywhere near as good as your reputation says you are, then that apartment is now your version of my brother. If that idiot has half the wit he's supposed to, then he'll be crawling back to you."

"So," she sniffed as she grabbed a napkin from the table. "What does this mean?"

"You two were adorable together, and I'm not going to let him mess things up because he's being an idiot. Only, that is, if you think you can possibly be in a relationship with my brother. Because maybe you don't want to, in which case that's fine. "

She met Naomi's gaze and sighed. "I don't know what to say."

"Right. You're as horrible as he is. Okay. So hold out. Because if you want this, if you want to be with him, there's a chance. I promise."

Chapter 9

Jon

JON HAD RETURNED to New York after a successful trip to Boston, and he'd followed his sister's advice. He also put on some music, a country song that reflected the tears that threatened to burst out of his eyes. The bottom line was that he didn't know what to do.

Because he'd spent the afternoon walking around the apartment, really looking at what Molly had done. It was beautiful. Not just beautiful, but *perfectly him*, as much as he'd described. It was the kind of apartment he'd imagined bringing her to, the kind of apartment where he could come home after a long day, a long flight, or a long weekend.

The living room couches were comfortable enough that he didn't have to go far inside of the apartment to relax. They were leather, and puffy like cotton. The wooden table at the corner, the elegant wooden bookcases that waited to be filled with his CDs, his stereo system. There were even mounting brackets for what he assumed would be a television on walls she'd painted dark blue.

She'd managed to create a room that screamed him, company, comfort, and calm.

He'd gone farther into the apartment to find more evidence of her care. The second bedroom had been painted white, with the logo of the label he worked for in beautiful, blue, Hebrew calligraphy. The desk, the filing cabinets, the bookcase, and what had to be the mounting block for his music player, were all open, ready, and waiting to be filled.

Which meant his bedroom was even more tailored to what he'd wanted. There was only a bed and a dresser, both open and waiting to be filled. In the corners of these walls, just below the crown molding, was a really cool design. He walked closer, intending to take a good look at it. He could smell the tail end of the new paint fumes, which meant it hadn't been here for long.

And when he saw what it was, he lost it. She'd managed to put an Empires logo on the wall, in a way that looked like a classic monogram. She'd put *him* on the walls of his apartment, and he'd been too stupid to notice. He had to get her back.

INSTEAD OF IMMEDIATELY calling to apologize, he needed to figure out what to do. Just bringing her a Chanukah present wouldn't cut it. Not for this. Which meant he needed brain fuel.

He headed to the garage, got into his car and drove down to Abe's deli. He parked in his usual spot, then headed into the deli.

There were huge crowds of people there. Chanukah, and a few other holidays, were coming upon them, so people spilled out of the deli, onto the sidewalk. They flocked to Abe's Kitchen because they wanted to taste the good stuff, deli food made as they remembered it.

He sighed, pulled down his hat and walked farther in. And yet . . .

It was as if the Red Sea had parted; the patrons stepped aside, leaving a path for . . .

"Jon," Abe said. "You. You wouldn't be here unless . . ."

"I love her," he replied, not leaving room for pretense.

"Good. You're a smart boy. So I'll tell you. You want to win back my girl? You tell her what she was trying to tell you. What she did for you. Out of love. She didn't just make you a space you fakacta bum. She made you a home. Now you show her you appreciate it. And her."

He nodded. And he understood.

"Now take this, for you, and go home to your space and think about it."

And based on Abe's tone of voice, there was only one thing he could do. He nodded. "Thank you," he said, taking the bag with one hand and shaking the man's hand with the other. "Thank you."

Then he left the deli.

Chapter 10

Molly

THE PARTY WAS amazing. Naomi, Uncle Abe, and Serena had outdone themselves. The plates, cups, and various candle displays looked gorgeous.

"I can't believe the quartet sounded so good," Mrs. Penkar from the penthouse said, smiling. "And they never sound good. The food was beautiful, too."

She nodded as she watched the partygoers mingling on the dance floor. Aunt Linda would have loved this, she thought

But Jon hadn't shown up. The anger in Naomi's expression had gotten more obvious the longer the party went, but Molly wasn't going to let him destroy her party. The building's party.

"Come on!" said Kelsea from the first floor, who grabbed her wife, Claire, and dragged her onto the dance floor. "They're playing music we can dance to. Let's *move*."

Finding herself without an option in the face of Kelsea's enthusiasm, she followed the couple onto the dance floor. Together, they danced to the string quartet's interpretations of various tunes. Some of them were questionable, some recognizable, and all fun.

She headed off the floor as the music slowed, leaving Kelsea, Claire, and the other couples who'd joined them to dance to a slower, more traditional song about being home for a holiday.

She smiled, watching the happy couples dancing, only to find her gaze drawn toward the handmade glass menorah. It was gorgeous. "Wow . . ."

When she got past how well the menorah reflected the light, she realized that she was looking into a pair of familiar brown eyes. Jon's eyes.

"You made me a home, Molly," he said. "I had a space. It wasn't very much. I wanted something that I could bring you into, so that I didn't worry about having a mess."

"I—"

He shook his head, but this time he looked sad. "You must have had a vision. So you asked me questions, and I answered them. I thought it would be good for me to take care of it, to take responsibility for my own apartment. I didn't want you to be in charge of decorating my apartment, because I wanted you to be able to relax there with me. It was horrible of me to assume you couldn't relax and really enjoy a space you worked in. But that's on me, not you. So anyway . . .

"Anyway, I've never been good with material change, and when I really think about it now, I think I would have procrastinated no matter how much I'd spoken about wanting a relaxing space. I was already making my own excuses, even thinking how having a pain in my back from that horrible futon was the reason I knew I was back in New York."

She heard a laugh, and knew it wasn't her.

"Yeah. It is funny. But the thing is, you saw through my excuses without even seeing them. You listened to what I said I wanted, and you gave it to me in a way that said 'me.' You made that space mine in a way I couldn't believe was possible no matter what I'd said."

"Thank you."

"The thing is, though, there's something missing, something that I couldn't add with my own stuff. And that 'missing' thing is you. The kind of you that would come over a lot, and leave things and let your stuff intermingle with mine, so I could smell your scent on the pillow when I come back from a trip, see your dishes in my fridge . . . that I'll let you into places that aren't just my apartment. Right now I heart you, but I feel like . . . I know there's more than that 'heart' between us. I want a beginning, a new one. Another chance."

"You trust me to respect your limits?"

He nodded. "Yeah. Because I think some limits are too silly to have and need to be challenged." And then he smiled. "I expect you to know the difference between the hard ones and the soft ones."

She nodded. "Okay."

He put his arms around her, and she felt the press of his lips on hers. He tasted like latkes, sufganiyot, and wine. And maybe the sweet hint of forever.

nothing [illegible] was the reason I [illegible] in New York."

She nodded, laughed, and knew it was true.

"Noah, this [illegible] the thing is that [illegible] [illegible] and I [illegible] you gave it to me in a way that [illegible] that made that space come in a way I couldn't believe was possible no matter what I did."

"Thank you."

"The other [illegible] though, there's something missing, something that I couldn't [illegible] with [illegible]. And that missing thing is you. The kind of [illegible] that would come over after and leave messages and let you [illegible] through with me [illegible] and could smell [illegible] on the [illegible] when I come back from a trip, [illegible] my [illegible] [illegible] places that [illegible] my apartment. That day I heard you on [illegible]. I know I want more than that. More between us. I want a beginning, a new one. Another chance."

"Doesn't the [illegible] your [illegible]?"

He nodded. "Well. Because I think [illegible] are [illegible] need to be challenged." And then he smiled. "I expect you to know the difference between the [illegible]."

She nodded. "Okay."

He put his arms around her and she felt his lips on her [illegible]. His [illegible] and [illegible] out of his [illegible].

All I Got

KK Hendin

Chapter 1

"Everyone has one place on earth that they connect to. They don't have to have ever been there to feel the connection, but for every person, there is a place on Earth that has their heart.

For every Jewish person, there are two places. One place of their heart, and one place of their soul. The place of your soul is somewhere in Israel. Sometimes the place of your heart is, too."

—R.K.

THE FIRST THING I do when the plane touches down in Israel is cry. Happy tears, streaming down my cheeks as the plane taxis slowly to a stop. The nice Christian lady sitting next to me is all sorts of confused, but too polite to say anything to a nineteen-year-old girl sobbing as the plane lands in Tel Aviv.

The Israeli lady sitting in the seat on the other side of the nice Christian lady would have said something, but she's already on the phone with her husband, telling him that we just landed.

I don't bother turning my phone on—Barbara is in

Italy for the next month, leaving her apartment empty, and Salome just got married. Also, I'd probably just end up sobbing incoherently to whoever it is I call, and the nice lady sitting next to me is already kinda traumatized by my sobbing.

I'm really not a pretty crier. Oh, well.

The plane hasn't come to a full stop yet, and already the overhead compartments have been opened, people taking their bags out, talking loudly on cell phones to various and sundry friends and relatives, letting them know their flight from New York had been okay, not so bad, just a little bit of turbulence, nothing to worry about, and they had just landed, don't worry, *motek*, I'll just take a *nesher*, it's late, don't worry.

I lean against the window and drink in the sight of the Tel Aviv airport for the first time since June. A month off of college means that the first flight to Israel I could find, I was on. Barbara on a month-long business trip in Italy means I had a free apartment in Chevron. Dream vacation? Basically.

The plane finally taxis to a stop, and the pilot's thick Israeli accent welcomes us to Israel, thanking us for flying with El Al, and Chanukah Sameach. The nice Christian lady smiles at me, wishes me a nice visit, and stands up to get her bags. The Israeli lady is already waiting in the aisle, chatting with the man sitting in the row in front of us, talking about the latest Knesset drama.

Walking into the airport threatens more tears, because I'm home. I'm tired, a little caffeine-deprived, I want a bed more than anything else right now, but I'm back and I'm home, and that's what counts.

And the airport is playing Chanukah music.

> "Taxi drivers are by far my favorite people. I used to ask them if they needed me to drive them anywhere, because I was bored and I missed driving. It confused the heck out of the drivers, mostly because they thought that I was asking for a ride somewhere but I didn't know how to say so in Hebrew. Sadly, none of them ever let me drive a taxi."
>
> —M.I.

THE RIDE TO Chevron is mostly quiet—the taxi driver is listening to the radio and grumbling about traffic and politics. I text my mom that I landed, but she's sleeping, so she'll probably text me later. I text Riva, letting her know I'd send her pictures the minute I get to Chevron. Or more accurately, whenever I feel human enough to do anything other than swan dive directly onto a bed. Riva doesn't have winter semester off, which is the only reason she hadn't been on the plane sitting next to me.

YOU'D BETTER! she texts back, because of course Riva is awake. Riva never sleeps. Well, she does, but Salome is convinced she never did. I've tried to convince Salome that I've seen Riva sleeping more than once, usually when we went away for Shabbos together. Riva was always awake when Salome was going to sleep, and was already awake when Salome got out of bed. Riva never sleeping had been a dorm room joke the whole year, and still continued with our group chat, when Riva is awake at hours that she shouldn't be.

The taxi pulls up in front of Barbara's building, and the taxi driver climbs out of the car to get my suitcases. "This is where you're staying?" he asks again in his heavily accented English.

"This is where I'm staying," I answer, rifling through my wallet for money. There should be some *shekalim* in here somewhere. I knew I saved some before I left Israel in June . . .

"Are you sure?"

"Yes . . ."

"It's not so safe here," he says. "You know this, right?"

I switch to Hebrew. "Don't worry about me. I've stayed here before."

"And now she tells me she speaks Hebrew," the taxi driver says, shaking his head dramatically. "It took you this long?"

"You started in English," I argue. "So I continued."

"Americans," he mutters. "Always so stubborn."

I burst into laughter. "Look who's talking," I say between giggles.

"Israelis are never stubborn," the taxi driver says, his mouth twitching. "Never ever."

"Right. Never." I honestly don't know how funny this even is, but I haven't slept in around forty hours. And I'm no Riva, which means I'm pretty sure I'm going to start tasting colors or something equally superheroish.

"Chanukah Sameach," the taxi driver says, climbing

back into his car. "Enjoy your stay, and don't forget to eat some sufganiyot while you're here."

"Chanukah Sameach," I say, and yawn. "Don't worry, I will definitely have a sufganiya while I'm here." I will be consuming all of the jelly doughnuts in the State of Israel, so if he wants to have any of his own, he should probably get on that sooner rather than later.

"Layla tov, motek," the taxi driver says, and drives off, leaving me on the quiet street.

This is the part where you schlep your things inside, I tell myself, but it's so beautiful out, and I'm not tired anymore.

Who are we kidding here? I am tired. I'm just too lazy to move.

Barbara's apartment is a ten minute walk from *Me'arat HaMachpeilah*, but it's a little too late to walk there alone. Tomorrow, I promise myself. I'll go inside now, unpack, light the menorah, eat something, and go to sleep. Tomorrow, I'll go to *Me'arat HaMachpeilah*, The Cave of the Patriarchs, and to get a sufganiya. The jelly doughnuts in New York just aren't the same as the ones here.

The thought of a bed finally gets me moving, and I manage to get everything that I want done before lighting the menorah and then collapsing onto the couch. The two little lights of the menorah twinkle by the window, and I watch them happily.

Sleep threatens to overtake, so I distract myself by humming Chanukah songs and eating some five percent cottage cheese on those crackers in the green wrapper.

Nice to know that my meal choices don't change that

much when given the freedom of someone's fridge. I go to put the cottage cheese back and discover a Shoko.

"Awww, Barbara!" I practically squeal. She doesn't drink chocolate milk, which means she bought it special for me.

I rip a little hole in the corner of the little bag of Shoko and drink happily. I don't care what anyone says, chocolate milk tastes best straight from the bag.

I check my phone. It's been half an hour since I lit the candles on the menorah. I blow them out and within minutes I'm face-planted onto the bed.

Beds are the best thing ever, I think as I settle in. Even better than chocolate milk in a bag.

> "I don't think I ever realized how real history is here until I went the Cave of The Patriarchs. I was standing only a few feet away from where Abraham is buried. Abraham. Like, father of Isaac and Ishmael. Who routinely spoke to God. I think my head exploded."
>
> —R.S.

OMGGGGGG CHEVRON I'M SO JEALOUS AND I KINDA HATE YOU, Riva texts when I send her pictures of the city decorated for Chanukah. *Daven for me, eat a sufganiya, and flirt with a* chayal, *okay?*

OBVS. But I won't be taking any pictures with any chayalim, no matter how cute they look, and no matter which unit they're in, I text back, and stuff my phone back into my bag.

Me'arat HaMachpeilah is fairly empty that morning, which makes me happy. There's something to be said about being here with crowds of people, like it was the first time I went, but the silence is nice. I take a seat next to Leah's burial site and begin to pray.

> "My favorite Israel story? I was on an intercity bus when it started raining. Not just a little drizzle, but RAIN. The entire bus started cheering. I don't think I ever appreciated rain as much as I did when I lived in Israel. Every drop of rain felt like a gift."
>
> —T.E.

THE SKY IS cloudy as I leave *Me'arat HaMachpeilah* and head to the bus stop. I had packed my umbrella in a bout of optimism, and it definitely looks like it's going to rain.

Awesome.

There's a *chayal* leaning against the bus stop as I cross the street and try to avoid getting hit by a donkey cart pulled by a little Arab boy.

The *chayal* calls something to the little boy in Arabic, who laughs with his friends and yells a very loud "SORRY!" in English.

"Are you okay?" the *chayal* asks me in English.

I smile. "I'm fine, don't worry. They're just little kids."

"Little kids with a donkey are a little more dangerous than just little kids," he says.

I shrug. "That's one thing you don't have to worry about in New York."

"Little boys driving donkeys? Yeah, not so much." He smiles, a little dimple showing on his tanned cheek. "Taxis, maybe. But little boys don't drive those."

"There is that," I agree, sitting down on the bench. He doesn't have much of an accent when he speaks in English, and the little accent he does have sounds vaguely southern. Also, he's really cute.

He leans back against the bus stop, content to watch and wait. There's another *chayal* across the street, standing guard, machine gun in his hands.

The first time I saw a soldier with a machine gun, I freaked out a little. Especially since he looked around thirteen and had bumped into me on the train by Mount Herzel. I was going to ask him if he wanted me to hold the machine gun and protect him, but I figured that probably wouldn't have ended all that well. I got used to the machine guns everywhere—on the bus, the train, in the shuk, at weddings, on the beach . . . you name it, the machine guns are there. Almost every eighteen-year-old in Israel is in uniform and has a machine gun. And so they go everywhere with them.

The sky looks darker and darker, and I check my phone. The bus should have been here by now.

"Excuse me."

Cute *chayal* turns to me.

"Has the 160 come yet?"

"Yeah, five minutes before you got here."

I sigh. Great. "Thanks."

"The next one will probably be here in around twenty-five minutes," he says.

"Gotcha." I've taken this bus plenty of times and know the schedule pretty well, but I don't have to tell him that. And honestly, a few months away could really mean the bus's schedule might have totally changed. Weirder things had definitely happened with the buses here. I pull out my phone and sent a quick text to Salome, to let her know I'd missed the bus and I'd be in Yerushalayim a little later than I thought.

Just this once. In the future, please make sure that you plan your trips better. Curfew is instituted for your safety, she texts back.

Thank you, Mrs. Meirovitz, I text back. Of course Salome would remember the exact wording Mrs. Meirovitz would use when we would text her and ask for late curfew.

Of course, Salome texts. *It's my job.*

Nicest. Dorm. Mother. Everrrrrrr.

LOLOLOLOLOLOLOL, Salome texts back, and I giggle. Riva is usually the queen of overenthusiastic LOLs in texts, which confused Salome for a while. But now she uses as many L's and O's as possible, and Riva will Google-translate all her messages to Salome to French.

How we managed to all live through a year of seminary without someone getting grievously injured, I'm still not sure.

A loud crack of thunder startles me, and it begins to rain.

The *chayal* across the road whoops and starts dancing. "Avi!" he yells. *"Bo l'rkod iti!"* Come dance with me.

Cute *chayal*—Avi, I guess—grins. *"Od regah, Asaf!"* He turns to me. "I'll be back in a few."

"Go dance," I say, smiling. "It's raining."

It's raining!

"Thank God," Avi says. "We need it." He takes off at a jog toward Asaf, who's full out jamming to the beat of the rain. The little Arab kids are back outside in front of their building, screaming and running in circles.

Asaf hoots as Avi begins to dance, goofing off as rain falls down in sheets. The Arab kids watch and giggle uncontrollably as Asaf grabs Avi and begins twirling him in circles, singing loudly. I lean back and laugh as the rain pours down.

Avi is cute. Really, really cute. Tall, tanned, and that little dimple that just makes everything so much better. Also, combine the uniform, his ombre kippah, and that southern accent, and whoo boy. On a scale from *chamud* to *chatich hores*, it's not much of a contest. Asaf is Ethiopian, I'm pretty sure, and approximately the size of a house. He should been terrifying with his shaved head and the scar bisecting his eyebrow. But Asaf's full out dancing here, all but inviting the little kids across the road to join them, and can't look terrifying if he tried. Avi is trying to get Asaf to waltz with him, which is a disaster of epic proportions, and it is glorious. Avi's trying to explain the steps to Asaf in a mixture of Hebrew and Amaharic, and Asaf is asking him where the spinning and dipping part happens.

"Now," Avi says, and tries to dip Asaf.

It's a good thing the rain is kind of blocking their view of me, because I am full out cracking up.

The little Arab kids from the building decide that they're not going to let two ridiculous *chayalim* have all the fun, and begin dancing, shouting in Arabic about rain. A few of them are trying to copy Avi and Asaf, which just makes me laugh harder.

It's a mess of shouting and dancing and splashing, and it's everything I missed about being here. I'm smiling so hard my cheeks hurt.

Ten minutes later Avi is back, soaked to the skin, brown hair plastered to his head, beaming. "You missed out on a good dance party," he says.

"I had a little bit of my own little dance party here," I say, because I did. It was hard not to. "Aren't you cold?"

He shrugs. "A little. It's fine." He grins. "But it's raining!"

"That it is," I agree. The rain is pouring down. I guess that bringing the umbrella was a good idea. "And not just a little drizzle, either."

Avi sits down on the bench. "I'm pretty sure the bus is going to take a little longer than usual getting here, because of the rain."

"I figured. It's pretty universal."

"You're from New York, right?"

"Yup. And when it rains, the buses all run late, too."

"Where in New York?"

What, like he's going to know? On one hand, his English is unaccented enough that it's possible he made *aliyah*. On the other hand, he seems to also be fluent in Hebrew, Arabic, and Amaharit. "Far Rockaway."

"By the beach, right?"

So he does know where Far Rockaway is. All too often when I tell people in Israel I'm from New York, they'll ask questions like how close I live to the Empire State Building. Or the Statue of Liberty.

"A couple of blocks away, actually."

"Cool," Avi says. "One of the guys in my unit lives there."

"Really? Who?" I ask. What guy from Far Rockaway is in the IDF?

"Chaim Stein."

"Of course," I say, smirking.

"I know," Avi says, clearly appreciating the irony. And whoo boy, he gets so much cuter when he smiles like that. "He has two eyes, a nose, and a mouth, too. Do you know him?"

"I know four of him," I say. "Maybe five, if I think hard enough."

"Yeah, it's hilarious listening to him talk to people from New York. No, not that Stein. Or that one. Or that one. The one on Reads Lane, but not that one, though. The one closer to Empire."

"Do you know his family's address, too?" I tease.

"Not offhand," Avi answers. "But all the guys in our unit know that he lives on Reads but not the other Steins on Reads Lane. There was one time we were all together on the bus and he met some guy from Far Rockaway. The whole unit informed the guy where Chaim was from. It was hilarious, especially since not everyone's English is that good."

"But they all know Reads Lane."

"Every single one of them," Avi agrees, and something about the way he says that just seems so familiar. Come to think of it, he just looks familiar.

Why? I don't know. Maybe I've seen him somewhere before. That's kind of how it just works here. You end up seeing the same people all over.

But I would remember seeing someone who looks like Avi.

I would. Really. And I would have mentioned it to Riva and Salome, who probably would have called me Mrs. Avi for like, a week or something, before finding someone else that they decided to marry me off to.

I don't ever remember being called Mrs. Avi. Or anything about a really cute soldier that speaks English with a hint of something southern. But he does look familiar.

I look up to see Avi waiting patiently for my answer. Right. Conversation. Which is not when you space out while staring at cute Israeli guys. Jewish geography.

"I think I actually do know who you're talking about, though," I say, after doing a mental scan of all the Steins I know on Reads Lane. "Is his sister a redhead?"

"I have no idea," Avi says. "Maybe? I'm pretty sure his sister is in school here this year."

"Elisheva! Yeah, I do know them. Our moms are friends."

"Small world."

"And you're right—he does have two eyes, a nose, and a mouth," I say.

"Amazing, isn't it?" Avi teases. "And do you know my friend's second cousin? He lives in America somewhere. Maybe New York? Maybe that place in the middle?"

"That place in the middle?" I repeat. "Which place?"

"I have no idea. A taxi driver asked me that one day. He was serious."

"Taxi drivers are my favorite. One tried to set me up with his brother last year."

"Did he?"

"Yeah. Apparently his brother works at the bank on Kanfei Nesharim in Jerusalem, and is only thirty-one. He also seems to like religious Americans, even though he's not religious or American."

"Is that so," Avi says, trying hard not to laugh. "I can definitely see why he would think the two of you would suit."

"Yes, because marrying a thirty-one-year-old guy would have totally not fazed my parents," I say.

"It's a bit of an age gap," Avi agrees. I wonder how old he is.

"Yeah, thirteen years is a bit much, I think. When I told my parents, my dad said that if I was thirty-one and he was eighteen, then we could solve the *shidduch* crisis."

"Some *shidduch* crisis group would probably give you a medal for single-handedly solving the whole *shidduch* crisis. The president would probably give you a medal."

"Shame that I was the one that was eighteen," I say. "Because it *would* be cool to single-handedly solve the entire *shidduch* crisis just by marrying one person."

"The newspapers would have a field day," Avi says. "All those letters to the editor."

"You guys get them here?"

"My mom gets them sometimes," Avi said. "I see them when I go home for Shabbat."

So his family lives here. That relieves me, that he's not a *chayal boded*. Not a lone soldier, without family here. I probably shouldn't be that worried about him, but here we are. "Were you born here?"

"Nope. I was born in Kenya."

Huh. "That's kinda random."

"My dad is a doctor, and my mom is a nurse, and they were there with a team of Israeli doctors after a huge flood. They knew they were going to be there for a long time, so my mother decided to go along with them. She said that she was going to be pregnant anywhere, so she may as well come and help." He shrugs. "And then I was born."

"That is significantly cooler than anyone else's birth story."

"Well, all the rest of my siblings were born in Sha'arei Tzedek. My mom said one dramatic birthing story was enough for her."

"I don't blame her." The rain is slowing down, but the bus still isn't here. It's a good thing I told Salome I would meet her by her apartment. If we had agreed to meet by the bus stop, she'd be sitting around in the Central Bus Station, doing nothing.

"The bus should be here soonish," Avi says, seemingly reading my mind. "We're lucky it's not snow. We'd be stuck here forever."

"You wouldn't think it would be so hard to buy a few shovels. You all already have sand."

Avi laughs, his dimple flashing. "This is the desert. We don't understand snow."

"I don't think it has feelings," I answer, standing up to stretch my legs. "But I don't know if anyone's ever did a study on whether it does or not."

Avi tugs on a sweatshirt he pulled out from his knapsack. There's a flash of skin as he wriggles it on. *Tamar, don't be a creeper. Stop looking.* "I don't know if you'd be able to find a way to test if snow had feelings or not. Like, how would you measure that?"

Good question. "I have no idea. Maybe if you whispered nice things to the snow, it would stay cold longer?"

"Snow, you are so pretty and white, and perhaps you'd like to build a snowman?" Avi jokes. "I don't know if that would work."

"I don't know if it even makes sense to ask snow if it wants to build snowman. I don't know how if it would be capable of building itself into something."

"Well, now you have to write a grant and see if the government wants to pay you to find out," Avi says.

His sweatshirt is safely on. I just keep on remembering my friend Sarah telling me about the time she went rafting with her brother and his friend when they were both in the army here. *I'm telling you, when Shimon's friend took his shirt off when they jumped in, I thought my eyes were going to pop out of my head. He was ripped. Peyos flying everywhere, and a six-pack. It was crazy. I'm telling you, never underestimate* chayalim. *Even the super* frum *ones.'*

Okay, maybe thinking about if Avi has a six-pack is a bad idea.

Okay, not maybe. It is. Bad idea. Stop. Conversation. Focus, Tamar.

"I mean, I'd love to make the government happy, but I'm not sure I want to do it like that. I'd never live it down."

There's a slight rumbling.

"*Shehechiyanu,* it's the bus," Avi says, hoisting his knapsack up. "I thought it would never get here."

The bus door opens and Avi waves me on. "I have to drop my bag down under the bus anyway. Go ahead."

I get on and pay for my ticket, making sure it's a round trip. I've forgotten, a lot more than once, and it's more expensive to buy two separate ones. "All the buses are running behind schedule, so make sure to check before you go to wait for your bus back," the driver tells me as he punches out change from the little change machine. "You don't want to get stuck in the rain later."

"Thank you."

"No problem, *neshama.*"

I slide into a seat on the surprisingly full bus. Avi climbs on and chats with the bus driver before heading down the aisle and sliding into the seat next to mine.

Not the seat across from mine, which is taken by an old man. Not the seat in front of me, where a Hasidic mom and baby are sitting. Nope. The one right next to me.

Well, this is quite the turn of events.

"I guess the entirety of Chevron is going to Jerusalem now," he says.

"Is anything happening there?"

Avi shrugs. "Well, my brother's bar mitzvah, but that's not why everyone is on the bus."

"Mazel tov! I was wondering why you were leaving Chevron."

"Yup, Baby Yaakov's bar mitzvah."

"Baby? If it's his bar mitzvah, he's not much of a baby, is he?"

"He's the youngest, so he'll always be the baby."

"I get that. My baby sister is eight, and she's always going to be my baby. Poor kiddo."

Avi grins. "They'll be okay."

"I hope so." Okay, so the thing about sitting next to someone on a bus is you sit next to them. *Next to* them. And it's really close. I shouldn't be enjoying this as much as I am. I lean against the window and try to snap out of it.

"So, how long are you going to be here?" Avi asks. "I assume you're visiting."

"Yup. For a month," I say. "Not long enough, though."

"Why don't you just move here?"

"I wish it was that easy. But college."

"We do have that here, you know."

"I know. But I have a scholarship. So."

"Ah."

"Yup." I sigh. Stupid money. "But when I finish, I want to make *aliyah*."

"What are you going to school for?" he asks. Genuinely curious.

"Occupational therapy."

"Cool. My older sister is an OT, also."

"Older sister? Where was she when you guys went to Kenya?"

"She was there," Avi says, stretching out in the seat. "She used to watch us when my parents were both working."

"Us? Wait, how many older siblings do you have?"

"Three. Aliza, Noam, and Ezra. Noam and Ezra are twins."

"Holy cow. Your mom is kind of a little crazy."

"A little bit. All the doctors who were there thought she was a little nuts for bringing all of the kids with her. While pregnant." Avi shrugs. "Well, more the other doctors there. Not so much the Israeli ones."

"That doesn't surprise me at all."

"Anyone who knows Israelis isn't all that surprised."

Well, that's true. "Do you remember anything from being there?"

"Not the first time," he says. "We left when I was around eight months, but we went back a bunch of times. My parents are close to a lot of people in the village we lived in, and go back every couple of years to visit and help out." He shrugs. "And I would go along with whoever went, because I picked up Swahili fairly easily."

"That's pretty impressive," I say. "There's a guy in my OT program who speaks Swahili, and apparently it's not easy to learn."

"So I've heard, mostly from the other doctors we used to go with." He laughs. "I was a ridiculous little kid. Some pipsqueak little Israeli kid, wandering around Kenya with a group of doctors, translating medical problems for my dad and his coworkers."

"Your childhood was significantly cooler than mine," I say.

"It felt regular to me," he says. "I mean, I knew at the time that not everyone went to Africa with their Abba. But Lior would go to Switzerland to visit his cousins, and Emanuel would go to Australia to visit his grandparents, and Yoram's dad lived in America most of the time. So me going to Africa wasn't that weird."

"Yeah, mine was still not nearly as cool," I say.

"Your childhood isn't over," he says.

"I'm registered to vote. I'm pretty sure that makes my childhood over."

"Well, your adulthood can be cooler than mine," he offers. "You still have plenty of time for that to happen."

"One hundred and one years is plenty of time," I agree.

"I have one hundred." He laughs. "When I turned twenty, Noam called me and wished me a happy one hundred years left of my life."

"Did you say thank you?" I ask, laughing. Riva would *so* do something like that.

"Obviously." He widens his eyes in mock horror. "My mother would be scandalized if I did anything less."

"And we don't want your mother to be scandalized."

"We try to avoid it if possible."

Chapter 2

"One of the best Shabbos experiences I had in Israel was when I met a girl on the bus. We'd seen each other a couple of times, and had always smiled at each other. Then on the bus back to Jerusalem, we started chatting. Her family had moved to Israel when she was younger, and they loved having guests. And so a friend and I went for the weekend, and adored every second of it.

And no, it wasn't weird to go to someone's house when you only met that someone on the bus. It's Israel. That's how it works there."

—N.J.

THE BUS FROM Chevron to the Central Bus Station in Jerusalem usually takes a little over an hour, but today it takes two and a half hours.

The only reason I know that is because Salome texts me, worried, an hour into the bus ride. But considering how the conversation flows, I would never have noticed the bus took so much longer than usual. I don't space out and stare out the window for even a minute, because talking to Avi is so much more compelling than the long stretches of sand that usually enthrall me.

I try not to overthink it all that much, but I find myself telling Avi things I wouldn't normally tell a mostly random stranger. Even a mostly random stranger in Israel. But so does he, and our conversations range from talking about our favorite thing to order on the crepes at Katzefet, (which leads to us arguing about whether actually call it Katzefet or Fro-Yo), to him telling me about growing up during the Intifada, and me telling him about my friend from preschool who died in a fire when she was five.

I laugh in those two hours more than I have probably laughed in the past month and a half. And when he makes a Veggie Tales reference, I'm sunk.

This is bad.

Very, very, very good. But very bad.

> "The *chayalim*? Best. Ever. It was a mutual party of fun—we thought they were adorable and they thought we were hilarious. We all kinda just flirted shamelessly with each other, bumbling over languages and just trying to understand each other. But we also worried about them, whether we had ever met them or not. They were the same age we were, and they were in the army while we were just goofing off in school."
>
> **—M.B.**

The bus pulls into the Tachana Merkazit, and it all comes crashing down. We've been talking for so long, and it has been blissfully awkward free, and I almost forgot that Avi's just a random *chayal* I met at a bus stop. And that upsets me a lot more than it should.

The bus parks and we all file off. Avi goes to grab his bag from under the bus, and I fidget.

Tamar. This is not nearly as serious as you want it to be.

Avi walks over to me, bag swung over his shoulder, and for the first time since I crossed the street in Chevron, everything feels awkward.

"Well," he says.

"It was nice to meet you," I say, rushing the words out. I don't want things to just end now, but what do I think is going to happen? "Mazel tov on your brother's bar mitzvah."

"Maybe I'll see you around Chevron. You're staying there, right?"

"Right."

"Well, I'll be there, too." Avi smiles.

"Bye." I can stand here and watch him smile all day, and oh my God, Tamar, you need to leave before you do something stupid. I turn toward the exit.

"L'hitraot."

I smile and wave like an idiot, and head out of the bus station, feeling like I've left something behind there.

Calm down, Queen Drama. He's just a guy.

But I've never felt this way about just a guy.

That's because none of the guys I've ever had any feelings about were tall, dimpled, sweet *chayalim* with slight southern accents and a wicked sense of humor.

I head out of the bus station. After the whole bus ride, I still don't know his last name, or where his family lived.

But what was I going to do, though? I ask myself as I hop onto the train to Bayit Vegan. He's a *chayal*. I'm only here for a month. It can't work out.

> "It's a wonder my roommates and I never killed each other. God knows why they thought of putting us all together in one room, but somehow, it worked, and I left school with another three sisters."
>
> —L.F.

"TAMAR!" SALOME SHRIEKS, throwing her arms around me. "I missed you!"

I hug her back as tight as I can. "Oh my gosh, look at you, all married and cute!"

"You were at my wedding, silly. You've seen me married." Salome pulls back and smiles. "Look at you!"

"I look the same as I did last time I saw you, silly. I'm not the one with a scarf on my head."

"Look at you, not saying that other word."

"*Tichel?* Because every time I would say *tichel,* you would tell me it sounded like some sort of old Eastern European cookie."

"Well, it does," Salome protests.

"It kind of does. *Kichel, tichel.* But one goes in your mouth and one goes on your head," I say. "Also, can we discuss that you live here? Did you ever think you'd end up living here?"

Salome shrugs, and manages to look classy while doing it. It's that French thing. It's practically impossible for Salome to look anything less than classy and infinitely cooler than anyone else. Covered in mud, sliding down the side of a cliff, flinging paint, you name it.

But it's Salome, and her Frenchness is just what makes her my Salome.

"Well, if I was going to live anywhere in Jerusalem, it would probably be here," she says. "Like what Riva used to say—all of the Frenchies all hang out together."

"Frenchies," I snicker.

"Like the girl from *Grease,*" Salome says, trying her best to imitate me, which sends me into gales of laughter. "Why are you laughing? Am I not American enough for you?"

"I love you, Salome."

"I love you, too. And I will not sing any songs from *Grease,* because I have pity on you."

"Oh, pfft. Where did that come from?" I demand. "You never had any pity on me before."

"Well, now I'm old and married, and so maybe now I have some pity on you," she says.

"I'm sure."

"I'm lying. I don't remember the words to the song."

I clutch my heart. "Salome. I feel so betrayed."

"*Nebach,*" she says, which makes me giggle.

"*Nebach?* When did you turn into such an Ashkenaz?" I demand.

"When I married my husband who went to all the Ashkenaz yeshivas."

I cackle. "Your husband is a Mir guy."

"I know. I was wrong."

Back in seminary on Purim, Riva and I had dragged Salome to the Mir Yeshivah for the reading of Megillat Esther. She asked why we had to go there. Really, it was because it was pretty close to the Kotel, where we had been that morning for davening, but we told her it was because we were going to find her a husband there.

"Like I'm going to marry an American Ashkenaz," she had scoffed, which made us laugh. "Fine. I'll go and then I'll go home and find you both French husbands."

"Why would you do that to the poor French guys?" Riva had asked, trying to keep her face straight. "Do you hate them that much?"

"No," Salome had said. "Never mind. Fine, we'll go to this Mir, and I'll find both of you husbands. So there."

And now she was the one who had married a guy who was in the Mir. An American who went to the Mir, which was an endless source of amusement for us. Riva and I ignore the fact that his parents are French when we tease her about her husband, like the excellent friends we are.

"How's Yoni?" I ask as we stand up and get ready to set up the menorah by the doorway.

"Thank God." Salome smiles. "He's happy you're here for a while."

"For a month," I say. "I don't know if he'll be happy by week three."

"No, he will. He's just a little worried about how much trouble we're going to cause."

"Us? Cause trouble? Never."

"I tried that on him. He didn't believe any of it."

I shrug. "Well, too bad that he doesn't believe the truth. And it's not like we've ever done anything that would make him think we'd ever cause trouble."

"Never," Salome says, her voice grave.

It takes us approximately three seconds before we crack up. Salome and Yoni met when we were in the midst of what some might call "causing trouble."

"So, have you had a sufganiya yet?" Salome asks as we step out onto the sidewalk.

"Sal, I've been here for less than a day."

"So?"

"Not yet. I wanted my first one to be from the shuk."

"Throwback Tuesday?"

"I regret ever encouraging you," I fake moan.

"You know you looooove me," she sings, and I remember just how devious Salome actually is. It's probably the only reason she survived the first month and a half of seminary with two crazy Americans as roommates, especially since she didn't speak that much English then.

She does now, and will deny it, which is hilarious.

I poke her. "I do love you, but not when you do weird things like this."

We're walking down Herzel because the sky is a clear blue and drastically different from this morning's rain.

And even though it's cold out, the cold is laughable in comparison to the polar vortex that will never end in New York.

"Oh my gosh, I forgot to tell you!"

"Tell me what?" Salome demands.

"About the *chayal* chamud that I met today," I say, trying to sound casual, because for real, I'm making it into too big of a deal. I am. It can't be as big of a deal as I want it to be.

"You're like a magnet, Tamarie. You can't go anywhere without making friends with cute soldiers."

I shrug. "I think that might be a bit of an over exaggeration."

"Excuse me, Miss All the *Chayalim* in Chevron Are My Best Friends?"

"They're not all my best friends."

"Only because there are new ones there now."

"Your faith in my *chayal* friending ability is a little much. If either of us would be the one making friends with all the *chayalim*, it would be you."

Salome rolls her eyes. "One time I get serenaded by a bus of soldiers, and you never let me live it down."

"Never ever."

"Wait, so what didn't you tell me?"

"So, this morning I was waiting at the bus stop by *Me'arat HaMachpeila*, and there was this *chayal* guy sitting there."

"Yessss. And now you're getting married to him?"

"Whoa there, Sparky. No. I barely know the guy."

"Uh-huh."

"Salome."

She raises her hands in defeat. "Okay, so there was a cute *chayal* sitting next to you at the bus stop. Then what happened?"

"Why do you automatically assume that something happened?" I demand as we walk by Yad Sarah.

She's right, but she doesn't have to be so smug about it.

"Tamarie. I lived with you for ten months."

"You make me sound so much more . . . I don't know, femme fatale-ish, than I actually am."

"Look at you, using French words correctly." Salome wipes away an imaginary tear. "I'm so proud. Now tell me what happened."

I give her the rundown of that morning. "And then we said good-bye at the Tachana Merkazit. And, yeah. That's it."

"That's it??"

"Yup."

"No. I don't like the ending."

Neither do I. I shrug. "Well, that's what happened."

"But you're going to be there for a month. I think you're going to see him again."

"Yeah, but . . . I don't know. I don't think anything can come from it."

"Have some faith, *chouchou*."

"Yes, Maman."

"Now you're making fun of me."

I hug her. "I would never. I love you too much."

"I don't remember things working like that," she says. "But you have to post this in the chat, and then you have to update me and Riva every time something happens."

"Okay, pumpkin. Don't worry." I pull out my phone. "Now?"

"Why not?"

Me updating Riva, and Salome adding in her two cents, lasts us until we get to the Machane Yehuda Shuk, which is both my favorite outdoor marketplace in Israel and also the home of all of the doughnuts over Chanukah. They sell sufganiyot everywhere, but for some reason, the ones here taste the best.

"Sufganiyotttt," I sing, pulling Salome along. "Let's go let's go let's go!"

"You're acting like this and you haven't even had any sugar yet," she says. "This can only end terribly."

"Oh, shh. It's not like I drank any coffee today."

"Of course you wouldn't drink any coffee! You should remember what happened last time you drank coffee."

"Nothing happened," I say as we weave around an old woman in pearls sorting through chicken livers.

"I don't believe you."

"I promise. I started drinking coffee in the beginning of the semester, and now I'm fine."

"I feel like some part of my innocence is gone," Salome says, steering us around a group of tourists. "You can drink coffee now?"

"I know. I'm a grown-up now and every—loooook, they look so good oh my God I want to eat all of them." It's sufganiyot, and dear God, I want to buy all of them. The powdered sugar ones, the ones with highlighter-colored frosting, the ones that have cream in the middle instead of jelly . . . all of the doughnuts.

"Eating all of them would make you sick."

"Shh, voice of reason. I will be ignoring you when it comes to doughnut advice." I turn to the guy behind the counter and switch to Hebrew. "Good afternoon."

"The bags are over there. Just let me know how many you plan on buying."

"All of them."

"She's lying," Salome interrupts. "Not all of them."

"All of them would be a lot to carry," the guy agrees.

"None of you have any faith in my ability to carry things," I huff.

"That's why you have a boyfriend," says Shuk Guy.

"I like the assumption I have a boyfriend," I say to Salome. "These Israeli guys. Always thinking about our marriage prospects."

"Such yentas." Salome shakes her head sadly.

"Look what seminary did to you," I tsk, taking two doughnuts. "You're practically fluent in Yiddish."

"Riiiight." Salome pulls out her wallet and pays before I can pull out mine. "That's why I went to seminary. Not to learn English. To learn Yiddish."

"Obviously. Why do you think I came to school?"

"To hang out with *chayalim*."

"You lie like a rug, missy."

"A Persian carpet," she answers, and then sticks her tongue out.

"Such maturity."

"Always." We start the walk toward the Old City, bickering and in general just goofing off.

And I can't stop thinking about Avi, which is kinda weird.

Maybe it's because I'm still kinda traumatized from going on the date that shall never be discussed again with you know who.

Going on a date with Avi would probably be a lot more fun. Also, less awkward, and would probably not end with me going home and telling my mom that I'm just going to buy a herd of cats, and too bad that Abba is allergic.

Which was how that other date that shall not be mentioned ended.

It was just buckets of fun.

"Tamarie."

"Huh?"

"You were out spacing."

"Sorry." We're almost by City Hall. "Ooh, wanna stop by the pillows?"

"For a picnic? Always."

"Yesss."

There's a little gardeny art exhibit behind City Hall, where all the seats available are pillows made of concrete. It doesn't sound comfortable at all, but I promise, it is. I've spent hours here, with friends or alone. It's usually empty, and it's far away enough from the street that it's a good thinking spot.

Salome sits down on her pillow and looks up at the sky. Cloudless. "Now all we need is Riva," she says. "And then it will be perfect."

I pull out my phone and take a selfie with Salome to send to Riva. "I kinda feel bad about sending her pictures," I say as I pass Salome a sufganiya. "You know? But on the other hand, she'd be really mad at me if I didn't send her all the pictures."

"Sometimes you have to pick the thing that hurts less," Salome says, taking a nibble out of her doughnut.

"True." Then I take a bite out of my sufganiya. "I'm moving to Israel. That's it. Forget my stupid college scholarship."

"If I remember correctly, you may have said something that sounded exactly like that around every other day last year."

"Don't rub it in, *giveret*. I'm going to enjoy my doughnut in peace and quiet and . . . other happy peaceful-sounding words."

"Whatever you say, dear."

"As I wish?"

"No. Not Princess Bride."

"Gasp."

"Nobody actually says 'gasp' instead of gasping," Salome says, licking sugar off her fingers. "Just you."

"It must be because I'm dead inside." I grin. "Also, don't think I haven't noticed you avoiding the Princess Bride problem here."

"I thought I was the one who was dead inside," Salome says. "But okay. And no Princess Bride because Buttercup shouldn't have been so obnoxious, and Wesley should have said something a little more aggressive than 'as you wish.' "

"Rebbetzin Samuels would be so proud of your critique on fictional character relationships," I say. "Although the movie part, maybe not so much."

Salome flutters her eyelashes. “It’s a book, Tamar.”

“You win.” I finish off my doughnut. “But you do have a point about Buttercup.” I ponder for a bit. “I’m kinda sad now, you know?”

“Romantic dreams are popped like balloons?”

“Something like that. Probably not that dramatic, though. More like a slow hissing of the balloon, and not so much popping.”

We both dust off the powdered sugar and head toward the Old City, to the Jaffa Gate. There are the usual two carts selling bread right outside the gate, and it’s the same guys who were here the last time I was by the Old City.

The Old City is decorated for Chanukah. Even the Arab shuk looks a little more festive than usual. We pass the church hostel, and Salome nudges me. “Look, Tamarie. You can stay here for Shabbat if you want to.”

“I told you, I already did,” I say, smirking. I haven’t, but we like to lie to each other about stupid things. Mostly if said stupid things involve places we claimed to have slept at. “Remember? That Shabbat you went home and Riva abandoned me?”

“Right. And you also slept on a park bench in Tzfat.”

“No, that I actually did.”

“Uh-huh,” Salome drawls, clearly still not believing me.

“One day you’re going to realize that Riva and I weren’t lying when we told you we slept on that park bench,” I say as we turn onto St. James. “I’m just saying.”

“Well, even if it is true, I will live in denial and pretend it isn’t.” Salome stops to chat with someone in French in front of the little grocery store on the corner. "Sorry, a neighbor."

"No problem." I pause. "Which way do you want to go?"

"Whichever way you want to go is fine with me," she says.

"Is the staircase to the courtyard down before the menorah open?" I ask. Chalk that up as yet another place for hiding with friends and having heart-to-hearts at three in the morning.

"It should be. I haven't been through there in a while. We can go check."

'We're walking through the Cardo when Salome pokes me. "Ooh, chayal chatich by the museum." She wiggles her eyebrows. "Even you would think he's hot."

"Tsk tsk, married lady," I tease. "Where?"

She laughs. "By the burned house museum."

I turn slightly to look, and squeeze her arm. "That's Avi!" I hiss. "Don't turn around. Don't you dare—"

Salome turns, and turns back. "Tamarie, look at you with good taste all of a sudden."

"All of a sudden. *Shtuyot.*" I glance back for a second. He's there with another two *chayalim,* and he's still cute. "But I know, right? Isn't he a *chayal chatich*?"

"As I said, *chouchou.* All of a sudden you have good taste."

"And which one of us saw Yoni first? Oh, wait, that was me. It's not sudden, *chouchou.*"

"You have a point," she concedes. "But other than Yoni."

The gate to the staircase is open, and we slowly make

our way down into the first courtyard. There's some Aish guy taking a nap on one of the park benches, and another two guys who seem to be trying to write a song. The second courtyard is empty, but the Kotel is right here, and as much as I want to twirl in circles through the courtyard and pretend I'm the Orthodox Jewish version of the music video for Taylor Swift's "You Belong with Me," I want to go to the Kotel more.

The Kotel is moderately crowded, and the minute I sit down to pray, I burst into tears. Again. I am a regular watering pot when it comes to Israel, it seems. There's an old Sephardi lady sitting next to me, and without pausing her Tehillim, she hands me a tissue, which only makes me cry more.

I curl up onto my chair, as close to the actual Kotel as I possibly can get, and pray. Salome is saying her Tehillim when I finish, so I lean against the Kotel wall and have a little conversation with God.

I can't stop thinking about him, and I don't know how seriously to take myself. It could be it's just a garden variety crush or something, but I don't know. I pause. *I'm not going to do the whole "show me a sign" thing, but I would love some clarity.*

The stones are sun-kissed and warm, even at this hour, and little notes are shoved into the cracks everywhere. I close my eyes and just stand there, soaking everything in and just breathing. There's nothing that centers me quite like meditating by the Kotel, and by the time I move back a few minutes later, I'm feeling more solidly here than I have been in a while.

Salome finishes her Tehillim and tucks it into her purse. We walk backward in silence and turn by the ramp.

"You look better," Salome says as we go to wash our hands again.

"I feel better."

"I'm glad." Her phone buzzes, and she pulls it out. "Yoni is running a little late, but he wants to know where we should meet him for dinner. I hadn't told him anywhere in specific before he left. Where do you want to go for dinner?"

"Nooo, don't make me decide!" I dramatically fling myself at Salome. "You know I'm bad at decisions."

"Do you want me to narrow it down for you?" she asks, patting me on the head.

"Obviously. Also, is there anywhere you know Yoni would want to go?"

"He's not picky. Okay. Milk or meat?"

"Either."

"Piiiiick."

"Well, it's Chanukah. Milk."

"Look at you, making progress. Okay. Ohhh, do you want to go to the tofu place?"

"Yoni eats tofu?" I ask, puzzled. "I didn't think that was his kind of thing."

"He loves tofu," Salome says, texting. "His mom is such a Californian."

I've met Yoni's mom, and "such a Californian" is not the first thing I would think of when thinking about her. Super elegant and classy and French is more it.

"Well, that's handy," I say as we walk back through the Cardo.

"It really is," she says. We skirt around a group of giggling seminary girls.

"Were we ever that little?" I ask.

"Yes. Last year." Salome shakes her head. "Sometimes you confuse me, *chouchou.*"

"Only sometimes?" I stick my tongue out at her. "Chronologically, I know that was us a year ago. It just feels like a lot more than just a year. I don't know. Seminary is the weirdest bubble of a year."

"It really is."

Chapter 3

"The best falafel I've ever had I bought by a gas station. This guy at a soccer game told me I should go to this place and get falafel, and I thought he was lying. He wasn't. Gas station falafel is hands down the best falafel ever."

—R.D.

BY THE TIME we get to Ben Yehuda, I remember that I haven't really eaten that much today, and I'm more than happy to take advantage of all the tofu and salady goodness that's there. Do normal people eat from the tofu buffet for dinner? I don't care, because my tofu and I are more than happy to spend time together at all hours of the day or night.

Yoni and Salome, without a doubt, continue to be the absolute cutest together. And because they have pity on my teeny tiny French vocabulary, they speak in English. Mostly, and then every once in a while one of them will say something to the other one in French and all the blushing will ensue and I can't even with their adorable, honeymooning selves.

I have a forkful of tofu in my mouth when Salome turns to Yoni. "So, Tamarie met a *chayal* today."

"Another one?" he asks, grinning.

I fake glare and wag a finger at him.

"In Chevron," Salome continues.

"I would assume so."

I continue to wag my finger and chew.

Yoni wags a finger back. "So. What happened this time?"

"Are you saying that like I did something wrong?" I ask.

"God forbid. But any time you end up making friends with a *chayal*, there's usually a story that goes along with it." He turns to Salome and flutters his eyelashes, making the two of us laugh. "I'm feeling the FOMO."

"I regret ever teaching you that," Salome says, trying and failing to be serious. "And anyway, Tamarie does a better job of telling her *chayal* stories than I do."

"Tamar, my favorite *shadchanit*."

"I'd darn well better be your favorite *shadchanit*," I say. "Did anyone else set you up with Salome that I should know about? I didn't know I had competition."

"Well, you and then that homeless guy when we were dating," Yoni says.

"But we were already dating when the homeless man told you that you should marry me," Salome says. "So that doesn't count."

"Shhh," Yoni jokes. "Don't tell her."

"Well, I guess I won't tell you about how I eloped with a *chayal* this morning," I say, pretending to look bored. "Whatever. It's a good story, though."

"If you had actually eloped with a *chayal* this morning, you would be wearing a *mitpachat* or something on your head. Also, I would assume that said *chayal* husband would be going out to dinner with us." Yoni smirks.

"Well, I am an American, you know," I say gravely, and then laugh when Salome starts to giggle.

"You should get a T-shirt with that on it," Salome says when she finally finishes giggling. "And wear it like Superman wears his . . . costume? Uniform? I don't know. And then anytime you want to say it, you can run into a phone booth or something."

"I don't know if there are enough phone booths around for me to pull off something like that," I say. "But I would love a 'Well, I am an American' shirt."

"And we'll get a matching one for your *chayal*," Yoni says.

"He might appreciate it," I muse. I look at Yoni's raised eyebrows, and fill him in on today's adventures with Avi.

"And then we saw him by the burned house museum," Salome says. "And I may approve."

"Approve of what?" I demand.

"Pretty much anything within reason, I think."

"Whoa," Yoni says. "That was honestly not where I thought the *chayal* adventures would end up."

"I know, neither did I," Salome says.

"Same."

"You do realize you're going to see him everywhere, right?" Yoni says. "That's just how these things work."

"Of course I'm going to see him everywhere," I agree. "Especially since he's stationed a ten minute walk from Barbara's apartment."

"I can't wait for all the *chayal chamud* updates," Salome says. "All the details."

"What kind of friend would I be if I didn't include all the details?" I demand. "Seriously, Salome."

"A terrible one," she says. "Which thankfully, you are not."

> "You see the same people everywhere you go. It's ridiculous. And you'll see people more often when you're both six thousand miles away from home than you will when you live around the corner from each other. I have no idea why, but that's just how it works."
>
> **—B.K.**

I'M SITTING IN the pizza store in Chevron, eating lunch and chatting with a few seminary girls who are here for the day. They're telling me about how their first Shabbos in Chevron, the week of Parshat Chayei Sarah.

"We slept in a tent," one of them is saying. "It was like sleepaway camp all over again, except that it was an actual tent and not a platform with a tent cover."

"Where did you even go to camp?" another girl asks, her very adorable British accent making it clear that she didn't go to the same camp. Or any camp in the Catskills, for that matter.

"Oh, no. We're going to let Miriam talk about camp again," Elisheva Stein groans.

"Um, excuse me, Miss I Am Obsessed with HASC?" Miriam demands.

"Well, I didn't sleep in a tent there," the redhead says, and this is déjà vu to so many conversations in the dorm's library at midnight when everyone was supposed to be doing homework. "I slept in a bunk with my camper, like a civilized human being. As one does when they work in a camp."

"Parshat Chayei Sarah was my first Shabbos in Chevron, too," I tell them. "But I stayed at someone's house, not in a tent. I kinda feel like I missed out on part of the Chevron experience."

"I'm sure if you really wanted, you could camp out here for Shabbos," says Miriam. "It's probably not the smartest idea, safety wise and everything."

"True. Also, I'm kinda into the whole having an actual roof over my head, you know?"

"Do I ever," Elisheva says.

"Is that some sort of Far Rockaway thing?" Miriam asks.

"Totally not," I say. "But maybe it's a Reads Lane thing."

A *chayal* standing on line turns around. "Reads Lane?" he asks.

"Yeah . . ."

"*At mekirah* Chaim Stein?" he asks. Do you know Chaim Stein?

"*Betach. Hu ha ach sheli.*" Elisheva says. Of course I do. He's my brother.

"You're the sister!" the *chayal* exclaims. "He told me

you were in Israel this year. He's right outside now. Hold on." He jogs to the door, machine gun bouncing, and yells for Chaim.

Five *chayalim* come into the pizza store and head straight over to the table where we're sitting. Things like this may be why Salome is convinced that I'm friends with the entire IDF. Mostly because things like this happen fairly frequently.

"Hey, Eli," Chaim says, reaching over and snatching a fry from her plate before she can slap his hand away. "Long time no see. What's it been, half an hour?"

"Give or take," she says, scowling. "Fry stealer."

He laughs. "I'm not eating your pizza. Be thankful for that, at least." He hip bumps her and slides in. Another two *chayalim* pull up chairs and prop their feet up as a third goes to order.

"Wait, you're not in seminary now, are you?" Chaim asks me.

"Nope. Just visiting for a bit."

"I was wondering. Especially since you brought me that duffel bag."

"Wait, she's Mezkaina Tamar?" one of the *chayalim* asks.

"Wait, what?" Mezkaina Tamar? Poor Tamar? What the heck?

The *chayalim* are cracking up. "It's Mezkaina Tamar!" one of them calls to the guy by the counter.

"Mezkaina Tamar!" he calls. "Thank you for the chocolate!"

"What the heck is happening?" Elisheva asks.

"Ima told me Tamar from down the block was going to be going back to New York for a week in November for a wedding, and she could bring me a bag of things. And so every time I'd remember something I wanted, or anyone else wanted, I'd think about poor Mezkaina Tamar, who was going to have to schlep the whole world to Israel to me." Chaim smiles, sheepish. "It kinda stuck."

"It wasn't so bad," I protest. "It wasn't like I had to schlep it on the plane or anything."

"Well, let's just say that my entire unit had decided that you were their favorite person for a really long time," Chaim says. "So, thanks."

"No problem."

The door opens, and one of the guys at the table yells. *"Avi, bo l'fgosh et Mezkaina Tamar!"* Avi, come meet Poor Tamar!

Avi. Of course it's Avi.

He strolls over to the table, looking just as excellent as he did when I saw him last. "Mezkaina Tamar?" he repeats. *"Aifoh?"* Where?

And then he sees me and breaks into a huge smile. "You're Mezkaina Tamar?" he asks.

"So it seems," I say, trying not to smile too big. "I didn't realize this was such a thing."

"Are you kidding? We thanked God every day for Mezkaina Tamar." He leans against Chaim. "I guess you do know Chaim."

"Wait, how do the two of you know each other?" Chaim asks, snatching another fry from Elisheva's plate.

"We were on the same bus to Jerusalem," Avi answers.

One of the other *chayalim* turns to me. "I'm sorry about their dancing," he says, all serious. "We try to stop them but they don't listen."

"Avi, you were dancing?" another *chayal* moans. "Oh, no. Avi. We talked about this already."

Elisheva's friends are confused, Elisheva is poking Chaim with a straw, and the *chayalim* are all tsking.

"Avi, Avi, Avi. How are you going to get married like this?" Short Chayal asks, doing an excellent imitation of some over worried mothers in my neighborhood. "Dancing in public? In front of a Bais Yaakov girl? When are you going to learn?"

"I assume you're going to have this conversation with Asaf next, right?" Avi asks.

"No, he's not looking to marry a Bais Yaakov girl," Short Chayal says.

"Shlomo . . ." Avi says, shaking his head. "What do we do with you?"

"Well, you don't keep dancing like that in the street," he says, trying not to smile and failing.

"Nah, I'm gonna keep dancing. You're just jealous that Asaf and I have sweet moves."

"Sweet moves?" Short Chayal repeats, confused. It doesn't have the same ring in Hebrew. "I don't know, Avi."

"I don't know, either, Shlomo." Avi grins. "But mostly you're jealous. It's okay. It happens."

Short Chayal mutters something to Avi and the whole group starts laughing.

Boys.

The table is overcrowded with people, but after fifteen

minutes of being thoroughly entertained by a group of ridiculous *chayalim*, they all get up and get back to work. I leave around the same time as them, because I have some errands I promised Barbara I'd run for her this week.

The rest of the guys are walking a little ahead of me, but Avi hangs back. "Sorry about that."

"About what?"

"Barging in on your lunch."

"It's fine. I wasn't planning on staying, and then I bumped into Elisheva." I zip my coat and shove my hands into my pockets as a cold gust of air blows by. "And now I know an entire unit of *chayalim* refer to me as Mezkaina Tamar."

"Yeah, about that."

I laugh. "It's hilarious."

"It's mostly kind of weird," Avi says.

"Yeah, well. Such is life. How was the bar mitzvah?"

"Nice. Weird, but nice." Avi waves a car by before we cross the street. "How was your friend?"

"So cute." And we spent a significant time talking about you, I don't tell him. She thinks you're cute, I also don't tell him. So do I, I definitely don't say. "It was really nice to get to hang out with her and her husband."

"That's good." We walk in companionable silence for a minute or two. "Can I ask you a weird question?" Avi asks.

"Sure," I say, having no idea what he wants to ask, and trying not to think too deeply into the question.

"Had we met before Tuesday?"

"You, too? I thought it was just me. I've been trying to figure out why you looked so familiar."

"Oh, thank God," Avi says, sighing in relief. "I've been trying to figure out why you look so familiar and I can't place it."

"I have no idea," I say. "Maybe we just saw each other around somewhere last year."

"Maybe, but you look more familiar than just some random girl I saw once or twice."

"I don't know. I spent a lot of time in Chevron last year, so maybe that is just it."

"Maybe. I don't know. Well, at least it's not just me."

"Definitely not."

"How was your sufganiya?" Avi asks.

"Delish." I grin. "Obviously."

"Good to know we haven't let you down in the doughnut department."

No complaints in the cute *chayal* department, either.

Tamar. Don't get too attached to people you're going to be leaving in less than a month.

Don't do it. It's only going to hurt you.

Chapter 4

"My friends and I used to have what we called 'Bus Stop Therapy Sessions' while we waited for buses. More often than not, other people waiting for the bus would somehow get roped into the conversation, and we'd end up getting some really incredible advice from total strangers."

—P.R.

I AM TERRIBLE at listening to my own advice, I realize as I begin my daily walk over to where Avi's stationed.

It's been a week and there hasn't been a single day we haven't seen each other. We can't pretend it's just casually bumping into each other anymore. Not when we ask each other what the other one's schedule is for the next day, with the intention of hanging out.

And I promised Riva and Salome that I would update them about what was happening, but I don't even know what to say. "Hey girlies, so remember that really cute *chayal* from the bus? I've spent more time with him than with all of the Hes Who Shall Not Be Mentioned in the past week than I did with HWSNBM the whole time we dated, and he's a *chayal* here and I'm going back to New York at the end of December and I really really really like him a lot and what are we supposed to do about this—I don't even know how he feels. P.S.: sufganiyot are an excellent thing to use when you want to eat your feelings."

Because that's how a message to them would go.

I promise, I never thought I was going to be that person, but this is why people use a *shadchan*. Because when you have someone to go between, you know where everyone is at. You aren't stuck in this limbo of "Am I the only one who feels like this," which is a terrible place.

"What happened?" Avi asks as I walk up to the bus stop.

"Nothing," I lie. "Why?"

"I don't know. You looked upset when you were crossing the street." He leans against the bus stop. "You sure you're okay?"

"Yeah, I'm fine."

"Hold on a second." He rifles through his pockets and pulls out a little bar of cow chocolate, and a small package of tissues. "For you, Tamar."

I don't want to admit that I get shivers when he says my name.

Too late.

"Um, thanks?" I take the chocolate and tissues. "Why, though?"

"You said the F word," he says. "Fine," he clarifies as I look at him, perplexed. "Saying you're fine is usually an indication that you aren't, according to my sister. And so just in case either of those are necessary ever, I have them on you."

"You seriously carry around chocolate and tissues just in case a girl tells you she's fine?"

"Well, I also carry them just in case anyone needs chocolate or tissues. Me included." He shrugs. "Boy Scout habits inherited from my dad."

"Thanks." I open the cow chocolate and offer him a piece.

"Do you want to talk about it?"

"Yes but no." *Mostly because it's about you.*

"You just let me know, okay? I'm doing bus station duty for a while today."

"Thanks."

The Arab kiddos are back out with the donkey cart, but this time, everyone's a little more decorated than usual. They drive by the bus stop and yell hellos to Avi as they pass, and I don't think there's a single human being that isn't entirely charmed by him.

Definitely not me. I don't think I have any hope of making it out without getting hurt.

"Oh, I forgot to tell you," Avi says. "I have a day off in two days. Want to go on a field trip?"

Yes.

No. Tam. Think.

Too bad. Yes, yes, yes, yes, and yes. "Sure. Where to?"

"I don't know. Wanna climb down the side of a cliff?" he teases.

"Do you have any flaming bamboo shoots I can use for my eyeballs instead?" I ask. "Because if you did, I may prefer that to climbing down a cliff."

"Even if the cliff ends in the middle of a herd of cows?"

"Even if. Though that did sway my vote just the tiniest bit."

"Really? How about ice cream?"

"A tiny little bit more." I grin. "Cliff climbing isn't per se my favorite thing to do, but I wouldn't mind it."

"I was kidding. Tzfat sound good?"

"Are you sure? That's like a five hour bus trip. I don't mind, I love Tzfat, but it's pretty far away from here."

"And how long are you here for?" Avi asks. "You should go to Tzfat before you leave. Where else are you going to get your fill of Israeli art hippies like you'd get in Tzfat?"

"You have a point, but . . ." I shrug hopelessly. "I feel bad. Don't you want to go home and spend the day with your family?"

"I just saw them, and I'm going to see them soon." He looks at me and his voice gentles. "Tamar, you don't have to feel guilty about doing something for yourself every once in a while."

"Yeah, I'm not so good at that." I twist my fingers around a tissue.

"Okay, try this. If I wasn't working, and I could see my family any time I wanted to, and we had a day we could go on a field trip, where would you want to go?"

Asaf calls for Avi, and he steps away from the bus stop. "Think about it, okay? I have a feeling you're a good person to field-trip with, and I'd really like to go somewhere with you."

He jogs across to Asaf, and I sink back to think.

> "Spontaneous field trip planning is the best. The geography of the country is so drastically different, depending on where you're going, that a two hour bus ride can make you feel like you're in a new country entirely. Sometimes we'd just go to the Tachana Merkazit (Central Bus Station), check out what buses were leaving in the next ten minutes, and pick one at random."
>
> —C.T.

"I'M BACK," HE says, leaning back against the bus stop.

"Hi."

"Hey." He grins. "So. Have you been thinking?"

"I'm always thinking," I say.

"I know. But specifically about field tripping."

"I . . . kinda want to go to Tzfat and try cheese," I mumble.

"Can I have confirmation on the request for Tzfat cheese tastings?" he drawls, his accent a little stronger than usual. "Because those are some magical words right there, ma'am."

"I'm not even going to try to ma'am you right back," I say. "It would be a rootin' tootin' disaster."

"Oy vey," he drawls, which is something I never thought about being a thing. But it is, and it is glorious.

"Indeed. But yes. That was a yes."

"Yessss. Excellent. Cheese in Tzfat. I am all for this plan." Avi pulls out his phone. "I realized I don't actually have your number. We should probably fix that."

I pull out my phone and give him my number. He types it in, and types something else.

My phone dings.

Message on WhatsApp from a new number. I open it.

You're my favorite person I've ever met at a bus stop.

I blush and stammer a little bit, and beam. And then text back, *That's such a coincidence, because you're also my favorite person that I've ever met at a bus stop.*

Chapter 5

> "Tzfat is a city of hippies and blue doors, but everyone is still Israeli. Israeli hippies are the funnest combination of humanity ever. They're super hippie, but they're Israeli. And even though climbing up into the Old City sometimes feels like you're climbing up Everest (okay, what I think climbing Everest feels like), the view is always worth it."
>
> —E.G.

TZFAT IS A magical city full of hippies, art galleries, blue doors, and burial spots for holy men. We wander through the streets of the Old City of Tzfat, because walking down is so much easier than walking up. And so instead of going to the cheese place first, we go eat lunch. Lunch is on the top of Tzfat, and the cheese is at the edge of the Old City.

We're sitting in a pizza store, this time with each other on purpose, when Avi turns to me. "Can I ask you a weird question?"

"Sure." I put down my slice. "What's up?"

"Have you ever bought the pizza vouchers in Chevron?"

"Yeah, lots of times. Every time I'm there, I buy a bunch." I brush the hair out of my face. "Why?"

"Were you in Chevron a little before Purim?"

I think back, brow furrowed. "I think so?"

"Well, there was this day last year, like a week or so before Purim, and I was working, when this American girl comes up to me and asks in her broken Hebrew if I was hungry. I told her—"

"I'm twenty years old. Part of my description of being a human being of the male variety is to be hungry," I finish. "Wait. That was *you*?"

"Thank you so much for that pizza," he says. "I was having a pretty frustrating day. The fact that some pretty girl went through the trouble to find me and let me know that she'd bought me lunch just because I was someone who was keeping her safe? It meant a lot."

"You remember what I told you?" I ask, flabbergasted.

"Tamar, two days before, there had been a shooting there."

I think back. "Right. That was why we went, I think. Thinking back, that was a pretty stupid thing to do."

"There were two people who died that day. A little Arab kid, who I used to see every morning on his way to school. And an old Jewish man who had retired and moved to Chevron when he was eighty-three. He used to give me a blessing every time he saw me, and he told me it was because I was helping keep him safe." Avi sighed. "I've been trying so hard to balance being a soldier and being a person, you know? Not that if you're a soldier you're not a person, but sometimes you have to forget you have feelings so you can keep going."

He looks so lost, and my heart breaks for him.

"And when they were killed . . . I tried so hard not to feel anything. I tried to just shove it to the back of my mind, to accept it and move on, because I didn't want to break. And then you showed up, all cheerful and happy and thankful, and I could see every emotion you experienced just flash across your face. And I thought that maybe I should try to find a way to remember that sometimes you're going to feel some very uncomfortable emotions. And maybe that's not a bad thing."

He looks up at me, his eyes a little glassy with unshed tears. "So thank you for the pizza. I can't believe I forgot your face. I'm so sorry."

I'm shaken, and I think my heart just grew five sizes. "Thank you for telling me," I say. "And I promise you, it was my pleasure to give you that voucher. Especially after you smiled at me."

"Why after I smiled?" he asks.

"Because your smile reached your eyes, and your dimples made me happy." I smile. "They still do."

> "Someone who loves me very much went to Israel and couldn't figure out what to buy me as a gift so all I got was a lame T-shirt."
>
> "Okay, maybe that's not actually what the shirt says, but that's probably what it means."
>
> —T.W.

We decide to skip the cheese tasting, mostly because we both ate more pizza than we expected to, and people whose stomachs have exploded due to an overabundance of dairy products aren't really something the city of Tzfat needs. And so even though there are plenty of things to do in Tzfat that don't involve tasting cheese, we end up in a goofy souvenir shop.

There are candles, there's art, there's various and sundry Judaic items, but best of all, there are the T-shirts.

All the cheesy T-shirts, which makes me cackle a little bit. "Let's have a lame T-shirt contest," I tell Avi quietly. Not all souvenir shop owners appreciate knowing we're mocking their merchandise.

"Is there a prize?" he asks.

"Well, obviously. What kind of terrible game would this be if there wasn't?"

"So, what is it?"

I smirk. "It's a surprise."

"Hmmm . . ."

I raise my eyebrows. "You in or not, dude?"

He laughs. "I'm in."

"Excellent. Okay, so three items with an overarching theme. The dumber or punnier, the better."

"Wait, how are we going to tell who wins?" Avi asks.

"We'll judge ourselves."

"You trust us that much?"

I shrug. "Who knows. I guess we'll find out."

Fifteen minutes later Avi staggers over to the corner carrying three T-shirts.

I'm also holding three T-shirts.

"Okay, who's first?" he asks. "I'm just saying, I picked out some winners here."

"I'm pretty sure I picked the winners here, but we shall see." I pick one T-shirt. "On the count of three, we'll flip them around."

"Three, two, one." We flip T-shirts. Look at the other person's T-shirt. Look back at the T-shirt we picked. ISRAEL ISRAELLY GREAT!! Mine on a purple T-shirt, Avi's on a green T-shirt.

"Well . . ." he drawls. "This is interesting. Flip over the second one on three?"

"One, two, three," I count, and flip over T-shirt number two. Look at Avi's. SOMEONE WHO LOVES ME VERY MUCH WENT TO ISRAEL AND BOUGHT ME THIS T-SHIRT. Both with a few words scribbled on the back in Hebrew that very obviously did not originally come with the T-shirt. "No way . . ." I mutter.

"If we have the same ones for number three . . ." Avi flips over his third T-shirt. "I don't know."

I look at his and start to full out laugh. Shoulders shaking, tears streaming, holding my sides laughing.

"No," Avi says. "So do we have the same brain?"

I flip over my third T-shirt choice. Some cartoon guy behind a car, with the words WILL BRAKE FOR MATZO BALLS on top. "It seems so."

"Wait, we have to explain the connection of all three," Avi says. "Maybe we can salvage this with that."

"You have a point," I concede. "Another brain like mine would probably be a very dangerous thing to have on the planet."

"That was kind of my thought, too."

"You know what? Maybe we shouldn't explain our reasoning behind these shirts," I say.

"Keep a bit of mystery here?"

"Well, mostly because I suspect that we have the same answers, and the world may not be able to survive with two brains."

Avi thinks for a bit. "You know, I think that may be a good idea. For national security and all."

"That was my thought process, there."

"Twin brains," he says soberly. "Quick, think something else."

"Um . . . am I now supposed to share said thought with you?"

"Do you think it's the same thing I'm thinking about?" Avi asks.

"I hope not." I look out the window. "I was thinking how the last time I was in Tzfat, I had a Joanie Mitchell song stuck in my head the whole time."

"Well, I can definitely tell you that wasn't what I was thinking."

I wipe my forehead. "Thank God."

"The world will spin another day?"

"I hope so."

> "I think I fell a little for every *chayal* I ever saw sleeping on the bus. It's then when you remember how young they are. How much sweetness is in a boy trained to protect if he needs to. How much

innocence is still in a boy who knows how to take apart his machine gun and put it back together without any assistance from anyone else.

I think that's when I felt the most protective of them. When they were curled up on each other on the bus, sleeping soundly."

—N.B.

WE LEAVE TZFAT, each of us carrying a bag with the ISRAEL ISRAELLY GREAT!! T-shirt. Complete with exclamation points.

I fall asleep next to Avi on the bus and wake up leaning on his shoulder. He's sleeping, snoring gently, and I sit up straight as fast as I can.

I was sleeping, I try to rationalize with myself. I wasn't doing anything intentionally.

But I was sleeping on him.

I wonder if he was up when I fell asleep on him.

I wonder how he feels about it. I look over to his sleeping face, eyelashes fanned and his face soft. He's got a bit of a five o'clock shadow, and for a guy who has the potential of looking dangerous if he needs to, he looks almost angelic as he sleeps.

And I think that's the minute I fall for him completely and totally.

Chapter 6

"The snowstorm in Israel? It was crazy. Oh my God. Like, I'd been in Israel when there was an inch of snow and the whole place shut down, and I laughed and laughed and laughed. But this was a real snowstorm. Everyone was off from school and were just outside building snowmen and having snowball fights everywhere you went."

—Y.C.

I WAKE UP in the middle of the night with four messages from my mother. Call me, call me, call me, call me.

I dial her number, heart in my throat.

Everyone's okay, thank God. But there's a snowstorm coming. A big one. Bigger than they've predicted in the past few years, big enough that schools are already thinking about closing for those days already and it's not for another two days.

She reminds me how school starts again for me in three days and they won't excuse me if I miss a day of school because the airports are closed but school isn't.

She reminds me about the attendance policy and how strict it is.

She reminds me gently that the fee for changing my ticket isn't so high.

"I hate this," I moan.

"I know, sweetie. I hate it, too. I wish you could stay longer. But you should call the airline to see what they can do."

I call the airline.

They have one available ticket before all of the snow potentially happens.

The flight leaves in seven hours.

I swallow hard.

I book the flight.

I pack in a daze, and wander through Barbara's apartment like a ghost. It's too early for me to go anywhere, but I need to. I have so little time left, considering how early I have to be at the airport and how long it takes to get there.

Avi isn't working by the bus station now.

I can't leave without letting him know. But he's on the base now and I can't bother him. If I call, he won't answer.

So I do the next best thing.

Well, really, the only thing I can think of to do.

I write him a letter. I'm honest. Brutally so.

I tell the taxi driver to pick me up by Avi's bus stop and drop the letter for him at the little security kiosk thing with a *chayal* whom I don't know. I ask him to make sure Avi will get it, and he says he'll try.

I hope he does.

The taxi driver pulls up just as the sun is beginning to rise over the horizon.

I watch the sky light up in color and wonder why I have to leave.

> "Leaving is always the worst part. It doesn't matter how many times you go and leave, it will feel like your soul is shattering every time the plane takes off from Tel Aviv."
>
> —L.H.

I CAN'T EVEN appreciate the sight of London at night as we land in Heathrow. Everyone in the airport is perfectly pleasant, but all of them have crisp British accents and aren't arguing with each other in Hebrew. The bathrooms are gorgeous and the seat that I end up falling asleep on while I wait for my second flight is super comfortable, but I don't want to be here. I don't want to be going back, I don't want to be here, I want to be back in Barbara's apartment, I want to be by Avi's bus stop, I want to be having dance parties with Salome in her Bayit Vegan apartment, I want to be sitting on my park bench in the Old City, I want to be riding the train through Jerusalem, I want to be floating on the Dead Sea, I want to be rolling around in grassy fields after climbing a mountain, I want to be anywhere but where I am.

There's nothing wrong with London except it's not Israel, and Avi isn't here.

Avi, who I didn't even have time to say good-bye to.

I cry myself to sleep in Heathrow Airport.

Chapter 7

"You'll be surprised what makes you happy when you go back home. That chocolate you used to eat, that cereal you used to bribe yourself with when you were studying, some cheap brand of shampoo . . . none of them feel particularly important until you're thousands of miles away and they remind you of sunshine on rooftops and grandmas telling you to put on a coat, sweetie, it's so cold outside. And it will make you so happy to have a connection back, even if it's just cheap shampoo."

—V.O.

I MANAGE TO beat the storm to New York by a day and a half. Snow falls outside, sticking to the ground in storybook piles of clean and white. It feels like we're in a snow globe for the first day, as snow falls and falls and falls, and cars haven't blackened the snow yet.

School is canceled for two days, and for two days I keep telling myself that I could still be in Israel if I hadn't decided to leave early.

My mom says it's me being responsible.

Riva and Salome agree with her, but also agree with me that it stinks.

They ask what happened to that *chayal* I met by the bus stop that day. Did I see him again after? Did I talk to him?

I don't know what to answer. Part of me feels like the time I spent with Avi was some sort of dream, or something. A fairy tale, of sorts.

Without the living happily ever after. Like some sort of deranged Cinderella tale without evil stepsiblings or balls, but dancing, and leaving way too early.

I did see him a bunch of times after that, I finally text them. I don't want to lie. I just don't want to tell the whole truth.

And? Riva demands.

And I left. He was really sweet, though. And funny. And kind. And compassionate, and smart, and, and, and.

Shame that you had to leave so quickly, Salome types.

It is, I reply.

I go back to school, and Sophia, who sits next to me, tells me I look great, but I look sad.

"What happened?" she asks gently.

"I think I lost my heart somewhere," I tell her.

She hugs me. "I hope you find it. Or it finds you."

> "Oh God, the adjustment period when I moved back to the U.S. was so bizarre. I tried speaking Hebrew with the taxi driver at the airport,

> who was super confused. And for the next three months, any time I bumped into anyone I would apologize in Hebrew. If someone asked me for directions in a language that wasn't English, I would answer in Hebrew. It took a while to retrain myself to make my default language in public English again, instead of Hebrew. But every time I hear Hebrew on a city bus, I am immeasurably happy."
>
> —D.N.

"TAMAR, GO GET the door!" my sister yells. "It's probably Chani returning the baking soda!"

It's Friday afternoon, and I'm cleaning the first floor bathroom and trying not to mope.

"You get it!" I yell. "I'm cleaning the bathroom."

"I can't, I'm making chicken!"

Ughhh. Raw chicken outweighs Fantastik and bleach. I strip off my cleaning gloves, give my hair a halfhearted shove off my forehead, and go to answer the door.

The Shabbos CD my sister loves is blaring, and I don't bother to even check who's at the door before swinging it open.

"Hey Chani—" I look up. My jaw drops. "Avi?" I whisper.

Because unless I've inhaled a little too much bleach and I'm hallucinating, I'm pretty sure Avi is standing at my front door.

Wearing a coat. And a scarf. His hair is windblown, and he's grinning, and I don't think I've seen something so beautiful as this. "I'm looking for this girl I met a few weeks ago," he says. "It's kinda funny, actually. I met her at a bus stop."

"That's a funny place to meet someone," I manage, clutching the doorway. What is he doing here?

"I know," he says. "But we were both waiting for the same bus. Seems God wanted us to meet, and He decided that the bus stop was a good place."

"There are worse places," I manage.

"Yeah, I liked it. And then we hung out almost every day until she had to go home. Went on field trips, ate suf-ganiyot, went on a scavenger hunt . . . lots of stuff." He shrugs. "It was really nice. And I got to hang out with her, which was the best part."

He toes a pile of snow on the front porch. "But then she had to leave a little earlier than she was supposed to, and I didn't have time to tell her how I felt about her before she left."

"So what did you do?" I ask, a lump forming in my throat.

"Well, I found out the day that she left that my job was being switched to something a little less patrol and a little more office related."

"Really?"

"So finally my months spent in Kenya come in handy," he says. "And my Swahili. Which means I've somehow managed to go from random *chayal* patrolling by *Me'arat HaMachpeila* to traveling for the Israeli government about foreign aid and other stuff that I can't necessarily talk about with people. But I'm in New York for the next three weeks, and the first thing I thought of when I was told about it was this girl I met. She lives here."

"I don't get it," I say. "I can't process anything."

Avi smiles, and shoves his hands into his pockets. "I didn't want to say anything," he says quietly. "I was scared that everything I was feeling was one-sided. And then you left early, and I thought it was too late. I wanted to call you, but I didn't want to get anyone's hopes up for things that may be a little too crazy to work." He pauses and looks at me, and I melt into a puddle of feelings. "But I wanted it to work. So badly. And so the minute they told me what was happening, I asked Chaim for your address." He spreads his hands. "And so here I am."

I may be full out crying now, but I will not admit it. "Hi, Avi," I whisper, which makes his face light up. "You're here."

"I'm here," he agrees.

"I have never wanted to hug someone so much in my life," I say.

"I know the feeling."

"I thought I was hallucinating on bleach fumes."

"I'm not a bleach dream, Tamar."

"You're real," I say, knowing I sound like an idiot, but not caring. Avi's here. He's here. He's here.

"I hope so," he says. "It would be really awkward if I wasn't real, wouldn't it?"

"Super awkward," I agree. "Here's the funny part, though. I started looking to see if there was a way for me to transfer my scholarship to an Israeli school. I decided I wanted to do something for me. Just for me, even if I never saw you again." I shrug, and smile slow. "Not that I would be okay never seeing you again."

"I'm glad. Because that wasn't a reality I wanted to have to live in." Avi laughs. "Other people can have my alternate reality. I like this one."

"I'm kinda into it, too."

"I brought you a present," Avi says, handing me a bag.

"You brought me you," I say. "That's enough of a present for me."

"Look before you say that."

I open the bag. Inside there are two T-shirts. "What the . . ." I pull out one of them: WELL, I AM AN AMERICAN, with a picture of a round of cheese.

"I cannot believe you," I say, laughing. He had laughed when I told him about it, one day at the bus stop. And even better, he remembered. "I love it."

"There's more."

I unfold the other T-shirt. I WENT TO ISRAEL AND MET A CHAYAL BY A BUS STOP, AND ALL I GOT WAS THIS T-SHIRT (BECAUSE HE THOUGHT A RING WOULD FREAK ME OUT).

I'm silent.

Avi shifts from foot to foot.

"So here's the thing," I say. "I don't know if a ring would really freak me out."

Avi smiles, smiles, smiles. "That's good to know."

"I thought it might be."

Chapter 8

"Would I say it was the best year of my life? Absolutely not. I'd like to think I haven't lived the best year of my life yet.

Would I say that it was one of the most life changing years I've experienced? Yes. One hundred percent. And I would relive it again in an instant. Making the same mistakes I made then, angsting over the same things. Because going through that year the way I did has impacted my life in more ways than I thought possible.

Was it the hardest year of my life? In some ways, yes. It was.

Was it a year I needed?

Absolutely. Without a doubt.

And I would do it all over again, if I could, knowing how different I would be on the other end. Knowing how after it was through, I would be a better person.

If becoming a better person included hanging out in a place you loved with people you loved?

Sign. Me. Up."

—R.F.

AND WE ALL live happily ever after.

Avi, me, and the T-shirts.

And the ring, that totally didn't freak me out when he gave it to me.

And because Avi is Avi, and I am me, the diamonds on the ring are in a circle, with a bigger stone in the middle. People think it's just the style, but I know it's a sufganiya.

Doesn't that figure.

I went to Israel expecting to just eat doughnuts and hang out with my friends, but all I got was an excellent husband and a doughnut-shaped engagement ring.

So much better than just a T-shirt.

About the Authors

MEGAN HART is a *New York Times* and *USA TODAY* bestselling author of more than thirty novels, novellas and short stories. Her work has been published in almost every genre, including contemporary women's fiction, historical romance, paranormal and erotica. Learn more at www.meganhart.com

JENNIFER GRACEN hails from Long Island, New York, where she lives with her two young sons. After spending her youth writing in private and singing in public, she now only sings in her car and has fully embraced her life-long passion for writing. She loves to write contemporary romance and romantic women's fiction for readers who yearn for better days, authentic characters, and satisfying endings. When she isn't taking care of her kids, doing freelance copy editing/proofreading, reading, or talking to friends on Twitter and Facebook, Jennifer writes. She's shocked her family hasn't yet staged an intervention for her addiction to social media. But the concerts she gives in her car and the dance parties she has in her kitchen are rumored to be fabulous.

STACEY AGDERN is an award-winning former bookseller who has reviewed romance novels in multiple formats and given talks about various aspects of the romance genre. She is also a romance writer. You can find her on twitter at @nystacey. She's a proud member of both LIRW and RWA NYC. She lives in New York, not far from her favorite hockey team's practice facility.

KK HENDIN writes books where people flirt awkwardly, make out, dish out a whole lot of sass and ridiculousness, and live happily ever after. She's the author of many books, including the Twelve Bears in a Bar series and the upcoming Undercover series. She also writes books as K. Hendin, where people aren't as nice and Happily Ever After isn't a guarantee. KK is currently writing way too many books, and is still waiting for the subway to run on a regular schedule. When she's not playing book Tetris in an attempt to fit everything onto the bookshelves in her tiny NYC apartment, she's probably wandering her neighborhood with her camera or drinking yet another cup of coffee.

Discover great authors, exclusive offers, and more at hc.com.